T0304818

THE WILD SWIMMERS

BY WILLIAM SHAW

The DS Alexandra Cupidi Investigations

Salt Lane
Deadland
Grave's End
The Trawlerman

The Breen and Tozer Investigations

A Song from Dead Lips
A House of Knives
A Book of Scars
Sympathy for the Devil

The Birdwatcher
Dead Rich
The Conspirators

THE WILD
SWIMMERS

William Shaw

riverrun

First published in Great Britain in 2024 by

riverrun

an imprint of

Quercus Editions Limited
Carmelite House
50 Victoria Embankment
London EC4Y 0DZ

An Hachette UK company

A CIP catalogue record for this book is available
from the British Library.

Hardback 978 1 52942 012 8
Trade Paperback 978 1 52942 013 5
Ebook 978 1 52942 014 2

10 9 8 7 6 5 4 3 2

Typeset by CC Book Production
Printed and bound in Great Britain by Clays Ltd, Elcograf S.p.A.

Papers used by Quercus are from well-managed forests and other responsible sources.

To Christine

PART ONE

ONE

It came down to a choice between two directions, north or south. If only Alexandra Cupidi had turned south instead of north, it would have been her who discovered the dead woman.

'I'm sorry to call so late,' the voice had said. 'Only, someone's reported a body on Dungeness. Drowned, by the sound of it.'

'Mum!' Zoë had put down the phone and called up the stairs. 'I think it's for you.'

Just ten minutes later, Detective Sergeant Alexandra Cupidi was in her old green Saab, bumping down the narrow track that led past the lighthouses and the scattered wooden cabins, and Detective Inspector Toby McAdam was back on speakerphone. 'I'm so embarrassed. Your daughter picked up. I thought it was you. She sounds so grown-up now. That was so unprofessional of me. Is she OK?'

'You can ask her yourself. Zoë's here with me in the car.'

Alex's daughter was there in the passenger seat. There was a pause before McAdam spoke again. 'She's in the car?'

'Say hello to my boss, Zoë.'

'Hello,' said Zoë.

'You think that's wise?' McAdam asked.

'It'll be a wild goose chase, Toby,' said Alex.

'What do you mean?'

'It happens about once a year. Somebody calls up, says they've found a body out by the old lookout station up at Pen Bars. And because it's been reported, we have to go and check – so they always call me up because I'm local. Before me, the same used to happen to Bill South when he was the neighbourhood officer round here, regular as concrete.'

'You mean clockwork?' Alex could hear hesitation in his voice. 'I know I called you at home, and technically you're not on duty, but . . . should you really be taking your daughter along to something like this, Alex? It's a report of a dead person.'

He was her senior officer and she liked him very much. She liked that she made him nervous. He was an inspector and she was only a sergeant, but she was older and more experienced than he was and he knew it.

'She's not a child any more, Toby, she's nineteen. And there won't be a body, Toby. At least, not a human one. Me and Zoë will have a mooch around and I'll send you a photograph.' Alex ended the call and turned onto the main road, heading towards Lydd.

At the back of the village was a pitted single track that led to Pen Bars, the south side of the shingle spit of Dungeness.

The body of the concrete man was a ghoulish thing to come across by accident. Nobody knew who had made the sculpture of the dead person and left it on that lonely expanse of stones,

4

out there on its own. There were more tourists coming here every year, but they only ever took in a small part of the vastness of Dungeness. They saw the beach with its rusty fishing boats and the crumbling wooden ribs of ones that had long been given up on; they visited Prospect Cottage, the famous artist's home, its walls black, its window frames bright yellow; they saw the crooked iron rails the fishermen had once laid to haul their trawlers up the ever-expanding banks of stones; they peered at the wooden huts, some inhabited, others locked shut, all in various states of repair; they trudged up the worn sandstone steps of the old lighthouse and gazed in awe at the bulk of the nuclear power station; but they never came here, to the huge flat expanse behind it all.

The concrete man lay face down, far from the shoreline – as if he had expired after crawling out of the sea. From a distance he was just a dark shape that looked like another pile of rocks, but the closer you were, the more uncannily convincing he became.

He was sprawled on the ground, legs curled, as if he had died in some desperate agony. People who came across him in recent years assumed he intended to represent the migrants who arrived here, risking their lives in small boats, but the concrete man was much older than these new arrivals.

Some said he had been made by an artist twenty years ago, as some kind of protest about the vast nuclear power station that dominated the shingle landscape. In fact, it was an even older generation who had left it there. Ravers from the New Age travellers had held huge parties here back in the 1990s. Back in those innocent days you took drugs and danced all night until you collapsed onto the stones like this man had. Ravers had made him as a kind of symbol of their own excess. Alex remembered the drugs. A daughter of a policeman, she had tried to pretend her friends didn't take them in the quantities they had.

Like a lot of things around here, the concrete man was disturbing and only half explained. Alex Cupidi was not from these parts. When she first arrived on Dungeness, she had found everything about this place strange. She had been here a few years now and was beginning to like it.

There won't be a body, she had promised DI McAdam.

The concrete man was still there. Even though they'd both seen him several times before, it took a few minutes for them to find him in this flat landscape. The pylons that strode across the land all looked identical. One gorse bush looked much like the next. Alex took a couple of photographs and messaged McAdam. *Body on beach*, she wrote drily.

'That it?' said Zoë.

Alex looked around. 'I should check the shoreline anyway. Just in case. It'd be stupid to come all this way only for there to be a real drowned person. Egg on face.'

'Mum,' scolded Zoë.

She was right. It was not wise to be flippant about the dead. Together, they walked down the track where she'd parked the car and from there made their way to the shoreline.

At the end of the track, she took her phone out of her jeans pocket and plugged in the earphones.

Zoë looked on disapprovingly. Sometimes Alex wondered

how she could have given birth to someone older and more judgemental than herself.

She looked one way and then the other.

'I'll head fifteen minutes this way, then come back.'

'Suit yourself.'

She picked north. 'What are you going to do? Look for long-haired bees?'

'Short-haired bees, Mum. And no, because they're actually extinct in this country as a matter of fact.'

But Alex already had her earphones in and was tramping northwards towards Camber and the shooting ranges.

The tide was high. Save for odd bits of green netting and the occasional plastic milk bottle, there was little to see on the waterline. There were no bodies at all.

She walked for a while, turned and headed back.

She reached the old coastguard lookout post and looked around for her daughter but couldn't see her anywhere. 'Zoë?' she called.

She paused her music for a second and listened for a reply, but none came, so she pressed PLAY and set off south this time, barely listening, thinking about the week ahead.

On Monday she was due to start back on the serious crimes unit. She had been on light duties for a year because of stress. There would be colleagues wondering if she was still up to it. The police were always changing. She would have a lot of catching up to do. There would be new systems to learn, new vocabularies and acronyms. The unit was short-handed, over-whelmed by work. Her life was about to become chaos again.

She stopped, looked around. Where was Zoë? Taking out an

7

earphone, she shouted her name, but nothing came back and she plugged the music in again.

When the next track finished, she thought she heard screaming. She snatched both earphones out.

'Mum!' The voice, blown on the wind, came from somewhere ahead.

'Mum!' Zoë wailed. 'Help me!'

Alex looked but could not see her. She set off running, but running on loose stones was hard and she could not run fast enough.

'Mum! Help me!'

She sprinted towards the sound. The spring tides had built a high bank of shingle. She stumbled down it to where Zoë lay at the bottom, soaked in seawater, her arms around the dead woman.

'I shouted,' Zoë bawled furiously, face streaked with tears. 'I called. For ever. Where were you?'

'I'm sorry,' said Alex.

'You didn't come. I have been trying to save her.'

The woman was dressed in a black swimming costume, her skin alabaster. A black rubber swimming hat pressed close to her skull.

'I thought if I could warm her up . . .' Zoë's eyes were red-rimmed, Alex saw, the skin around her mouth red, too. She realised that her daughter had been trying to give the woman mouth-to-mouth resuscitation, though even a brief glance told Alex it was pointless because she had long been dead.

Zoë lay alongside her, clutching the cold body.

'I'm so, so sorry,' said Alex. 'I thought it was just a hoax. I would have never brought you.'

The phone in her trouser pocket buzzed. She ignored it.

Alex waded into the water beside her. 'You can let her go now,' she said gently. 'If you like.'

'I called and I called,' her daughter wailed, still clutching the dead woman, 'and you didn't come.'

TWO

'You seen Alex?' When Bill South opened the front door to his small cabin, Jill Ferriter was standing there, her voice loud in his face. 'Only, I been to her house and she's not there. You see her?'

Bill had oil on his hands, his shirt and even in his hair. Jill Ferriter wore a pink shirt, coral pink lipstick, and carefully applied eyeshadow to emphasise her pretty bright-blue eyes.

'She's not in. Neither's Zoë. And I really really need to speak to her, urgent. I was going to tell her something important.' A pause. The young woman sniffed, leaned in. 'Bill? Can I smell petrol?'

'Yes,' said Bill. 'You can.'

'Everything OK in there, Bill?'

Constable Jill Ferriter was Alex Cupidi's friend and colleague. Alex always insisted to Bill that she was a good copper, too. Bill found her brash. Half an hour in her company left him drained.

'I saw her driving off about half an hour ago,' said Bill. 'Her and Zoë. They were in the Saab.'

'Oh,' Jill said, disappointed. 'I'd called to tell her I was on the way but she didn't pick up. Mind if I wait?'

Before he had the chance to answer that he was busy, she had pushed straight past him and made her way into his domain.

'Why would I mind?'

Bill South lived on his own. It felt like he always had. His wooden cabin sat by the side of the small concrete track. Further up from the shore, Alex and Zoë lived in an older, much more solid house than his. Bill bristled when the tourists who crowded the place in the summer called his small home 'sweet'. It was practical; red weatherproofed cedar with white-painted windows. It had two symmetrical gables that faced the track and a front door between them. He kept it warm and well-maintained.

'Oh.' Jill stopped when she saw the outboard motor, fixed to a rusty metal stand in the middle of the room. A tin cup sat beneath the propellor, full to the brim with dirty oil.

'I wasn't expecting company,' he said. He looked down at his hands; they were filthy. Blackness had worked its way beneath his nails, into the crevices of his fingers. He had been replacing the spark plugs, preparing it for the coming summer. Screws were laid out in a tin lid in the exact order he'd removed them. He hated stopping a job like this when he was half way through.

'I'll put the kettle on, then.'

'Oat milk, if you got it,' she said.

'I don't,' he answered.

Bill picked up the nailbrush by his sink and started cleaning his hands of grease and dirt.

★

11

When he'd made the tea in a small brown teapot, he took it to the table by the back window. It was a good lookout post. From there he could see the road that passed by the lighthouses and spot Alex's car when she came back, whenever that was. He knew already that he wouldn't be able to get on with the job until then.

'Aren't you going to ask me what's so urgent?' Jill demanded eventually. 'Why I needed to speak to Alex?'

'No.'

Jill was remarkably thick-skinned. 'Only, I've had the weirdest shitting few days imaginable. You're never going to believe this. Starting at the beginning, Thursday I go out on a Hinge date with this bloke called Malcolm.' She paused. 'You know what Hinge is, don't you? It's a dating app.' Like he was so old he wouldn't know that. 'We meet in a wine bar, drink a bit too much and then catch an Uber back to his place, which is in Hythe. Only, first thing that's obvious when we get there is that he's not bloody single. There's women's stuff everywhere. Like, bras drying on the radiator.'

Bill tried not to listen.

'I said, "You're not single." He said, "Who said I was?" But you know, I'm a bit pissed, so I don't pay attention. I know. I'm so ashamed.'

'You sure you want to tell me this?' Bill was almost twice Jill's age.

'No. Listen. This bit is funny; it's the other thing that isn't. Well. Not funny really. Tragic.' She flopped down into his leather armchair. 'I don't know why I end up doing shit like this, time

12

after time. I reckon there's something wrong with me. Do you think there is?'

'There's something wrong with most of us,' said Bill.

'OK, so anyway. We're in the bed about twenty minutes and he's actually not that bad, but that's beside the point because just when it's getting somewhere . . .'

Jesus Christ.

'. . . just when it's getting somewhere, there's a key in the bloody door.'

'His girlfriend?' he said, in spite of himself.

'Yes. His bloody girlfriend. And she comes straight in and we're both lying in her bed, bare asses and everything. I could have died.'

'She chucked you out?'

'Actually, that was the funny thing. She chucked *him* out, and then just gave me a bit of a talking-to. Not in a bad way. It was, like, quite tender. It was as if she knew exactly who I was. She could see into my actual soul. She said I could do better than this if I tried. Suggested I go for counselling and advised me not to mix alcohol and internet dating. Asked me why I indulged in risky behaviour. Kind of humiliating. There I was, breaking up her relationship, and she had her arm around me and I was in bits, bawling her place down.'

He put a strainer over a mug and poured.

'Wow. You use loose tea?' She sounded surprised that people still bothered. 'So anyway. His girlfriend was right. What the hell was I thinking, Bill? I'm a bloody mess. I mean. Getting drunk and having sex with someone else's boyfriend. I do need counselling. It's like some psychological defect.'

13

'That's what you came to tell Alex about?'

'God, no,' said Jill. 'I told her all this already. It's just, like, context.'

'Oh God. Context for what? You mean there's more of this?'

Jill took a breath. 'You knew my mum, right?'

'Yes, Jill,' Bill said, his voice softening. Anyone who had served in the police force around this area twenty years ago had known Jill's mother. She had been a substance abuser and a sex worker. She had been a handful. 'Of course I knew Sandra.'

'It's no surprise, is it, I'm a fuck-up? She was a fuck-up too.'

She was looking at him with those needy eyes. 'She wasn't a bad person, Jill. She just had the wrong people around her.'

'A million per cent. She was a fuck-up and that's why I ended up in care. You know that. The apple falling close to the tree.' She stood and joined him, sitting either side of the small table at the rear window, looking out towards the lighthouses, watching out for Alex to return.

'So anyway. Big surprise. Context. Like the woman said, I do a lot of stupid stuff too, like get drunk and have inappropriate sex. I never grew up normal exactly, did I?'

Bill sighed. 'Maybe not. But you're not like your mum, Jill. I knew her. She was damaged. She was sad all the time. You're full of life, Jill.'

'Too full?'

He smiled at her. 'Maybe, Jill. I can't judge.'

'I spent so long wishing I had a normal family. Mum and dad. You know.'

'Normal mums and dads can mess you up too,' Bill said.

'I really wanted a dad, 'cause I never knew who he was. I always thought if I had a father – someone like you – I've have not been so bloody needy all the time.'

'I don't think I'd have ever been much of a father, Jill.'

'Shut up and listen, Bill,' she said. 'I'm getting to the point. I always wanted to find out who my dad is, and now I think I know.'

He had lifted his cooling tea to his lips. He put the cup down again. 'Oh.'

'Mum never let on who my dad was. See? That's what all this is about. And then she died, obviously, and I never got to ask her. It's always bugged me. I mean. Wouldn't it bug you?'

Bill looked straight into her big, sad eyes.

'So yesterday,' she continued blithely, 'I got this email at work. *You don't know me but I think I'm your father.*'

'Sorry?'

'That's right. *You don't know me but I think I'm your father.*'

'You're serious?'

'I know. Spooky as shit, but kind of exciting too. That's what I need to talk to Alex about. She'll tell me what to do.'

'Was that it? Just an email from someone saying, *I think I'm your father?*'

'Pretty much. And where he was.'

Bill lifted the teapot to top up his cup. 'I don't want to come over as insensitive, but you're on Facebook and all that stuff. Hinge. Not that difficult to find out a few things about you. What makes you think this isn't some kind of con?'

15

'My mum shagged around. I know that,' said Jill. 'She wasn't a saint. Why would anyone want to pretend to be my father?'

'Why wouldn't they? You're down on yourself, but look at you. You're a successful young woman. You've got a good job. You've got your own place. You're something.'

'Successful,' Jill snorted.

'Did your mum have any idea who your dad was?'

'I always thought she did, but she didn't let on. Maybe she didn't. She didn't know very much at all half the time.'

'Sadly true.' Bill had been a neighbourhood officer. In that role, only a handful of people were responsible for ninety per cent of your work, and Jill's mother had been one of those. He rubbed his chin with a hand that still smelt of oil. 'Best speak to Alex. She'll know what to do.'

'Yeah. She'll know what to do.'

It was a fresh day. After a long winter in which it felt the wind here would never stop, the sun was warm. Bill wanted to finish work on the engine and try his dinghy out on the water, but he couldn't resist asking, 'So, this person who says he's your dad. Where is he living, then?'

She stared out of the window and seemed to shiver, though the day was warm. 'Yeah. Well. That's a bit of a problem.'

'What?'

'He's at Ford.'

It took him a second. 'Ford Prison?'

She nodded.

'Oh. Right. He emailed you from prison?'

16

'It wasn't him, obviously. He got a mate on the outside to do it.'

'What's he in for?'

She looked down at her mug of tea. 'That's the thing,' she said. 'It's murder.'

THREE

Alex could just make out the words Zoë was saying: 'It's OK,' Zoë was telling the dead woman as she stroked her forehead. 'My mum is here now. She'll know what to do.'

It was a rising tide and the dead woman lay at the waterline, limbs shifting in the waves.

'Where were you, Mum?' Zoë cried.

Alex had had her earphones in and had not heard a thing. 'I'm so sorry,' she said, and reached out to her, but Zoë flinched away. Alex's daughter remained next to the body as the sea rose around them, slowly pushing the dead woman up the beach as the water crept up the stones. Zoë stayed holding the woman, refusing to move, until the place was alive with light and motion.

The young man taking notes wore white coveralls. 'Your daughter moved the victim, you said?' He sounded disapproving.

'She tried to give her mouth-to-mouth,' she said. 'Though there would have not been much point.'

As soon as she had seen the body, the job had taken over.

Joining her daughter in the water, she had felt for life signs, though she had known there would be none, and then called the emergency services. Only once she had known that blue lights were on their way had she gone back and put her arm around Zoë, lying beside the dead woman in the freezing water, refusing to leave her.

Now the police and the paramedics were here. 'Cause of death drowning, I suppose,' said a police constable.

'That's not our call, obviously,' Alex said.

'Stands to reason though.'

She looked down at her daughter sitting on the stones in soaking clothes, arms clutched around her knees. The foil blanket that a paramedic had put around her had not been intended as a criticism of Alex's mothering skills, but right now it felt like it.

Alex sat down beside her and said, 'I'm sorry.'

The paramedic said, 'Your daughter's in shock. She needs to get out of those wet clothes. You should take her home.'

'I can, but my car is blocked in by your ambulance.'

'Right,' said the paramedic. 'We'll finish up here. Not a lot for us to do. We've called a HART team in.' A Hazardous Area Response Team. They needed a specialist team to remove the body. It would be some time before they arrived, so in the meantime the paramedics had covered the woman in a damp blanket. Police officers stood on the beach to the north and south, warning walkers away.

Eventually the ambulance began to move, taking an age to turn in the narrow track. When it had finally rumbled away towards Lydd, Alex called out, 'Are we OK to go?'

The constable lowered his phone and nodded.

'Come on,' said Alex, 'let's get you warm.' She lifted her daughter onto her feet and turned to go, but after a couple of steps she realised that Zoë was not following her.

'I should go and say goodbye,' said Zoë.

'Right. OK. You should.'

When Alex explained to the woman officer who had been stationed near the dead woman that her daughter wanted to have a moment with her, the PC seemed at a loss to know what to do.

'It's fine,' said Alex. 'She won't disturb the body and she was in contact with her anyway.'

Reluctantly, the officer stepped aside.

Alex took Zoë's hand and led her forwards. Zoë stopped short of the body and knelt down beside her silently for a minute, then stood again, staring out to sea, silver blanket still wrapped around her, shining pink in the evening light.

'Zoë?'

Her daughter didn't move.

'Are you OK?'

She stepped back and took her arm. Zoë shook her off, her eyes focused on the sea.

'What are you looking at?'

'Porpoises,' she answered. Alex stared in the direction she was looking at, but could see nothing at all in the movement of the waves. Sometimes she wondered if her daughter just imagined these things.

FOUR

'Where are they anyway?' Jill looked at the screen on her phone. 'You had no idea where Alex was going? Was it some kind of emergency? She's not picking up. I really, really, really badly need to talk to her.'

Bill stood, crossed the room and picked up the pair of binoculars that hung by the front door, then returned with them to his seat by the back window and scanned the scrubland to the north. He spent hours looking out of this window sometimes. He was a birdwatcher. He loved to wait quietly, simply observing the world. 'This man who says he's your father. What makes you think he's a murderer?' he asked, raising the glasses to his eyes.

'He signed his actual name. I googled him.'

'Ah. And he was definitely convicted of murder?'

She nodded. 'You're not going to like this.'

'Why?'

'He said his name is Stephen Dowles,' she said quietly.

The name was a jolt of electricity. He lowered the binoculars.

21

Jill had known he would recognise it. Any officer who had served around here in the 1990s would have. He looked at her, appalled. 'Jesus. Stevie Dowles says he is your dad?'

Jill jutted her chin out a little. 'Yep.'

'*The* Stephen Dowles,' he said.

'How many are there?'

Most criminals were, by and large, victims of circumstance. Putting most of them away never felt like much of a victory. But every now and again you came across a double murderer like Stephen Dowles and putting someone like that behind bars felt like you were making the world a better place.

'I looked him up. I seen what he did,' Jill said, not meeting Bill's eye.

'And this man says he's your dad?'

'He said, *I knew your mum. We slept together in 1994*,' Jill Ferriter said. 'I mean, that would be possible. That's the year I was born.'

They still sat in the window, looking out at the big blue sky and the sun that was starting to paint the pale shacks to the east pink.

He raised his binoculars back to his eyes, but he couldn't find the small brown bird he had noticed on the gorse outside. His hands weren't as steady as they should be. It was probably a willow warbler, thought Bill.

'You have your birthday on Facebook, don't you?' Bill considered. 'He could have worked that out.'

'I know you think I'm daft, but I'm not,' said Jill. 'I think it's legit.'

'I'm sorry,' he said. Bill had met Dowles. Now that he recalled his face, he knew that what she was saying was true. She looked the spit of him.

'Why?'

'A man like that . . . Ford Prison, you said?'

Jill nodded.

Ford was a Cat D prison, the least strict category. Some prisoners were allowed out at weekends. It was where they sometimes put prisoners who were on the journey back into the community. If he was in a Cat D prison, it meant that Stephen Dowles would probably be out soon.

'So you know what he did, then?' asked Bill.

'I looked it all up,' Jill said. 'Looked at all the newspapers. Yeah. I read it all. I spent my whole life wanting a dad and he turns out to be this monster.'

Jill stayed there, watching the road that ran past the lighthouses, waiting for Alex's car to drive down it, all nerves.

He returned to his engine, cleaning the plugs, replacing them, refilling the driveshaft with lubricant, then putting the cowling back in place.

He took a cloth and wiped an oily fingermark off the cowling. 'Looking forward to Alex being back at work, I suppose?'

'God, yeah,' said Jill.

Bill busied himself, unclamping the engine, hoisting it from its metal stand and lugging it to the front door. He propped it against the wainscotting for a second to open the front door and felt the chill evening air in his face. He stood there a while, then turned, picked up the engine again and hefted it outside.

'Look. She's coming!' Jill's voice called.

She joined him at the door, waiting for the car to round the bend by the nuclear power station fence.

There were two people in the car, Alex at the wheel, and Zoë, much smaller, beside her.

The car pulled up, the passenger door opened and Zoë, covered in shiny silver, jumped out and ran towards Bill.

Next thing she was on him, her spindly arms around his neck, sobbing. 'Bill,' she was crying. 'Oh Bill.'

Her clothes were damp and he could smell the salt on her.

'What's on earth's wrong, skinny one?' Bill asked, hugging the girl back.

'There was a dead woman,' said Zoë, talking through her sobs.

Bill looked up at Alex, alarmed.

Alex said, 'There was a body up at Pen Bars. Zoë came across her. She's in shock. It was my fault. I left her alone for a while . . .'

'Washed up on the beach? A drowning?'

'Looks like it.'

Jill threw her arms round Alex. 'I've been trying to get in touch. I got something real important I got to talk to you about.'

Alex untangled herself from Jill's grip and said brusquely, 'God's sake, Jill. I'm sorry. Not now. I don't have time to listen to another of your dating catastrophes. Can't you see Zoë's upset?'

'Oh.' Jill stepped back, mortified. 'Sorry.'

Alex pulled Zoë away and led her back into the car. Jill stood in the middle of the track, watching her. She saw Alex glance back at her in the rear-view mirror before the car turned.

'I'm such a selfish idiot,' wailed Jill.

'You best come back inside,' said Bill. 'She has a lot on her mind, what with work starting tomorrow and now this. I'll make more tea. Maybe you can talk to me about it all instead?' And he took her gently by the arm and led her back inside the cabin.

That evening they talked until it was dark and he told her everything he remembered about Stephen Dowles and the two people Dowles had murdered in 1994, one a small-time drug dealer, the other a woman who had run a local post office in Brenzett. He told her about what it had been like around here then. How the drugs had arrived, first in the massive raves that had gone on all night pumping out music, full of joyful dancing, and then as something much darker that lurked on stairwells and in children's playgrounds, and how from that point on, many of the things that had been good around here had started to go downhill. And they were still talking early next morning, when the sun started to creep back into the sky.

FIVE

Ashford was more building project than police station. The grey 1960s block had been declared unsafe. Instead, Serious Crime had use of three Portakabins while they were waiting for the refurbishment work to finish. Despite the chaos, it felt good to be back here. Alex Cupidi had missed it.

'OK. First things first,' said Toby McAdam. 'Most of you will know Alexandra Cupidi who's back with us after . . . a short break. She'll have a lot of catching up to do, so let her know what you're up to.' McAdam went around the room naming everyone, just in case she had forgotten.

First day back and she was exhausted already, though. Last night, Zoë had cried for hours.

'Where's Jill?' demanded McAdam, realising that she was not in the room.

'I'm sure she'll be here any second,' Alex said. She had not heard from her since seeing her outside Bill's house. She wished she had not been so abrupt with her yesterday evening. She wished too she had not been so irritated that it was Bill her daughter had run to and thrown her arms around. She tried to concentrate. McAdam had moved on to discussing the preliminary autopsy report on the unidentified dead woman who had been found yesterday evening at Dungeness.

'We have serious cause for concern. Cause of death is drowning. However, there is pre-mortem bruising on the face, breasts and shoulders of the victim,' said McAdam. 'They are not caused by sharp objects like being hit by a boat, or rock. The pathologist suggests they are more likely to have been caused in a struggle.'

'She was killed?' someone asked.

'We're going to have to proceed on that assumption,' said McAdam, pinning a photograph of the dead woman's face onto the board.

'Bruising on her face, breasts and shoulders?' Alex said. 'Like someone had been punching her?'

'Very possibly.'

'Anything on the lower body?'

McAdam pulled out another sheet of paper and pinned it to the board. An outline of a body, with pen marks circled on the face, the shoulders and the chest. 'Just a preliminary report, but no. All on her upper body.'

'And nothing from Missing Persons?' asked Alex.

In the photo, the dead woman's eyes were closed. Apart from the brown bruise on her cheek, her skin was pale yellow, like the inside of a cockle shell. 'No reports of a white woman, aged between thirty and forty, being reported missing.' McAdam turned back to Alex. 'The body was discovered by Alex's daughter yesterday at around six p.m.' His voice became less official. 'Is your daughter OK?'

27

'Yes, thank you,' said Alex, though she didn't know whether that was true at all.

McAdam eyed her for a second. 'OK.' He nodded, continued. 'We're treating this death as suspicious, obviously, given the bruising. Our first priority is to simply discover who she is and to understand the circumstances surrounding her death. I've asked the Press Office to circulate her description to see if we can get an ID.'

'What about the person who called it in?' Alex asked.

'A juvenile, the dispatcher believes. Didn't give a name or any other details,' answered McAdam.

'Kids go down there to smoke weed and drink,' suggested Alex. 'Probably one of them.'

'OK. Still no sign of Jill?' asked McAdam, looking at his watch.

Just as he said that, the door banged open. 'Sorry, sir,' mumbled Jill Ferriter, closing it with her behind, bag in one hand, cup of coffee in the other. 'Something came up.'

'Happy you could join us,' McAdam said – and if it was meant as sarcasm, it didn't work. McAdam's voice was always too positive, too chirpy. The first thing Alex noticed was that Jill was wearing the same shirt as she had been yesterday, a little more crumpled.

Jill pulled up a chair next to Alex's and lowered her voice. 'Well? First day back. How are you feeling?'

'Tired.'

'Have it.' Jill caught the envious glance and thrust the coffee cup towards her.

'You sure?'

28

'Go on. I want you to have it.' Jill insisted. 'So, come on then. What's it like being back?'

'I'm fine, obviously.' Alex took the coffee gratefully.

'And Zoë?'

'Still upset. I wasn't sure I should even leave her this morning, but you know – first day. I think part of it was that she's nervous about me coming back. Not surprising, I suppose. We're used to things like that, she's not. Is that the same shirt you were wearing yesterday?' Jill never wore the same shirt two days in a row unless she'd hooked up. 'Were you out on the tiles again last night?'

'God, no! The opposite. I was with Bill. Seriously. Listen, Alex. I'm sorry I ambushed you yesterday when Zoë was upset. That thing I needed to talk to you about, it's kind of sensitive . . .' Her voice trailed off.

Alex waited for Jill to finish the sentence. She had stopped halfway through a thought, staring at the board on which McAdam had pinned the two pictures of the dead woman.

'What was it you wanted to talk to me about, Jill?'

Jill was standing now, walking over towards the wall. She reached up and touched one of the photographs.

'Ah, right. Jill,' McAdam was saying. 'Now you're finally here, I want you to liaise with the Press Office. They're putting her picture out online as we speak. We may also need to find someone who can tell us about the tidal—'

'Mimi Greene,' said Jill quietly.

McAdam stopped what he was saying. 'What?'

'Mimi Greene,' said Jill. She yanked the paper off the wall

and looked at it. 'What happened to her?' She looked around the room.

The Portakabin went quiet.

'How do you know she was called Mimi Greene?' asked McAdam. And everyone was looking at Jill Ferriter, waiting for her to answer.

SIX

'How do I know Mimi Greene? I just do.' Jill Ferriter smoothed her eyebrows. 'Hinge, actually.' Jill looked around. 'What happened?'

Nobody spoke.

'Oh God. Somebody going to tell me?'

Alex stood and reached out a hand towards her.

'I'm afraid she drowned, Jill,' said McAdam. 'You knew her?'

Jill shook her head. 'I can't believe it. That's so awful.' She looked down at the paper in her hand.

'I'm sorry,' said McAdam gently. 'Was she a good friend of yours?'

'No, no. Not at all. That was the thing. I hooked up with an ex of hers. Just last week.'

The room was quiet, everyone listening to her.

'It was a date,' she said, still staring at the image of the dead woman. 'Catastrophe. A guy. It turned out that despite what he'd said to me online, he wasn't actually ex at the time, this woman Mimi was still his girlfriend, and that was a bit of an issue. Guy called Malcolm,' she said bluntly.

31

'Oh my God!' interrupted Alex. 'That story you told me about that date where you . . . That was her?' She looked back at the photograph of the dead woman.

'Bit awkward,' said Jill. 'Claimed he was single at the time, which was a total lie. I don't like them coming to mine so we had gone back to his place in Hythe. Studio flat, you know? Right on West Parade. Quite nice. Sea view. As far as Malcolm knew, this woman was supposed to be away at her mum's, only she come back early.'

'God,' said Alex. 'This was the woman who let herself in halfway through you and him—'

'I wasn't going to tell everyone that,' said Jill.

'Sorry.'

'Yeah, but you're right. Literally halfway through,' said Jill. Again, that nervous finger on her eyebrows.

McAdam's mouth was wide.

'Anyway, Mimi – that was her name – she was nice about it. To me, anyway, not to Malcolm. She was just . . . nice to me. Concerned, you know? Actually told me I should be aiming higher.' Jill stared at the picture. 'I can't believe that. She's dead?'

'Definitely her?' asked McAdam.

Jill nodded. 'Shit. Yeah.' She raised her arm up to her eyes and wiped them with her bare forearm.

There was silence in the Portakabin as she cried.

'It's OK,' she said, turning. 'Go on. Ask me stuff. It's the job, isn't it? Just a bit fucking weird.'

'We'll need her full address,' said McAdam quietly.

'Sorry. Yes.'

'Take your time,' he said gently. 'This must be a shock.'

32

McAdam pulled his phone out of his pocket and called the Press Office. 'Hold that call-out on the dead woman,' he said. 'We've just ID'd her.'

Alex looked around the room. 'Anyone else wondering why this Malcolm hasn't reported her as missing?'

'Exactly,' said McAdam, nodding.

'That's the thing,' said Jill. 'She kicked him out. There and then. She told me she'd deleted his contacts and everything. He probably doesn't even know. Jesus fuck. I'm sorry. It's just a bit of a shock because she seemed like a really cool woman. You know you get that feeling about someone? I really liked her.'

'And what was Malcolm's last name?'

'I never asked,' said Jill miserably.

McAdam, married with kids, ironed shirts and family photos on his desk, seemed flummoxed. 'You went to bed with him?'

'I was drunk.' Her voice was quiet.

'Description?'

'Tall. Thirty-ish. Fair hair. Good-looking. Really nice teeth. A bit like Charlie over there, to be honest.' She pointed to a young constable whom Alex hadn't seen before who was standing in the corner. Alex looked round at the new constable. Right now he looked like he wanted to disappear into the earth beneath him.

'What about phone numbers? You must have his number?' Alex asked.

'We never got that far. We just used the app. I think I probably sent him my number but he never called me on it. He seemed to prefer it that way.'

Alex suddenly felt a lot older than her friend. 'And you never got a clue about where he lived?'

'I thought he lived in that apartment in Hythe.'

'Tattoos? Scars?'

'Be honest, I wasn't paying attention to that.'

Someone tittered and McAdam turned and glared and there was silence again. Then McAdam turned back to Jill. 'Right. Our friend and colleague Jill Ferriter is now a witness in this investigation, OK?' He looked around. 'You understand what that means?'

Alex did. She dug in her huge shoulder bag for a tissue to pass to her colleague, but Jill had already found one herself.

McAdam looked around the room. 'Once this meeting is finished and she has been formally interviewed, Jill is going to be excluded from being part of this investigation.'

'Christ,' muttered Jill. 'Jesus bloody Christ.'

'I'll ask for her to be reassigned to work elsewhere. I don't want any members of our investigating team to be in contact with her now, for obvious reasons.'

'Jesus.' Jill was shaking her head. 'I don't actually believe this.'

'It's vital to protect the integrity of the investigation. Given the bruising on the victim's body, we are proceeding on the assumption that this is an unlawful killing. Right now, the main person of interest is her boyfriend . . .' He looked over at Jill.

'Malcolm,' Jill said again.

'A man who Jill has had –' McAdam paused and looked down at his shoes – 'close relations with.'

'I'm the fucking idiot, aren't I?' Jill whispered.

'So we are going to have to exercise extreme caution. Under no circumstances do I want anyone in this team contacting Constable Ferriter. Do you understand? If for any reason you do meet her, socially or at work, there must be no discussion at all of this case.' He reached out and took the photo from Jill. 'We have to treat this as murder. Obviously we need to find this person, Malcolm. However, a word of caution. At this stage we keep our suspicions strictly to ourselves. We don't want the public and the press jumping to conclusions that will prejudice this enquiry. Understood?'

'OK.' There were nods. 'Yes, boss,' said one officer.

Last year, somewhere in Lancashire, a woman had drowned accidentally in a river. Her body had not been found for weeks. Fuelled by contradictory statements from the local force, the true crime social media world had speculated that the woman had been murdered by her husband. The press had gone crazy. Events had spun out of control. Officers had ended up losing their jobs as a result. DI McAdam was a cautious man. He would not want a repeat of that scenario.

McAdam turned to Jill, still sitting at her desk, tissue in one hand. 'Do you have any reason to think why this man, Malcolm, might wish this woman . . .'

'Mimi Greene,' Jill supplied the name.

'. . . Ms Greene any harm?'

'I don't know,' Jill said, still whispering. 'I barely know him.'

'Do you have a photograph of him?' McAdam asked.

'Just a screenshot of his profile picture. It's not bad though.'

'Mail it to Alex.'

Jill nodded.

'Thanks, Jill,' he said. He paused. 'That will be all.'

She looked around, puzzled. 'So? You want me to go? Now?'

'We need to recuse you from the investigation,' said McAdam.

'Go home. Someone will be in touch with you to arrange a formal interview and to assign you to other duties.'

Jill stood, awkwardly, knowing all eyes were on her. 'Fuck this,' she said.

The room was oddly silent, so Alex stepped forward and gave her a hug. 'Are you OK?' she asked.

McAdam stepped forward and said, 'Look. I know you two in particular are friends, but maybe it would be better if you didn't speak to each other for a few days.'

Jill looked shocked. 'But . . .'

'I need Alex to lead on this one, Jill. If Mimi Greene was killed by Malcolm, a man who you had a sexual relationship with, there can be no suggestion at all that you have had any part in the investigation. If he is our man, his defence would be able to argue that you were trying to get your own back on him by putting him in the frame. You do understand that, don't you? Hopefully, it's just for a few days. But don't phone each other. No messages. We need total radio silence.'

Alex watched her friend silently pack up her bag, unplug her phone charger.

Outside on the concrete step, Alex held Jill's hand and said, 'Are you going to be OK?'

Jill's eye make-up was smudged. 'I feel like I'm being punished for shagging around. Everybody thinks I'm a liability. I'm such a bloody loser.'

'It's not that. It's just procedure.'

Jill nodded. 'Yeah. Right. Do you think I had sex with a murderer, Alex? Right now, that would be absolutely bloody rosy.'

'We don't know anything yet.'

'Maybe I'll take some leave. I got some owed. I don't think I can bear being around while everyone laughs behind my back.'

'They won't be laughing behind your back, I promise.' They stood there on the step together for a few seconds. Jill didn't make a move. 'Right then. I better go. Lots to do,' said Alex.

'Course you bloody have.' Jill nodded and pulled her hand away. 'I get it.'

'By the way, what was it you wanted to talk to me about?'

Jill paused, then seemed to make up her mind about something. 'Nothing, actually,' she said. 'Nothing at all.'

SEVEN

Alex sat behind the wheel, with the constable she had never worked with before at her side. Charlie Reed was the good-looking young PC Jill had said looked like Malcolm. It was a dull half-hour drive from the station to Hythe, to the address Jill had given them. She would have preferred to have gone out with Jill but as McAdam had underlined, Jill was now a witness. She couldn't be part of the investigation.

Charlie took silence as something to be filled. On the short drive, he had already told her how he liked hang-gliding, running and tennis, and that he had recently bought a new gas grill for the garden of the house in Folkestone that he shared with his brother and how he was looking forward to using it if the weather kept improving. 'That Jill Ferriter,' he said now. 'She's a bit . . .'

Alex stayed quiet.

'I mean. Sleeping with some guy in his girlfriend's flat. It's not very safe behaviour, is it?'

'Safe behaviour?' Alex couldn't help herself responding.

'Going back to someone's flat when you're drunk – someone you just met on a dating app. It's a bit much, isn't it?'

Alex clamped her mouth shut.

'So, you came down from the Met, I heard,' said Charlie finally, when the last conversation had gone nowhere. 'Bet you found all this a bit . . .'

'Different doesn't even begin to cover it,' said Alex.

They had pulled up in front of a small block of flats on the seafront. An agent from the management company was outside with a bunch of keys.

They suited up in the hallway outside the second-floor apartment, added overshoes and gloves, and when they were ready, the man turned the key and let them in. 'Look after my stuff, will you?' Alex asked the man, handing him her orange shoulder bag.

The apartment was small and tidy, with the exception of the bed, which was not made, and a half-drunk cup of tea on the small kitchen table next to an open laptop. A row of novels were stacked on the shelf above the TV. There were a few literary prizewinners' names she recognised, a couple of books about art, a few romances, a light smattering of poetry and a weighty-looking volume of local myths and legends.

'Look for anything that might give us a clue to who Malcolm was,' she said.

The walls were covered in large photographs, printed on canvas, not of people, but of the sea in all its moods, some with it wild, froth flying off the top of the waves, others taken in mornings when the winter sun rose over the Channel. There was only one photo of Mimi herself, standing on a snow-covered beach. She was dressed in a robe, one of the ones sea swimmers wore; her legs below it were bare and her skin glistened with water, as if she had just emerged from the sea. There was a big friendly smile on her face.

'The computer's password protected,' called Charlie, who had been going through her desk. 'I can't find an address book or anything with Malcolm's name in it,' said Charlie.

Alex was going through her cupboards and drawers. 'She's wearing a dryrobe in the photo. It's missing.'

'So maybe she left it on a beach somewhere?'

'Exactly.'

Alex bagged up an electric toothbrush she found in the bathroom and a hairbrush she found on the woman's bedside table. Jill had identified the dead woman as Mimi Greene, but the surest way to confirm that was Mimi Greene's DNA.

'Any post?' Alex called out from the bedroom.

'Something from a pension company. A couple of bills. Nothing personal.'

She stuck her head out of the bedroom door. 'What about anything addressed to Malcolm, the ex-boyfriend?'

'Nope.'

'Any sign of a phone?' Alex called out from the bedroom.

'Haven't found one.'

'Car keys?'

'No. She didn't drive, apparently.'

She hadn't found anything of particular interest, either. When she returned to the living room, she noticed Charlie looking out of the window at a woman in a blue bikini. She was slim, but curvy; the kind of woman some men glanced at for a little too long.

'Well?' she asked.

'Sorry. Nothing much,' he said.

'I meant her.' She pointed out of the window.

'I was just . . .'

'Making very sure she's behaving safely, I know.'

'What?' he said.

'Stay here,' she ordered him. 'Don't touch anything until I'm back.' Picking up her bag from the letting agent, she walked down the stairs and out onto the street, scrambling over a low wall to get onto the beach.

The woman was drying her hair with a towel, her skin pale. She looked up, startled, as Alex marched towards her. 'Do you swim here often?'

'Not really. My first of the year.' She leaned her head on one side and shook it, trying to dislodge water from her ear.

Alex delved into her shoulder bag and pulled out her wallet. 'I'm a police officer,' she said. 'Do you know the woman who lives in that flat there?' She turned and pointed towards the window where Charlie was still standing.

The woman followed her finger, then frowned. 'Why?'

'She swam from this beach. In her thirties, dark hair, quite athletic-looking.'

The woman pulled her towel tight around her, starting to shiver. 'Maybe. Don't think so.' The light on the sea was special today. The shine on the ripples of water made the water look deceptively inviting. 'I'm not a regular. Water's still

41

bloody freezing. I'm dying here. Mind if I carry on getting dressed?'

Alex looked away as the woman sat back down on the pebbles, trying to tug jeans up her wet legs. 'I'm not that brave, but there's a gang of women who do. Coven, I should say. You see them out here in all weathers pretty much every day. I've seen them when there's mammoth waves and everything.'

Alex was gazing north, towards the grey bulk of the power station. 'You don't know how I can find any of them, do you?'

'They swim a bit further up the beach by Marine Parade.' She pointed southwards. 'First thing in the morning, mostly. Sunrise. Crazy early. Sometimes in the evenings. Rain or shine. Makes me exhausted just to watch them.'

'Sunrise, you say?'

'Yeah. It can be beautiful here some winter mornings, sun coming up, but Jesus. Hardcore. What's the fun in that? Why are you asking all this?'

Alex looked away. 'Just a routine enquiry about a possible missing person.'

Back at the car, driving back to the office, Charlie said, 'I was being a knob, talking about Jill Ferriter, wasn't I?'

'Yes, Charlie, you were.'

'When I'm nervous I talk a lot,' he said. 'That's all. I don't mean anything.'

'So I make you nervous? That's good,' she said, and pulled out onto the M20, heading back to the station.

EIGHT

That night, on her way to bed, Alex saw the light under her daughter's door and knocked.

'Yes?' Zoë's voice was curt.

'I just wanted to ask if you were OK.'

No answer.

'Sorry I haven't seen you all day. Busy first day back.'

There was a pause. 'I'm fine,' Zoë said eventually.

'Because I know it must have been pretty awful for you yesterday.'

'I'm fine, Mum.'

Alex stood her ground outside the door. 'What did you do then, today?'

'Bill came round.'

'That's nice.' She waited for her daughter to say more. She didn't. 'Well then. I'm going to bed.'

'It's only ten o'clock,' Zoë said.

Alex looked at her watch. Zoë was right. It was only a few

43

minutes after ten o'clock. One day back at work and she was absolutely shattered.

Alex's alarm went off at four in the morning. She rubbed her eyes and forced herself awake.

In the kitchen, she made herself a flask of strong coffee, dressed, then jumped in the Saab. Rolling past Bill's cottage, the sky was already turning purple. Bill's light was on; he, too, awake early, for some reason.

The coast road was empty. She pulled up close to Mimi Greene's flat shortly after quarter to five, wandered up to the promenade with her coffee and found a bench. The stars of the Great Bear were fading ahead of her.

She hoped Jill was OK. Alex was used to a constant stream of messages from Jill appearing on her phone, chatter about her colleagues, her latest crushes, comments on the news headlines, talk about holiday destinations, anything at all. Since yesterday morning, she had been silent. It felt odd. She missed her. She checked again to make sure, wondered if there was any harm in just sending her a message to ask if she was OK, but decided against it.

The early morning chill hung in the air. She took the coffee from her shoulder bag and filled a cup, hunching to keep warm. The seawater was still. The ripples that nibbled the steep shingle were barely waves.

Sometime after five, a crack of sunlight broke over the hills at Sandgate, and just as it did so, three women appeared, all dressed in swimming robes: one thin with grey close-cropped hair, one tall with dark hair, and the third shorter, rounder, with braided black hair. Alex watched them for a minute as they crossed the promenade and then dropped the few belongings they had with them onto the stones. They descended the deep slope, then discarded their robes. The tall one was balancing with poise on her left leg, pulling the other up behind to stretch her quads. The youngest of the three was jumping up and down on the spot, warming herself.

Alex waited and watched.

They chattered in low voices, inaudible at this distance.

The first into the water was the thin, dark-haired woman. In this light, it was hard to make out any faces. She walked a few steps, then dived in. The others followed her. They swam out, away from the shore, so that soon all Alex could see were black heads against black water. As they swam, the sun rose over the horizon and she began to be able to make out faces.

All three faced the rising sun for a little while, then all set off swimming again, as if on a signal. A couple were strong swimmers, slicing through the cold water, front crawl.

They swam for about ten minutes before the first of them turned and headed in. The others followed.

Alex approached as they were putting on their dryrobes. The woman with grey hair looked up, frowned. 'I'm a police officer,' said Alex. 'Do you mind if I ask you a few questions?'

The youngest was sitting on the stones, tugging off her swimming shoes. 'Can we help you?' she asked, puzzled.

The tall one who had been doing stretches stepped forward. 'Is there a problem?'

'Not at all. I was just wondering if any of you knew a woman called Mimi Greene?'

The youngest woman blurted, 'I *knew* there was something wrong. I *knew* it.'

'Why are you asking about Mimi?' asked the grey-haired woman.

'You were friends?'

They all nodded.

'I'm afraid there's been a body found on Dungeness. We're pretty sure it's Mimi's.'

At once, the youngest woman burst into tears. 'I knew it was her. They said they had found a body. I knew it was.'

All three looked shocked. The other two knelt next to the crying swimmer and put their arms around her.

'Can I ask when you last saw Mimi?'

'Three days ago,' said the grey-haired one. 'We were hoping she would be here this morning,' she said. 'She drowned? I don't understand. It's nuts.'

'So Mimi Green swam regularly with you?' asked Alex.

'If her shifts coincided. Do you know what happened?'

'Were you worried when she didn't appear?'

The older two women seemed to looked at each other, shocked, as if they realised now that they should have been worried, until the tall one said, 'Mimi worked shifts. A few days on and a few days off. We were hoping that this was just her having to change her rota unexpectedly for a few days.'

Alex nodded and started to take their names and details.

'You said, "It's nuts."' Alex addressed the grey-haired woman – Isobel. 'Why did you say that?'

'Well . . . because she drowned,' Isobel answered. 'The idea is ridiculous.'

'I don't understand it,' said the smaller woman, whose name was Rose. 'Mimi was a strong swimmer.' She wiped wet eyes with the back of her hand.

'She swam so far out sometimes though,' said the third. 'Maybe she just got swept out.'

'And your name is?'

'Kimaya.' The woman introduced herself formally, holding out a slim wrist to shake. Kimaya had smooth brown skin and striking pale eyes. She could be a model, thought Alex.

'So Mimi swam on her own sometimes?' Alex asked.

'Yes. We all do. She'd swim with us when she could,' Kimaya answered. 'Other times she went out on her own, you know, if we weren't around. She loved water.'

'We weren't there for her,' wailed Rose.

'You'll forgive us,' said Isobel, who seemed to feel it was her role to speak for them all. 'This is a shock.'

'And you swim in the mornings?'

'It depends on the tides and the weather,' said Isobel. 'I always try to swim with the rising sun, but it's not ideal for everyone. Sometimes the evenings are better.'

'Isobel organises us,' said Kimaya. 'She puts out the call and we come.'

Over the next twenty minutes, as they dressed and took sips from flasks, Alex took details, watched them absorb the shock of the news, thanked them and said she would be in touch.

Alex's car was parked about fifty metres away, so she strolled down towards it. The sun was up now, sparkling on the sea. She sat in the driving seat for a while, watching the morning sky change to blue.

The indicator lights of the car in front of her flashed. She looked up to see Kimaya opening the door of one of those new electric Audis.

Kimaya was about to get in when she spotted Alex and closed the door again.

Alex wound down her window.

'You think something's wrong, don't you?' said the swimmer. 'Otherwise you wouldn't have come here.'

'Just due diligence, really,' Alex fudged. Kimaya seemed in no hurry to leave, so she asked, 'Tell me, how long have you been swimming together?'

'Four years. No – five. We got together before lockdown and somehow lockdown kind of really cemented us together. You know . . . being in the outdoors after being cooped up for so long. Rose is more recent. She just joined a few months ago. Isobel inspired us. She's kind of our guru,' Kimaya said earnestly. 'You do know who she is, don't you?'

'Should I?'

'Isobel van Wees? The poet.'

Alex looked at Kimaya blankly.

NINE

Charlie marched up to the door with her.

Alex paused. 'Actually, I think I'll do this on my own, Charlie,' she said.

'Oh. Right.' He looked crestfallen. 'I'll be in the car, then.' She watched him retreat down the pavement, then pressed the doorbell. It was a pretty old cottage, one of a symmetrical pair that had been built at some time in the nineteenth century, with arched brick windows and a grey front door, close to the sea end of the street.

A huge man answered almost at once, filling the door frame. 'And you are?' he demanded.

'Detective Sergeant Alexandra Cupidi. Is Isobel van Wees in?'

He was well over six foot tall. Even Alex, gangly as she was, felt small next to him. 'It's about the poor woman from her swimmers' group, isn't it?'

'May I talk to Isobel?' she asked.

He stood to one side. 'She's working, but I suppose you best come in.'

49

He led them down a dark panelled corridor to a bright kitchen dining room. At the back, a large glass room had been added to the house. Isobel van Wees was sitting in a black office chair at a pine dining table, piles of books spread out on the table in front of her. She was dressed in loose cottons that hid her skinny frame.

'Ah,' she said. 'You're back. I was trying to write something about poor Mimi now. Victor, put the kettle on.'

'What are you writing?' asked Alex.

'A meditation. In memory of poor Mimi. We women who live by the shore and long for the sea,' said Isobel. 'Mimi was one of those. I think women have a strange and profound attraction to the sea. Or to the coast, to be precise. Men are attracted to the sea, women to the coast. Men try to conquer the sea in ships. Women wait by the shore. Mimi loved the coast and the waves. It consumed her in more ways than one.'

The kitchen was cluttered and lived-in. At the right end of the room, hanging from a dark wall, was a print of the coast around Folkestone. The land was the pale yellow of summer wheat, the sea blue by the coast, then white where the water became deeper. The sea was covered in carefully etched lines and numbers. There was also a gaudy nineteenth-century print of the Virgin Mary framed in dark walnut wood. Mary was dressed in white, standing on a churning sea, waves breaking against her legs. She gazed upwards towards a light in the sky that spelled out the words 'STELLA MARIS': *star of the sea*.

'May I call you Isobel?' asked Alex, still standing.

'What can I do to help?'

'We're trying to establish the circumstances surrounding Ms Greene's death.'

There was a second's silence, broken by a loud yelp.

Alex looked round to see Victor holding up his right hand. It was dripping blood.

'Fuck,' he said. 'Cut myself.' And he stood there, hand raised, blood dripping down his palm, down his wrist, onto the tiled kitchen floor. 'Slicing a lemon. Knife slipped.'

Alex was the first to react. She moved across the room, took his hand and raised it above his head to lessen blood flow, then pulled a piece of kitchen roll from the roller and wrapped it around the wound while Isobel watched.

'I thought you said she drowned,' said Isobel, still sitting at her desk, her face white.

'She did,' said Alex, clutching Victor's arm. 'But we still need to try and understand the circumstances.'

Isobel stared at her for what seemed a very long time. 'You mean, you think there is a prospect that someone killed her?'

'It's just routine.' Alex ducked the question.

'My God. The thought.'

Victor wiped his eyes with the forearm of his injured hand. 'Bad enough she's dead,' he said.

'Can we talk about when you last saw her?' Alex addressed Isobel.

'We already discussed this when you met us on the beach . . .'

'In detail this time.'

Isobel frowned, then reached among the pile of books and found a black desk diary. After a few seconds looking through it, she pointed at a page. 'As we said, we swam together on Friday evening. Around 6.15.'

'How was she?'

51

Isobel thought for a second. 'Subdued, I would say. She had been having some issues with her boyfriend, she said. They had broken up.'

'She talked about that?'

'Not much. She told us that he had brought another woman to her flat and that she had found him out and asked him to leave. She seemed very matter-of-fact about it.'

'Malcolm.'

'Yes. That was it. I don't think it was ever much of a relationship. I don't want to judge her, but I think the whole thing was a mistake.'

Alex waited for her to elaborate, but she didn't. 'What else?'

Isobel peered at her handwriting. 'There was a low tide. One point seven metres.'

'You keep a record of every swim?'

'I make notes and observations. There had been a storm the week before and the seawater was still quite milky. It was a calm day, much like this morning. We swam for about twenty minutes. The water was cold but it was beautiful.'

'Milky, you said?'

'There is chalk in the water here, from the white cliffs. It means that the light on the shore here tells a very different story from the light on other places. You must have noticed. Do you live around here, Sergeant?'

'I live on Dungeness.'

'Another woman who lives by the sea,' said Isobel. 'We have an inhabitant of Nanny Goat Island with us, Victor.'

'Sorry?' Alex interjected.

'The original inhabitants of Dungeness had no running water

or gas and most of them kept goats for the milk,' explained Isobel. 'Hence the name. Victor is big on local history. He is writing a novel based around the wrecking of the Spanish galleon the *Alfresia*.'

'You know that there were wreckers on Dungeness in the seventeenth century?' Victor announced, clutching kitchen roll on his wounded thumb. 'In the 1630s they lured a Spanish ship onto the ness, wrecked it, stole the cargo and murdered every one of the survivors who made it to shore. Slaughtered them. It was brutal. The Pilot is built from timbers from the wreck.'

It was the pub Alex went to on evenings when she was disinclined to cook. She tried to imagine it being constructed by bloodthirsty locals. 'That will need a plaster,' Alex told him.

'I'm afraid we don't have milk,' Victor announced. 'That's why I was cutting the lemon. For the tea.'

'Do you swim too, Mr van Wees?'

'Harris. My wife is van Wees. We kept our own names. Do I swim? Only when the weather is much warmer than it is now.'

'Men are less good with pain,' said Isobel drily. 'How is your thumb, my love?'

Victor finished cutting the lemon and brought cups of tea to the table, thumb still wrapped in paper. It was blotched with red. 'I'll make myself scarce,' he said, pulling open the glass door at the rear of the kitchen. He closed it behind him and disappeared up a narrow garden path.

'He has a writing shed,' explained Isobel. 'I bought it for him for his fiftieth birthday. It was a hit. Now he seems to spend most of his life in there.'

Alex could just see it behind the buddleia. A square,

modern-looking thing clad in red cedar. 'Is it OK if I talk to you some more about Mimi?' she asked. 'We need to try and discover a little about what she was like.'

'Was.' Isobel looked sad. 'Your use of the past tense. This is all just so shocking. This kind of thing doesn't happen in our community.'

'I don't suppose it does,' said Alex.

'I'm trying to adjust. To get used to the idea that Mimi isn't here.'

'You swam regularly with her? And Kimaya and Rose did, as well?'

'Yes. We meet whenever time and tide allow. We swim all year round together, the four of us.' Isobel dropped a slice of lemon in her tea and shook her head. 'Mimi was the kind of person it was impossible not to like. She shone niceness. Too nice for her own good. I've never met anybody who didn't warm to her. That's why her death is so terrible.'

'Too nice for her own good. What do you mean by that?'

'Please don't read too much into that.'

'Did men take advantage of her?'

'Oh. You mean Malcolm? I don't think he took advantage of her at all. She knew exactly what she was doing with him.'

'Really?'

'He was a very good-looking boy, and apparently very good in bed,' she said, in the way a farmer might talk about a bull, 'but it was never going to last.'

Alex looked around. There were hand-thrown pots on the shelves and the fridge was covered in the kind of postcards you buy in art galleries.

'You're a poet, I understand,' said Alex. 'What do you write about?'

She tilted her head back a little. 'That's a strange question to ask.'

'I'm sorry. I don't often ask poets questions,' said Alex.

There was something very precise about Isobel. She seemed to pause a little moment, weighing her words before she spoke. 'Are you questioning me now? Is there any reason why you need to ask me that?'

'Just curiosity. I'm just trying to learn a bit about who Ms Greene was by finding out who her friends were.'

'By asking me about poetry?'

Alex said, 'By conversing with you. Informally.'

Isobel raised her eyebrows. 'Very well. A critic once described my poetry as "neo-folkloric mystical feminism", if that helps.'

'Not in the slightest,' said Alex.

'I'm with you there,' said Isobel. She broke into a small grin.

'Did you ever meet Malcolm?'

She peered over her books at Alex. 'Why are you so interested in Malcolm?' She divided his name into two very distinct syllables.

'We need to find him,' said Alex. 'Did you know him?'

Isobel scowled. 'Not really. He moved in on her, quite literally. They had been together a week and he moved his underwear in. She tolerated him for as long as she wanted a nice-looking man in her bed.'

'He's no longer at the flat. We've been there.'

'As I said, the night before we last met, Mimi came home and found Malcolm in bed with some awful woman. She said

55

she had told him to get out and that was that. Easy come, easy go.'

Alex held her tongue. 'You weren't curious about the details?'

Isobel looked disapproving. 'Of course not. It was her business, not ours.'

'Do you know where we can find him?'

'Why do you need to find him?' She was becoming suspicious now. 'As I said, she had thrown him out.'

'Whether the relationship was finished or not, we have a duty to try and inform him. Did you know him?'

'Not really. He never joined us on the beach. I don't think Mimi encouraged him. She knew I disapproved.'

'You disapproved?'

'He was no match for her intellectually. Or even spiritually.'

Alex took a sip of the tea out of politeness. 'Did she seem different over the last few weeks? Did she seem preoccupied by anything? Worried about something, perhaps?'

Isobel was not an idiot. 'What are you suggesting?' she asked.

'It would be useful to know her state of mind. You said she was subdued.'

Isobel van Wees looked shocked. 'Are you concerned that this might have been a suicide?'

She leaned in to examine Isobel closely. 'I'm sorry if that's upsetting.'

'It's not upsetting. It's just extremely improbable. She wasn't that kind of woman.'

Alex nodded. 'OK.'

'But now you say it, there was definitely something on her

56

mind,' said Isobel. 'Over the last two weeks or so, she was quieter than usual. I hadn't really thought about that until now.'

'Perhaps it was related to some kind of issues with her boy-friend?'

Isobel wrinkled her nose. 'Maybe. She missed a couple of sessions in the last couple of weeks. But that was before she kicked the leather-headed boy out of her life.' Isobel lowered her head. 'I wish I had asked her what was wrong, now you mention it. Sometimes I'm so wrapped up in my work.'

'You have no idea where we can find him?'

'I have no interest in him at all,' she said.

'All I have is "Malcolm". Do you have a last name?'

'No. Like I said, I barely knew him.'

At the door, after Alex had given her a card with her contact details on it, Isobel took Alex's hand. 'I am grateful for your questions, even if I don't sound it. I feel I let her down somehow. You will keep me up to date with what you find, won't you?'

Alex didn't like to make promises. 'I will try.'

Isobel held the door open for her. 'By the way, do you swim?'

'Me? Yes. I do.'

'Good,' said Isobel with a smile. 'I would very much like you to join us one day. You will enjoy it. I promise.'

Charlie was outside, waiting in the car.

Alex opened the passenger door, sat down, pulled out her notebook and started to jot down details. 'Anything useful?' Charlie asked keenly.

She held her finger to her lips. She didn't want to be inter-rupted until she'd completed her notes. He sat in awkward silence. After five minutes, she put her pen back into the bag. 'You ever heard of the Pilot Inn in Dungeness?' she asked.

'Yeah. It's OK.'

'Did you know it was built from timbers from a seventeenth-century shipwreck?'

'Oh yeah,' said Charlie, looking out of the window. 'I knew that.'

TEN

Malcolm was a puzzle.

Nobody seemed to know his last name.

'Look,' said Charlie, holding up his phone at his office desk. 'I can't find him anywhere on Hinge.'

'What do you mean?' asked Alex, halfway through a late lunch of an egg salad sandwich from Pret.

'I invented a couple of profiles to try and see if I could find him. One is me, Charlie, the other was a woman, Charlene. Been swiping for the last twenty minutes but he doesn't come up.'

'You invented profiles?'

'Well . . . yeah.'

'That's covert surveillance,' said Alex. 'What do they teach you these days? You know you're not actually allowed to do that?'

Charlie looked horrified. 'Serious?'

'Turns out you don't know everything, then. I won't tell if you won't. Just don't log on again, OK?'

'I didn't realise,' he said. 'I was just trying to help.'

Alex knocked on McAdam's door. 'We need to get in touch with Jill,' she said. 'She was linked up with him through the dating app. I just realised we need to check if his profile's still active. She's the quickest way we can do that.'

McAdam nodded. 'Why not? Get Charlie to do it though.'

'Right.' Alex had to admit it made sense, even if she didn't like it. She and Jill were friends. Right now they had to keep everything as clean as they could.

Instead, she listened as Charlie called her up. 'No. We've not made any progress. No idea what his last name is or where he lives. Yes. She's fine. She's sitting right next to me. Listen . . . We're trying to see if Malcolm is still active on Hinge. Can you check for us?'

Alex watched as he waited, doodling on his notepad.

'Yeah. Thought so,' he said triumphantly.

Alex could hear the bubbling of her voice, tiny, impossible to make out.

'Really? OK. I'll make a note of that,' said Charlie, and then he put down the phone and turned to her. 'Turns out that yes, Malcolm deleted his profile, which explains why I couldn't find him.'

'When?'

'She wouldn't have been able to tell that – just that it's gone. You seriously think he was the one who killed her?'

'What does that mean, deleting your profile?'

'Could mean anything. Could mean he's found the woman of his dreams. Could mean he's figured out we're looking for him. Could mean that he knows he's done something bad. You can request the records from the company that run the app, but it'll probably take for ever.'

Alex thought for a while, then asked, 'How did she sound?'

'What do you mean?'

'Was she upset? Did she sound relaxed?'

'Don't know, really,' said Charlie. 'Just normal, I guess.'

Alex turned back to her work, frustrated. 'Wait. What was that you said you needed to make a note of?'

Chris looked back at his notepad. 'Oh yeah. She said she had forgotten something when she was interviewed. She remembered he had a scab on his palm. And when she asked him what it was, he told her that a chisel had slipped.'

'A chisel?'

'Yeah. Sorry. Should have mentioned that, shouldn't I?'

'Yes. So he might be a carpenter?'

'I suppose so, actually,' said Charlie brightly.

Rose lived in an ugly new-build flat in a four-storey block on the east side of town, a little way back from the seafront. Dark streaks were already showing on the white render. The sea was not kind to buildings.

Alex rang the bell, once, then a second time. Rose took an age to answer.

'Sorry,' she called through the intercom. 'Just got back from work. I was changing into something more human.'

On the phone, Rose had told her she worked for an accountancy firm in Folkestone. She had only started there recently. Would it be OK if they talked after work? Alex had arranged to visit on her way back to Dungeness.

'Isobel says you were asking funny questions,' Rose said, opening the upstairs door.

'It's just routine,' said Alex again, though nothing ever was. The place was plain and small. She walked into a square living room, a single window looking northwards, towards Folkestone and a narrow glimpse of the sea.

'It's all just horrible,' said Rose. 'I keep crying, all the time.'

Apart from a small shrine of family photographs on a shelf, there was little that felt very personal, apart from a row of books tucked onto a windowsill and an unhealthy-looking weeping fig plant.

'Were you close?'

'Was I close?' Rose gave a shy smile. Alex pulled out a dining chair and sat at it. Rose settled on the sofa opposite the window that faced the sea. 'I don't know. I saw a lot of Mimi. She was very kind to me. She's a health worker – was a health worker – and looked after me when I was down.'

'In what sense, down?'

Rose seemed unsettled by the directness of Alex's question. 'I have periods when I am quite down. I've had depression most of my life. I lost my job in London before Christmas so ran away here. Mimi works for the wellbeing charity I was referred to. She has experience dealing with mental health issues. Had. It was her who suggested I come swimming in the first place.'

'Did it help?'

'Yes. I mean, I don't know if it's all the swimming or just the routine and the company, but I've certainly had to resort to medication much less since I started.' She smiled shyly, then the smile disappeared. 'It's just so horrible to think she's gone. She was a very good woman.' Her crying was quiet, self-contained, but oddly unapologetic.

'Was Mimi ever depressed herself?'

'Mimi?' Rose's hand flew to her mouth. 'God. Why would you ask that? You don't think she deliberately did this to herself, do you?'

'We don't know anything at all, that's why I'm here.'

'She was way too well balanced for anything like that.' She considered. Shook her head again. 'No. She wouldn't. Would she?'

'How did she seem these last few weeks?'

'That's the thing. There was something off about Mimi – the last three or four weeks.'

It was what Isobel had said. 'She acted differently in some kind of way?'

'For a start, she'd missed a couple of swimming sessions, which wasn't like her. And she seemed a bit frosty, you know?' Hand in front of mouth again. 'God. That's an awful thing to say about her. Not frosty. Just distant.'

'What do you mean?'

Rose seemed to go through agonies trying to express herself. 'It was probably me, not her. I mean, I can be a bit needy sometimes. I just wanted to talk to her, because she could always say the right thing when I was feeling down, but recently it felt like she was pushing me away.' She started weeping quietly. 'I think I was just trying too hard to be close to her. I was a bit in love with her, to be honest.' She squirmed in her chair. 'She probably found it too much.'

'You think she was avoiding you?'

'Maybe that's why she went swimming on her own. That would be awful, wouldn't it? Like it's my fault there was no one there to help her.'

63

Alex leaned forward, reached out a hand and laid it gently on Rose's knee. 'None of this is your fault, Rose.'

Rose gave an uncertain grin. 'Sorry. I have issues.'

'What about Malcolm? Do you think her behaviour had anything to do with their relationship?'

'Malcolm?'

'He cheated on her.'

Rose said, 'I doubt that had much to do with it. It wasn't anything big. She once told me that he was gorgeous, but not a very good person. I don't think she expected him to stick around. Or wanted him to, really.'

'They were living together,' objected Alex.

Rose wrinkled her nose. 'He moved in. She never asked him. He wasn't there much anyway. I think he had another place of his own. You know she came back one night last week and found him with a woman in her bed?'

'Yes,' said Alex quietly. 'I did know that.'

Rose scrunched up her eyes and dried them with a tissue. 'He was an idiot to do that to her.'

'Would you know any way we can get in touch with her boyfriend? Ex-boyfriend, in fact?'

Rose looked horrified. 'You don't think he was to blame, do you?'

'It's just we have no idea where he is or whether he's even aware of what's happened.'

'I didn't like him much.'

Alex was getting nowhere. 'I believe he may have been a carpenter or a joiner. Did he ever say who he was working for?'

'That's right. I think that's how they met. He came to put up some shelves for her. But no . . . I have no idea.'

So at least she now knew he was a carpenter, or a builder of some kind. Alex rose from her chair to stand next to her, looking out of the window. 'Nice view,' said Alex.

Standing there, Alex noticed that one of the books propped on the windowsill was a slim volume of poetry.

She picked it up. It was a book called *Kalypso* by Isobel van Wees. She picked it up. 'Is it any good?'

'I think she's a genius. The poems are amazing.'

'Really?' said Alex. When he was drunk, her father had shyly recited Yeats and MacNeice from memory, but Alex had never had the patience for poetry.

She turned the book over. On the back cover, the black-and-white author photo of Isobel showed her standing on a beach. With a shock, Alex realised she recognised exactly where she was standing. Behind her was the gloomy rectangle of the lookout station at Pen Bars. She was standing almost exactly where Zoë had discovered Mimi Greene's body.

ELEVEN

Thursday was Alex Cupidi's fourth day back at work. Malcolm was no longer a particularly common name, so it shouldn't have been that hard to find Mimi Greene's ex, but Alex wasn't getting anywhere. It was driving her nuts.

Google didn't help. There was a Malcolm Ashe, cabinet maker, but he turned out to be in his sixties; a building company called Malcolm and Sons in Rye (strike two, because that was a surname); and a bespoke carpenter called Malcolm Soutar who lived in Margate, but when she called, he said he had been married twenty years and had never heard of Hinge. Their Malcolm was not old enough to have been married for twenty years.

Beyond that, nobody.

Alex had already set her staff the task of calling up building contractors in the area, but that had turned up a blank too. No one seemed to know anyone called Malcolm.

'I mean. How many people are actually called Malcolm these days?' Charlie whined. 'It's one of those names. Like Nigel.'

'Sooner or later, we're going to have to share this with the public, you know?' Alex told McAdam. 'They could help us find him.'

McAdam looked uncomfortable. It had been his decision to proceed cautiously, not to release Malcolm's name to the public. 'I know.'

She was going to press the point, but her phone went. She answered it: 'Detective Sergeant Alex Cupidi.'

'Kimaya Boyes,' said a woman's voice. 'You called me. Left a message.' Kimaya's voice was low and quiet. 'It's shaken us up, you know. The idea of her drowning. It seems so wrong. All of us love the sea.'

'I'm sure it has. I would like to talk with you about Mimi – what you knew of her. Is there a time that's convenient?'

'Isobel said you're a swimmer. Listen. It's high tide tonight around six. Why don't you come out with us?'

'Me?' said Alex. 'Swim?'

'Sure. You'd love it.'

'Was this Isobel's idea?'

Kimaya laughed. 'Of course it was. She put me up to it. The water's still cold but it's starting to warm up. It only hurts a little this time of year.'

Alex thought about it for a second. 'Six, you said?'

After the call, Alex stood. 'Leaving early, boss,' she said. 'I've got an appointment with a witness in Hythe.'

Back at the cottage, she pulled the swimsuit she hadn't used since August out of the airing cupboard. It would do for another summer. 'Have you seen my swimming shoes, Zoë?'

Everyone on this part of the coast wore swimming shoes. The beaches were too hard on your feet without them.

'Why?'

'I'm going to go for a swim.'

'In the sea?' Zoë's eyes widened.

Alex was puzzled. 'Yes.'

'Don't, Mum,' her daughter wailed. And Zoë was falling against her, arms around her mother's neck, sobbing. Alex realised with a shock that just because she was so used to this world of dead bodies, there was no reason for her daughter to be. Zoë had lain next to the cold body of Mimi Greene on the beach, trying to bring her back to life. She had smelt the seawater on her pale, dead skin.

'I'm sorry, Zoë,' said Alex, hugging her back. 'I didn't think.'

'Don't. Don't. Promise me.'

'It really shook you up, didn't it?'

Zoë nodded.

'OK, love. OK.' And she patted her daughter's head as she hugged her. Her fierce daughter was still trembling with anxiety. 'I promise. I won't swim. But I still have to go and sit on the beach and watch them. You understand that, don't you?'

Alex arrived just before six and recognised Kimaya's Audi parked on West Parade.

She was there about twenty metres down the beach, black hair wild in the wind.

Alex got out and joined her. 'You came.' Kimaya smiled. 'Good for you. Where are your things?'

'I'm not swimming. My daughter didn't want me to.'

Kimaya looked puzzled, until Alex added, 'We live on Dungeness. My daughter, she was the one who found Mimi Greene's body. She was alone with her for some time before . . . before the rest of us arrived.'

'My God. Poor girl.'

'I didn't realise how badly it had affected her. She's afraid of me going in the water.'

'Of course it would affect her,' said Kimaya. 'So she's become afraid of the sea?'

'And afraid of me going into the sea.'

'How terrible.' Kimaya stepped forward and gave Alex a hug.

Alex stood there, a little awkwardly, smelling the rich linen scent of her perfume, until Kimaya felt it was time to disentangle herself and step back. 'Mimi would have hated for that to happen. Come and join us down on the beach anyway. We're just going in. Can we chat after we've swum?'

Alex nodded, took her towel and sat down on it while, on the beach, Kimaya did some stretches. She was tall, strong-looking, lithe-limbed and at ease with her own beauty in a way Alex had never known.

The wind was blowing across the shore, and dark clouds were building up towards the west.

Hearing the crunch of footsteps, she looked round. 'You again,' said Rose in a shy, friendly kind of way. 'Isobel not here yet?'

'She texted,' said Kimaya. 'She's on Zoom with her literary agent. She'll be here any second.'

'Not coming in?' Rose asked Alex, pulling off her trousers.

'Maybe another time,' said Alex, not wanting to explain again.

In another minute Isobel was there, towel around her shoulders, dressed in a black swimming costume and a black swimming hat, just like the one that Mimi had been wearing. She nodded at Alex. 'I thought you were swimming.' She made it sound as if Alex had disappointed her.

'Maybe she will another time,' said Kimaya, 'but right now is not good for her. I'll explain.'

The other women seemed to be waiting for Isobel to get in before they did. As soon as she was there, they worked their way down the shingle, all three of them, and walked into the water – then plunged in without pausing.

Alex watched. Isobel held her head above the waves, doing a steady breaststroke back and forth. Kimaya did the same, alternating with backstroke. Ungainly out of it, Rose was an athlete in the water, slicing through waves with a strong and graceful front crawl. Sweaty from work, Alex wished she could join them.

After they had swum for a few minutes they gathered together and chatted, heads bobbing. The conversation was sombre, their voices low. At one stage, as if on a signal, they all turned and looked at Alex, and she wondered what they were saying, because it was obviously her they were talking about.

TWELVE

Alex watched them, their skin goosebumped, towelling themselves down, putting on dryrobes. Out of the water, Rose became shy again, awkward in her body. Kimaya, on the other hand, blossomed. Isobel remained angular, commanding, businesslike as she tugged off her swimming shoes and replaced them with ordinary household slippers. 'Good swim,' she said.

'But not the same without Mimi,' added Rose.

'No,' agreed Kimaya softly.

'Out there, we were talking about our memories of swimming with her.' Isobel tugged off her swimming cap. 'How she was always at one with the water. She was very much the one who held this group together.'

'I thought you were the one who organised it?'

'I am, but she was the life of it.'

'Will you keep going?' asked Alex.

'We talked about that too,' said Kimaya. 'How she would have hated it if we stopped. We talked about maybe having a memorial swim for her. And we talked about your poor daughter. I hope you don't mind.'

'How awful. I didn't realise,' said Rose. 'Is she OK?'

Isobel said, 'Perhaps she could come and meet us one day? She might want to swim with us too. It would be wrong for Mimi's legacy to be making another woman afraid of the sea.' Isobel took Alex's hand. 'Will you ask her? Please?'

'I don't think this is really her, this kind of thing,' Alex answered.

Isobel looked at her disapprovingly. 'Perhaps you could ask anyway? You never know. It'll be a Sunday night swim. It will be a full moon. Perfect, really. It might be good for her in terms of saying goodbye to Mimi.' Isobel seemed to stare her down.

'I'll ask. I can't promise,' said Alex.

When she was dry, Kimaya joined her in the Saab. Alex put the heater on because Kimaya was shivering gently in the chill of the early summer evening.

'You're cold.'

Kimaya laughed, rubbing her legs to warm them. 'Just because we swim every day doesn't mean it isn't fucking freezing. Are you talking to me because you think someone killed Mimi?'

'What makes you say that?'

Kimaya paused, then said, 'Because you seem so interested. It doesn't seem like you're treating this as if it was a ghastly accident.'

The Saab was warming up slowly. It was four days since Zoë had found the body and there was still nothing definitive from the pathologist to say it was foul play. Frustrating, but not unusual for a body found in seawater. 'It's unexplained at the moment. So we have to investigate.'

'Go on then.' Kimaya shook water from her ear. 'Ask away.'

'Tell me about yourself,' Alex said.

Still rubbing her legs, Kimaya explained she lived in Salt-wood, in a large house above Hythe. 'I don't work, I'm afraid,' she said. 'Isobel doesn't approve of that, but I married well, as they used to say. My husband is in dry bulk shipping,' she said, as if slightly embarrassed by the fact. She was rich. It explained a lot. There was a reason she always looked so elegant and drove an expensive car.

Alex offered coffee from her flask. When Kimaya shook her head, Alex poured one for herself. 'Both Isobel and Rose said that they thought Mimi seemed a bit preoccupied. That she may have had something on her mind.'

'Actually, that's what we were talking about, out there.' Kimaya nodded towards the sea. 'We had all noticed it, I suppose, but none of us said anything. Looking back, I wonder how could we have been so selfish as not to ask her what was going on? We act like we're so close to each other, but we fail to act like real friends when something like this is happening. It's something we feel bad about now.'

Alex looked at the sea, darker than it had been, now the cloud was building over it.

'Do you think it was to do with her splitting up from her boyfriend?'

She snorted. 'He wasn't her boyfriend. Not really.'

'Nobody likes being cheated on.'

'Honestly? She was OK about that.'

73

'Really?'

'Relieved, I think. I think she'd been on the verge of asking him to leave for days.'

'I find that strange.'

'Not really. He was just a bit cheeky, moving in on her. He wasn't her type at all. Bit of a lad, you know. Younger than her. Fast, you know what I mean?'

'Do you think he might have been upset by her chucking him out?'

'Probably,' she said lightly. 'My impression of him was that he was very vain. Men don't like being rejected much, do they?'

'But you think there was something else worrying her?' said Alex, steering her away from the topic of Malcolm.

Kimaya shrugged. 'Yeah, I do.' She rubbed her hair with a corner of her towel. 'She had missed a couple of swims recently, and when she did come she spent most of the time just swimming off on her own, like she was deliberately not wanting to engage for some reason.'

'So her behaviour was different?'

'The last time I saw her was that evening swim. Looking back, I realise I didn't have a chance to say a word to her. She even changed separately from the rest of us. So I messaged her afterwards and asked if she was OK.'

'On Friday evening?'

'Isobel doesn't approve of gossip, of us talking about our relationships. She's very proper, you know? But I thought Mimi might want to unload. And I admit it. I was curious. I mean, wouldn't you be?'

'Did she get back to you?'

'She sent me this.' She picked her phone out of her sports backpack and scrolled through her messages, then held it up.

Let's meet. Need to talk to u xx

'What did that mean?'

'I thought it was just she was apologising for being stand-offish. Or wanted to say something about Malcolm. I really don't know.'

'But you never got to meet her?'

'No. Pretty awful, really.'

'If you don't think it was her boyfriend that was troubling her, what do you think it was?'

Kimaya looked directly at her and said, 'Honestly? I don't know. That's the thing with Mimi. She was a good listener, and the most empathetic person I know, but I only realise now that she wasn't a great talker. She kept herself to herself. So I don't know what the hell was going on in her head. I wish I had, because I think there must have been something.'

Alex nodded. 'Well, we need to track him down. Do you have any idea where he is?'

Kimaya shook her head. 'I barely saw him when they were supposed to be living together.'

'You were her friend. Why not?'

'Because we're a group of women who swim together. That's how we know each other. That's the important thing to us. We're girl friends. My husband came a couple of times back in the early days,' she said. 'He said we intimidated him, and if you'd met my husband you'd know he's not an easy man to intimidate.'

'Your husband, Mr Dry Bulk Shipping?'

Kimaya laughed delightedly. 'Yes he is. He runs a company

worth gazillions, hires and fires, does deals with governments and businessmen around the world, but he couldn't cope with us.'

'He was scared of Rose?'

She laughed. 'No. Not me either. Or Mimi. It's Isobel mostly. She's a warrior queen. That's why we love her. The day he came with us, Isobel told us all about a poem she'd written about wounds and lunar cycles and menstruation. My husband was out of the water quicker than if there had been sharks.' She grinned.

Alex's phone buzzed. It was six in the evening, around the time of day Jill would text to say she was coming over with a bottle of something cold.

'Thanks for the offer of the swim at least,' said Alex. 'And for the chat. Rose thinks he may have been a carpenter. It would be a real help to know what Malcolm's last name was. Or where he worked.' She pulled her phone from her pocket, but it wasn't a message from Jill. It was from Zoë.

Just checking what time you're back x

She should have messaged her to reassure her, she chided herself.

'Malcolm? Honestly. I have no idea about his name or anything else about him,' said Kimaya. 'None at all. Come to think about it, that's odd, isn't it?'

THIRTEEN

When Alex knocked on the door of Zoë's bedroom the next morning on the way out to work, her daughter was still half asleep.

She sat on her girl's bed and stroked her short hair. 'What did you do yesterday?'

'Nothing,' said Zoë.

The curtains were closed and the room was dark despite the bright morning sunshine. 'You can't just stay indoors all day in weather like this. It's not like you.'

'I don't even know what I'm like,' said Zoë.

Alex tried to sound positive. 'Why don't you go and hang out with Bill or something?'

Zoë shook her head. 'He's out all the time now.'

'Probably got some work, I suppose.' Bill was a self-taught naturalist, a birdwatcher, a man who seemed to know the name for every bug and plant in this place. In recent years he had found work doing ecological surveys with a company who were based in Rye.

'No,' Zoë said. 'He's up to something but he won't talk about it.'

Alex frowned. 'Up to something? What do you mean?'

Zoë shook her mother's hand away. 'Him and Jill.'

Alex was baffled now. 'What do you mean, him and Jill?'

'She's been round there. She stayed over. It's like something intense that's taking all his time. It's pretty weird.'

'Jill stayed over?'

'Her car's been parked outside. Didn't you see it? You're supposed to be the detective.'

'He doesn't even like Jill much.' Alex was puzzled. 'He says she talks too much. What's she doing with him?'

'I don't know, Mum. Don't ask me. Ask her.'

'Maybe I will.' Alex leaned forward to kiss Zoë but she pulled away. Alex stood and opened the curtains.

'Mum!'

It was strange. She was used to Bill disappearing for days at a time, but she had expected Jill to be in touch, whatever McAdam's orders. 'You know those women I was going to go swimming with yesterday? I told them about you and about how you were scared of the sea now.'

'Mum! Why did you tell them?'

'They were the woman you found's friends. They're sad, just like you.'

Zoë turned her back, lying with her face to the wall.

'Listen,' said Alex. 'They said, why don't we both go swimming with them? Together. They're experienced. That has to be safe, doesn't it? They're doing a special swim in Mimi's memory on Sunday night.'

'I don't want to go swimming with them. I don't want to go in the sea.'

'They're OK. They're interesting.' She waited for Zoë to say something, but she didn't. 'Quite a cool bunch of women, really. All different. I think you'd like them. And one of them said that it would be sad if Mimi's death meant it ended up that someone like you was afraid of the sea, because Mimi had loved it so much.'

She couldn't see the expression on her daughter's face.

'Well?'

'I'll think about it,' grunted Zoë.

Friday, and the Portakabin was roasting. A fan swept from side to side in the room, ruffling paperwork each time it blew onto Alex's desk. The end of her first week back at work and she was anxious. She had made little progress.

At her desk, she messaged Jill. **I miss you**, she wrote. **Everything OK?** Where was the harm in that?

Just as she pressed SEND, McAdam put his head around the door and said, 'Anything new?'

'No.' Hurriedly, Alex looked up from her phone. 'Nothing at all. No leads at all on Malcolm.'

Alex's phone buzzed. She ignored it, turning it face down so the screen was hidden.

McAdam looked weary too. 'The fact he's become so hard to find doesn't look too good. Actually, it's not just that he's hard to find. Do you think he's actively hiding?'

'Or maybe he's a victim too?'

'I've been considering that too. In retrospect, I think I was

79

mistaken not giving out his details straight away. I've cleared it to release his profile photograph from Hinge to the press this afternoon.'

'Right,' said Alex, relieved by that at least. 'I was thinking. What about other women?'

'What do you mean, other women?'

Caught by the breeze from the fan, a duty roster half tore itself from the board and started flapping, until the fan moved away, leaving it hanging limply. 'Malcolm was on Hinge. We know he dated at least two women. I bet there's more.'

McAdam nodded. 'Hopefully they'll get in touch when they see his picture on the news.' While his attention was diverted by the flapping paper, Alex turned her phone over. Three was a reply from Jill.

You cracked first!!! I win. Lol. Any news on Malcolm?

Grinning, Alex turned her phone back over. 'What if we go catfishing?'

McAdam was repinning the roster. 'What do you mean?'

'Charlie has a profile on Hinge. He looks a bit like Malcolm, according to Jill. He's not exactly hideous. I bet he's had a few enquiries, too. And I bet some of the women who'd message Charlie are the same ones that would have messaged Malcolm. Nice fair-haired young man. Single, or so he claims.'

His back was still towards her. 'It's a bit risky, isn't it?'

While he wasn't looking, she thumbed her screen:

Nothing on Malcolm.

'You mean, use Charlie's profile to contact women who might have been in touch with Malcolm?' McAdam was saying. 'We'd have to do that through the covert investigation team.'

A bit weird. He's just vanished.

'Obviously. Yes.' Alex put her phone down to concentrate on the conversation with her boss. 'Why not though? Besides, if Malcolm's the murderer and we may need to show a pattern of behaviour, it would help secure a conviction. We need to find other women he dated. Plus, the more it looks like he's gone to ground following the death of Mimi Greene, the more we have an issue of public safety. I think we have a duty to warn other women that he may have been in touch with. And you never know, there might be someone out there who knows what his last name is, or has a number for him at least.'

On her lap, Alex's phone buzzed again. She tried to keep the smile from her face.

'Yes,' McAdam said. 'Yes. Good. That's an idea. Have you spoken to Charlie about this?'

'I'll call him now if you like.'

When he'd gone, she picked up her phone again. She read the last message from Jill.

I had sex with a murderer, then. Right now that's all I fucking need.

Alex stared at the angry message, puzzled.

Charlie was in the cafeteria unwrapping a protein bar when Alex ordered a coffee, sat down beside him and asked him to hand over the logins to his Hinge account. 'What you said on the phone. Is this a joke?'

'Not at all. You're a very, very good-looking young man. I'm sure all the girls will swipe,' said Alex.

'You think?' He didn't sound unhappy about it.

81

'Of course. Your hair's right. Apparently you have gorgeous eyes.'

'Do I?'

'Your girlfriend ever tell you that?'

'I don't have one, right now.'

'Didn't anyone get in touch with you when you put your profile up on Hinge?'

Charlie coloured. 'A couple. But I didn't answer them because you told me not to.'

'There you go then. But you'd need to hand over the account password to the covert intelligence team, and it's important you don't reply to any of the contacts yourself.'

'I wasn't going to anyway,' he protested. He broke off a bit of the bar and chewed on it.

'Look at it this way. You're our honeytrap,' she said.

'I feel I'm being objectified,' he said.

She smiled at him. 'Poor love.'

When she had finished the coffee, she stood and walked out into sunshine that was too warm for May.

Bill picked up his phone straight away. 'What?'

She heard the noise of traffic in the background. 'Where are you, Bill?'

'Out and about,' he said vaguely.

'You're up to something, Bill. I can tell,' she said. 'You and Jill. What is it?'

He said nothing.

'No. Don't tell me.'

'I wasn't going to,' said Bill. 'Jill asked me to do a favour for

82

her.' Alex thought about that last message. *Right now that's all I fucking need.* 'Is Jill in some kind of trouble?'

'It's up to her to tell you all about it. Just put it this way though. I've had an interesting couple of days. What is it you wanted?'

'I wanted to talk to you about Zoë. Have you seen anything of her?'

'I've been sort of busy,' said Bill.

'Me too. This thing I'm working on is taking a lot of my time. I was just wondering, if you see her, could you have a chat with her? I think she's . . . I think she's upset with me for going back to work.'

'Yep.'

'What do you mean, yep?'

'I think you're right. She is upset.'

'OK. Well. Will you talk to her?'

'Right,' he said.

'Thanks.' She leaned back against a hot brick wall. 'What is it you two are up to, then you and Jill?'

'Like I said, Alex. You really need to ask Jill about that,' said Bill, ending the call.

83

FOURTEEN

On Saturday morning, Alex set up a table in the mess garden she had at the front of the house and sat in a large straw hat, drinking her third coffee. 'Come on out, Zoë. The weather is gorgeous,' she called.

'Sun's bad for you.' Zoë was just inside the front door, sitting on the floor of the hallway.

'Come on. We need to talk.'

'You come inside then,' Zoë answered.

'Bill says you're worried about me going back to work,' said Alex.

Zoë stood up, walked towards her and flopped down into one of the garden chairs. 'Bill said that? To you.'

'Yes. You are worried, aren't you?'

'What did he say?'

'Nothing. Just that you're worried.' Alex felt that she was no good at this kind of thing. She had spent her life resenting her own mother for being so off-hand a parent, only to realise that she was no better. 'Listen. Those friends of Mimi. The

84

ones who swim. You know I mentioned to them that you were taking the whole thing badly—'

'I'm not taking it badly! I'm taking it for exactly what it was. I found a woman who was dead, Mum.'

'Yes. Obviously . . .'

'Doesn't that stuff even affect you any more?'

'Of course it does,' Alex said quietly. 'Of course it does.'

'Really?'

'It's my fault you had to see her. I should have never taken you there. I was careless and stupid.'

'That's not the point at all, Mum. A murdered woman. Here. Where we live.'

Alex blinked. 'You don't feel safe?'

'No. No I don't.'

'This is hard then. This woman, Isobel, really wants you to be there with them when they swim for Mimi. She thinks Mimi would have wanted that. She really is worried about you becoming afraid of the sea—'

'I'm not afraid of the sea, Mum. I'm afraid of . . . I don't know.' She picked up a glass of orange juice and took a cautious sip. 'Right now, I feel it's swallowing me up.'

'Oh, love,' said Alex. She leaned across to put her arm on Zoë's, and for once Zoë didn't jerk away. Her daughter, who had spent so many hours on her own here, looking for birds and bugs, was afraid of the place.

'Well? Do you think you'd like to come?'

'What's this Isobel like?' asked Zoë.

'I think she's a little bit fierce,' said Alex.

★

85

She left Zoë sitting under the shade in the garden and went inside. Even though it was supposed to be a day off, she called up Toby McAdam. 'Any news?'

The covert team were operating Charlie's profile on Hinge and the photo of Malcolm had gone out on the morning's news. Alex wanted to know if there had been any progress.

'Eleven women already,' said McAdam. 'It's wild. All of them slept with him. Eight from the public. Three people who messaged Charlie's profile on Hinge. All of the others met him on dating apps as well.'

'Eleven? Jesus.' She heard the noise of shouting in the background. 'Where are you?'

'I'm at this indoor climbing centre in Maidstone. My day looking after the kids. Zoë should try it. I'm sure she'd love it.'

She saw Zoë sitting up under the umbrella, watching some kind of bug crawling on her arm. 'She would hate it.'

'But this is the weirdest thing,' said McAdam. 'Malcolm kept in touch with everyone via apps. None of them had a phone number for him. None of them knew his last name. So far, none of them have been able to confirm a workplace or anything that can help us find him.'

'You're kidding me?'

'Turns out Charlie has a lot of admirers too.'

'Please don't tell him. He'll explode. So – this hiding behaviour. It didn't start after the death of Mimi Greene. It's something he's been doing a while.'

'So it would seem,' said McAdam. 'Well done, Lulu!' he called out to one of his children.

'You're right. That is weird. I mean, right now he looks

86

like he's the guilty person because he's so hard to find, but it turns out he's been hiding all along. So what has he been hiding from?'

'We're interviewing the women formally next week,' McAdam said. 'We should be able to see if there's any pattern of violence.'

She would not be back at work until Monday herself. The weekend seemed too long.

'And what about you?' McAdam asked. 'Are you OK? You were away a long time. Are you fitting back in all right?'

'Me?' she said as reassuringly as she could. 'Absolutely fine.'

She returned to the garden with a pair of shears and started on the bramble that had appeared in the lawn.

'What are you doing?' asked Zoë.

'Gardening.'

Zoë watched her for a while, with a skeptical expression, then went back inside. As soon as she'd gone, Alex put down the shears. She was so bored.

She walked up to Bill's house and knocked at the door but he was out. His motorbike was gone. He seemed to have been busy this week. She hadn't seen him at all. It was strange.

Back in the house, she called up to Zoë's room, 'Do you want to go for lunch at the Pilot?'

A muffled voice from behind her bedroom door. 'OK.'

They walked, because the afternoon was long and Alex could have a drink if she didn't take the car. The small road along the spit was busy. They kept stopping to talk to people. The painter who lived in the old first-class carriage was out rebuilding the path to his small studio. He stopped and had a long conversation with Zoë about the foxes who lived on Dungeness. The two designers who lived a couple of doors down were out too, painting their carriage, and greeted her like an old friend. Everyone they met smiled when they saw her, but nothing seemed to lift Zoë's dark mood.

'Did you know that the Pilot was originally built from the timbers of a seventeenth-century Spanish galleon?' Alex asked Zoë as they passed Prospect Cottage.

Zoë sniffed. 'Looks more like it was built from the remains of a twentieth-century service station.'

At lunch, Alex gorged on chips. Zoë pecked at a salad.

Back home, after three glasses of wine, Alex fell asleep on a lounger in the garden. When Zoë woke her at seven in the evening, she opened her eyes groggily.

'I decided to go swimming tomorrow,' she said. 'With those women.'

'You did?' Alex sat up.

'By the way. I think your arm is sunburned.' Alex looked down. Zoë was right. Her skin was bright red, already sore to the touch.

She slept badly that night, partly because of having slept too much during the day, partly because the skin on her arm stung. She found herself puzzling over the elusive Malcolm and the equally elusive Bill, who seemed to have been absent from Dungeness all week. In London, as a working single mother, she had little time for friendships. She hadn't realised how dependent she had become on the few friends she'd made since she'd moved here. The place had changed her.

She fell asleep as light was beginning to seep through the crack in her curtains and seemed to be woken only minutes later by her phone ringing.

'What?'

'Sorry,' said McAdam. 'There's a situation.'

Alex blinked. She held the phone away from her to try and tell the time. It was 5.17. 'What situation?'

'Somebody torched Charlie's car in the early hours of this morning, and then put a burning rag through the door of his house. Him and his brother – they were lucky to get out alive.'

The room seemed suddenly airless.

FIFTEEN

Alex was fully awake. 'Is he OK?'

'Fine. But a little shaken.'

'Give me the address,' she said. 'I'll be there in half an hour.'

'Thanks,' McAdam said.

Before he could put down the phone, she said, 'The honeytrap. That was my idea. What if it was the worst one I ever had?'

It was dawn by the time she reached Charlie's house on the outskirts of Folkestone. The fire services had put out the burning car and a woman in a white coverall was combing the tarmac on all fours, knees covered in foam pads. Blue tape stretched across the road.

The remains of a Citroën Berlingo stood by a hedge, which had partly caught fire too. She hadn't imagined Charlie drove a car like that. She had thought he'd have wanted something more flash. A German model, maybe. The bare metal was exposed, and the windows that hadn't shattered had turned opaque from the heat.

She looked around. On the far side of the hedge was a playing field of some sort. Charlie's house was a little way further down the street, a new-build, red brick and white windows, a short pathway between a low-clipped hedge to the door. The uPVC front door had melted a little above the letterbox, into which the burning rag had been stuffed, but was mostly intact.

'Anything?' Alex asked the crime scene investigator.

The woman leaned back, upright, still on her knees. Alex didn't recognise her and had to hold out her warrant card to her to prove she had a right to ask. 'Two people,' answered the woman. 'Stood behind the hedge there, I reckon.' She pointed. 'Set fire to the car then went up and shoved a cloth through the letterbox and set that alight too. Footprints everywhere. Trainers of some kind.'

'Kids?'

'Size nine or ten, so teenagers at the very least, or older.'

Alex turned back towards the house. 'Can I go in?'

'Yeah. We did that zone first.'

When she got there, Alex noticed that there was a short rubber ramp leading up to the door. She rang the bell, and then, realising it might not be working, knocked.

'Oh. It's you,' said Charlie, opening the door wide. He looked pale and tired.

'Sorry, Charlie. Not a great night for you.' Alex stepped inside. The hallway still smelled acrid.

In the kitchen, sitting in what looked at first like a rather elaborate office chair, a second young man looked up at her. 'This is my brother, Guy,' Charlie explained.

'I didn't know you had a brother.' Alex took in the wheelchair he was sitting in, and the grab bars on the walls.

'Twin brother,' said Guy. It took a second for Alex to understand what he was saying. 'Identical in every way,' added Guy.

'Are you OK?' she asked them.

'Guy woke me when the car went up. He's got an alarm by his bed. Luckily, they put in fire extinguishers when they did the place up for us. Car's a total write-off though. It's going to take for ever to get a new one, unfortunately.'

Guy said something, spittle flying from his mouth, but the words tripped over each other.

'He said, "Fucking bastards,"' explained Charlie automatically.

'Fucking bastards,' said Guy, nodding his head.

'Fair enough,' said Alex. 'It was a special car?'

'Wheelchair ramp. Winch. All that,' said Charlie.

Alex looked around. There were piles of cups in the sink. The uniformed coppers would have been around first thing. 'Any idea who did this?'

'People who don't like the police, I guess,' said Charlie.

'Can't blame them,' his brother added.

Automatically, Charlie put the kettle back on. 'We're going to have to move out. It's not safe. I don't know where the hell we're going to go, though.'

'Do people around here know you're a police officer?'

'Of course they do. This is Folkestone. Everybody knows everyone else's business round here.'

'So you've had trouble before?'

'Actually, no,' said Charlie quietly. 'Never.'

'Apart from him next door,' Guy added, jerking his head towards the next house in the terrace.

'That's different,' said Charlie. 'We have this next-door neighbour,' he explained, 'who complains that he can't sleep properly. You know what the job's like. You get in late. If ever I'm parking the car after dark, he'll say I woke him up. I've stopped bringing it into the close – I park it outside, otherwise he complains about the noise of the engine. It's not worth the bother.'

'That's why it was by the hedge?'

'He's always there, looking out of the window,' said Guy.

Alex smiled. 'Nosey type?'

'He's a fat bastard. Probably gets no sex.'

'Unlike you and your twin brother?'

'Are you patronising me because I'm in a wheelchair?' Guy asked.

'Ignore him,' said Charlie. 'He's just trying to wind you up.'

Guy laughed.

'But whoever did this knew you, because they knew both your house and your car. The car wasn't outside but they knew which one they were going for.'

'Yeah, I realise that,' said Charlie.

'There's a hedge between the road and . . . what is it, a field?'

'The recreation ground.'

She thought for a while. 'You think it may be something to do with us using your picture on Hinge?'

'What picture?' Guy turned to his brother.

Charlie explained that they'd used his profile in an effort to contact women who might have been in contact with a suspect in a murder case.

93

'The swimmer?' Guy asked.

'Apparently, quite a few women got in touch,' Alex said. 'They'd have been told that it wasn't real, that it was a police officer, and that we're trying to contact a man called Malcolm.'

'Quite a few women got in touch because of his photo?' Guy was laughing. 'They want to date him?'

'Well. You are identical twins, after all,' said Alex. 'It's probably you they were after.'

'Are you patronising me?' he said again.

This time she laughed.

She drank Charlie's coffee and sat with them for a while. Guy was treating it like a joke, but Charlie was clearly shaken. It wouldn't be easy, finding a new place that was suitable for a wheelchair.

The sun had risen now, catching the white of the cow parsley in the hedge. On the pavement opposite, a woman in a tracksuit was walking a Yorkshire terrier. She paused for a moment while her dog peed against a post that held a street sign. Behind the hedge, children played on a slide. Everything looked nicely suburban and perfectly normal.

Alex made up her mind, approached the house door and rang on the bell. The door opened almost straight away. As Guy had said, the man was large. He wore a white shirt, untucked in, hanging down over a pair of shapeless trousers. 'Yes?'

'Detective Sergeant Alexandra Cupidi,' she introduced herself. 'Are you aware of the arson attack that took place here in the early hours of the morning?'

'Already been asked about that,' he said. 'Coppers came round knocking on all the doors. Awake all night.'

94

'I apologise for disturbing you a second time.'

'Oh no. Just happy to do my bit,' he said earnestly. 'You probably want to know who round here might have had something against Charlie Reed?'

'Exactly that, yes.'

'I can tell you exactly. I told the other coppers. The Johncock boys over there at number 105, they have a van that hasn't been taxed in a year. Charlie shopped them for it. They were fined and everything.' He stepped outside the house and pointed to the terrace hidden behind the hedge.

Alex smiled at him. She knew his sort and were grateful for them. A lonely man who just wanted to be part of things, and who, in trying, just ended up pissing off everyone around him.

She strolled across the road to 105 and knocked on the door, but there was no one in.

The front garden had been paved to make a parking space, but the van wasn't anywhere to be seen.

Alex peered through the living-room window. The house looked uncared for. Inside, a front room with a huge TV, a sofa and some empty cans on the floor. There were magazines too. She peered at them and realised they weren't just magazines; they were catalogues from builders' merchants.

SIXTEEN

'You sure about this?' asked Alex.

'Yes,' said Zoë quietly. 'You were right. I need to do this.'

'You love this place. It made you as much as I ever did.'

'Shut up, Mum.'

It was dusk when they got out of the car at Hythe and collected their things from the back. Further along the beach there was a plume of smoke rising, and a flicker of flame. Isobel had brought a fire pit and was adding logs to it while they took off layers and prepared for the swim.

Five women went into the water at around quarter past eight, just in time to watch the fat sun dropping into the South Downs. The sky to the west became magnificently purple. The five women paddled together in a circle as the cold water under them grew dark. 'We all look out for each other, Zoë,' said Isobel. 'Are you OK?'

'Yes. I'm fine. Thank you.'

'A sunset for Mimi. She was our blazing light,' said Isobel.

'Warm and magnificent. And now look the other way. This one is specially for you, Zoë.'

And, paddling in gentle waves, they turned to look towards the south-east.

'What?' demanded Kimaya impatiently.

'Just wait. One minute.'

At first, just a pale hint in the sky, then a dull sliver of moon showed at the horizon.

'Oh, wow,' said Zoë.

Within a few minutes, a fat pink disc had risen above the sea.

'It's special,' said Isobel. 'I can't remember a night where they've followed each other like this, sun and moon.'

'Specially for Mimi,' said Rose.

As it turned to yellow, the moon seemed to lay down a pathway of light that made its way across the surface of the water, from the horizon right up to each of them. 'It's so beautiful,' said Zoë.

'It calls to you, doesn't it?'

Alex rotated slowly in the water. Lights had come on along the shore, a line that dotted the whole sweep of the bay from Folkestone all the way to the dark, distant bulk of Dungeness B power station. It was magical.

'Time to come in now,' Isobel said. 'You'll get cold. I just wanted you to see it.'

By the time Alex got out, Rose was putting a towel around her daughter. Zoë's teeth were chattering. 'Get close to the fire,' Rose ordered.

Isobel was adding new logs to the fire pit.

'I don't understand why there weren't hundreds of people doing what we were doing,' said Zoë. 'That was fantastic.'

'Because it's bloody cold, for one,' Kimaya laughed.

Isobel and Kimaya laid out blankets around the fire and they sat, faces lit by flames. Isobel had brought a bottle of Spanish red and she poured tumblers for everyone except Alex, who had come in the Saab.

Isobel raised a glass. 'We should drink to Mimi,' she said.

Alex watched Zoë raise a glass too, then take a healthy gulp from it, dribbling a little down her chin as she shivered. The fire warmed them. When one of the logs shifted, sparks rose up into the night sky.

'That was amazing,' said Zoë. 'Thanks for asking me.'

Shy Rose put her arm around her again and gave her another hug. 'We're sorry, for what happened to you, you know?'

Zoë nodded. 'I've been dreaming about her,' she said.

'Really?' Isobel was sitting up, knees hugged to her chest.

'She told me she had been killed.'

The women looked at each other. From further down the beach came a sudden blare of music – teenagers having a barbecue.

'Dreams are important,' said Isobel. 'How was she in your dream?'

'She was dead. Cold and wet. Just like when I found her. Except this time she opened her eyes and spoke to me. She was weirdly calm. She said someone else was going to drown.'

Nobody spoke for a while. Alex held her tongue. Isobel asked gently, 'Do you believe that dreams can be true?'

'Yes. I mean. I don't know. It seemed so real at the time.'

Isobel nodded.

Rose began to cry quietly, then she half laughed. 'Sorry. I can't help it,' she said. 'I miss her.'

Kimaya had her back to the town. 'Look at the moon,' she said. 'It's so small now. It was so huge before.'

They all looked. 'It's an illusion,' said Zoë. 'It just seems bigger when it's closer to the horizon. Optically it's exactly the same, just our brains play a trick with us, making it seem bigger.' It was a very Zoë-ish thing to say, thought Alex.

Kimaya nodded. 'Wow. I never knew that.'

Everyone looked at Zoë. Eventually, Isobel spoke. 'I think to find her must have been a terrible thing for you – finding Mimi there, being alone with her. Shorelines are so strange. The image for me of Mimi on the edge of the shore – I can't get it out of my head, either.'

Rose wiped her eyes with her forearm. 'Sorry,' she said again. And Alex watched as Zoë reached out a hand and laid it on top of Rose's.

Isobel was reciting something:

> '*There was a young woman who lived all alone,*
> *She lived all alone on the shore-o,*
> *There was naught she could find to comfort her mind*
> *But to roam all alone on the shore-o.*'

Alex felt out of place among them, and, oddly for her, wished she didn't. She was not a fan of poetry or mysticism, but the women seemed happy with it, and that was OK. She was not good at enjoying herself sometimes. If it was just her, she might have stood and left them to their woodsmoke and wine, but Zoë seemed comfortable in their company so she remained.

'Shingle is full of colour,' Isobel was saying. 'Pale blue and

99

grey, and the orange of a wheat field in high summer. The closer you look, the more extraordinary it seems. Here' – she held one up triumphantly – 'I have a hag stone.' She handed it to Zoë. 'Look through it.'

Zoë held the stone to her eye. There was a hole through the middle of it.

'Druids used to think them magical,' Isobel was lecturing them. 'The tradition endured. Fishermen used to nail them to their boats to keep evil away. People hung them outside their doors.'

Kimaya and Rose began talking about how they thought they'd seen sharks a few days ago. 'Might have been,' said Zoë. 'More likely a porpoise. I've seen a lot of them. They were swimming off the shore the day I found Mimi.'

'How do you tell the difference?'

And Zoë was off, completely in her element, discussing the shape of dorsal fins and rattling off names of sharks like the porbeagle and the smooth-hound.

'You must write me a list,' said Isobel.

Despite the fire, it was getting chilly now. Alex pulled on a pullover. In the pocket of her jeans, left on a pile on the beach, her phone buzzed again.

Isobel's husband appeared at around 9.30, with more logs and another bottle of wine.

'Intruder, intruder,' said Isobel.

'I've brought fresh samosas. And chocolate.'

A cheer.

'And more wine. Mind if I join?'

'This is Zoë. Alex's daughter,' said Isobel. 'She's a fantastic naturalist.'

And he joined them, and Alex was worried it was going to turn into a much longer night, but almost as soon as he sat, Kimaya stood and said, 'I hate to say it, but I better call a cab.'

'Stay,' begged Isobel. 'It's a special night. We have two new swimmers.'

'Sorry. I have an early start tomorrow.'

Alex was grateful for the excuse to go, and she was about to stand and announce that she too had to be up early, but then she glanced over to her daughter and saw that Rose and Zoë were still close together, talking.

They were not so different in age, Alex realised with a shock. Her daughter, so young and yet all grown-up too. Alex should stay and let them talk, she realised, so she remained sitting on the beach, conscious of the cold at her back.

She noticed Zoë had put her arm around Rose. She caught a little of what Rose was saying. 'I feel I was so selfish, just talking about myself all the time to Mimi. That's all I did. I should have been there for her. I feel worthless. I mean . . . what is any of this for if someone like that can just disappear?'

Alex's phone was buzzing again, insistently now. Someone was calling. She reached over and picked up her jeans and took the phone from the back pocket.

Jill's number, she realised. There were missed calls too from her. She had been trying to call for the last twenty minutes, over and over again. She was clearly ignoring McAdam's order not to keep in touch.

She stood and swiped the screen to answer, walking away from the group so she could talk in private.

'Jill?'

'Thank Christ I found you.' Her voice wasn't steady. She sounded spooked.

Alex's skin prickled. 'What's wrong?'

'It's Bill. He's in hospital,' she gabbled.

'Bill?' At the mention of his name, Zoë looked round.

'He was in the water.'

'Stop, Jill. I don't understand. Take a breath.'

'Somebody pulled him out of the water up in Rochester. They're saying they don't know if he's going to make it, Alex. I think he might be dead. This is all my fault.'

Alex clutched the phone tightly. She turned. Zoë and the other women were staring at her, faces caught by the glow of the fire.

'What was he up to, Jill? What the hell was he doing?'

'Just come. Please.' Jill's voice was desperate.

PART TWO

PART TWO

SEVENTEEN

It was Sunday – exactly a week ago. Jill had gone looking for Alex, but Alex had not been at home.

'Look. She's coming!' Jill's voice called.

Jill joined Bill at the door of his cottage, waiting for Alex's car to round the bend by the nuclear power station fence. Next thing, Zoë was flinging her arms around his neck and telling him about the dead woman up at Pen Bars.

And when Jill embraced Alex and told her that she had something really important to tell her, Alex just snapped, 'God's sake, Jill. I'm sorry. Not now,' and had left with Zoë.

Watching Jill's head drop, Bill had felt sorry for her. For all her bluster, he had always thought there was something child-like in Jill Ferriter. He approached her and said, 'You best come back inside. I'll make more tea.'

She stood for a second, still stung, then seemed to snap out of it. She followed him back into the cabin. 'Not more bloody tea, Bill, please. It's coming out of my ears. You have anything stronger?'

'Sorry. Can't keep alcohol in the house any more.'

She sighed and sat down in his leather chair.

'Poor Zoë. What a thing to happen.'

Bill pulled one of the dining chairs close to her and sat down. 'How much do you know about Stephen Dowles?' he asked quietly. She had just told him about the man who had emailed him, claiming to be her father.

'Too much. I looked up the stuff online.' She dug in her shoulder bag and pulled out a large brown envelope. 'Double murderer, back in 1994. He killed some petty drug dealer and stuffed his body in the boot of a car, then he held up the post office at Brenzett with a shotgun. That was the worst. What made it extra bad was, after the poor woman at the post office had given him all the money, he just shot her dead. She had done everything he asked and then he killed her in cold blood. No reason at all. Thought my mum was pretty bad. But you know . . . all this.'

She opened the envelope, took out a photocopied sheet of paper from it and handed it to Bill. He unfolded a copy of the front page of the *Kent Messenger* dated November 1994. The headline read: 'FINALLY COPS NET POST OFFICE MONSTER'. There was a black-and-white photograph of a man underneath it. The caption read: 'Dowles killed TWO in cold blood'.

'Weird, in't it? I always thought I looked the spit of my mum, but seeing that . . .' She chewed on her lower lip. 'It's me.'

Bill looked from the photograph to Alex's friend and back again. The likeness was in their big round eyes, and the round-ness of their foreheads. And in the set of her mouth, too.

'So why did he contact you, Jill? Why did he contact you now?'

Jill took back the cutting. 'Don't know.'

'Has he asked to meet you?'

Jill shook her head. 'No. Nothing like that.'

'Even if this man is your father,' Bill said, 'and I'm not saying he is . . .'

'Except he is.'

'. . . you don't owe him anything at all.'

Jill was quiet for a while, then spoke. 'I was fostered, you know. Good people, most of them. People I loved who loved me. But all the same I wanted to be normal, you know? Normal. And some nights I used to fantasise that my real dad had called up and was coming to take me away with him. I invented him. He was always dead rich, obviously.' She smiled. 'He smelt of nice aftershave and had a stubbly chin, and bought me pet hamsters and stuff. For a while I convinced myself he was a billionaire who lived on an island in Scotland . . . Didn't really expect him to be a double murderer serving life. I'm not sure I can really cope with all this.'

Bill looked at her. 'Family is a weird thing,' he said. 'We don't ask for it. It just happens to us.'

'I can't cope, but at the same time, I have to know who he really is. You understand that, don't you?'

Bill nodded. He got up. 'You should eat something,' he said. He went to his small galley kitchen and looked in the fridge. 'I've got sausages. We could have them with beans and eggs.'

'Honestly? I'm not hungry, Bill,' Jill called from the living room.

He peered at her through the doorway. She was looking at

107

the picture of the man who said he was her father. 'I'll cook it anyway.'

He stood by the cooker frying the sausages in an old pan, blackened on the outside. The cooker was propane. None of these cabins were on the mains.

Jill came and stood by the door. 'You must remember him, Bill. You were a neighbourhood copper at the time.'

'Oh yes,' he said. 'I only saw Stephen Dowles in the flesh the once, but I remember him well enough.'

He turned the sausages in the pan and it came back to him. The clear blue sky on the autumn day he had been posted on duty outside the post office in Brenzett. That was after the second of Stephen Dowles's murders. In those days the post office was a small village shop, with bags of coal and newspaper stands propped outside, postcards advertising church groups and bring-and-buy sales in the window. Bill had been sent to keep bystanders away while the forensics team did their work. The locals were angry and frightened, demanding to know what was going on. Things like this did not happen around here. A well-loved woman had been killed for no reason at all.

He remembered the craning necks of passers-by. He remembered the brightness of the low sun, standing there on the tarmac outside the shop.

'Like I said, I only saw Stephen Dowles once.' He cracked open a can of baked beans. 'It was a few weeks after the murder at the post office. I was at Ashford police station the night they brought him in. A copper, a DI, had found him living rough in a vacant council estate east of the town. According to Figgy, he hadn't put up any resistance.'

'Figgy?'

'The DI. Everyone called him Figgy. He was a good man. A grafter. I liked him. Figgy was the one who brought Stephen Dowles in, and I ended up with the job of checking his pockets, taking his belt and shoes. I just remember he gave them up without a whimper. It was almost like he was barely there. Then I asked for his watch. It was some cheap digital thing. When he took it off I remember seeing the scratches up his arms. Scabs.'

'Heroin?' Jill asked.

'Then Figgy took him in for an interview and it was just twenty minutes later he came out to say, "Full confession. He admitted to murdering Mary Spillett." That was the name of the postmistress.'

'I read it in the paper,' said Jill. 'He killed her at point-blank range with a shotgun.'

'Of course, we all cheered. You do when things like that happen.'

'Hurrah. My dad is a murderer,' said Jill.

'It's what you do, Jill. You're a detective. You know how good it feels when your team catches a bad one.'

'Yeah. I know,' said Jill sadly.

'Only, Figgy told us all to shut up. "Wait there, lads. Save the cheering. I've got something else bloody major hidden up my sleeve. You're not going to believe what happens next! Just put the kettle on and send out for custard creams." That sort of thing. The interview room was on the second floor back then. A couple of coppers waited outside, trying to hear what was going on the other side of the door. It was one of those days when people's shifts ended but they all stayed on just to find out what Figgy would say next time he emerged from the room. Then about eight in the evening Figgy finally came out, punching the air. "Wayne Jordan," he told us. "Full fucking confession." We were stunned.'

Jill said, 'Wayne Jordan was the drug dealer he'd killed a couple of weeks earlier. That was in the papers too.'

'Exactly. Two of the county's worst murders solved at a stroke. You know what it's like, Jill. A small weight had lifted.'

All Bill's pans were battered and old, black on the outside, but he didn't see much point in buying new. He plopped the beans into a small one and carried on talking. 'Know what? I had been the copper who had to go and tell Wayne Jordan's mum that her son had been found dead in the boot of a car. Katie, her name was. You've had to do that kind of thing, Jill. You know how hard it is.'

Jill nodded. 'Turn the sausages down. They're burning,' she said.

'So I remember that night I volunteered to go with the family liaison officer and tell her that we had found the man who killed him – so she found out about it before it was in the papers. You never get over something like that, but it's a little better when you know what happened.' He stared at the sausages in the pan a while longer, then pulled out a couple of eggs. The first hissed and spat when he dropped it into the fat.

'Why did he do it, Bill?'

'I don't know,' Bill said. 'Just that he did. He was taking a lot of drugs. I wouldn't be surprised if that had a lot to do with it.'

He put a plate down in front of her. 'Sorry. The food is a little basic.'

'No,' she said. 'Looks great.'

They ate in silence. It was Alex's first day back on Serious Crime tomorrow, thought Bill. He would be seeing less of her now.

Jill cut the sausage into small pieces and dipped them into her yolk. 'Thing is, I feel I have to know who he is now. I need to know why I'm his daughter.'

'Or you could just forget about him,' said Bill.

'I can't, Bill. What do you think will happen if it gets into the papers that he's out? What do you think will happen if he tells someone that his daughter is a copper, serving in the same force that put him away? You think the papers are going to forget about him too?' She looked up from her barely touched plate. 'You see? I need to know, Bill. For my own protection as much as my own sanity.' She pushed the beans around a little with her fork. 'I was going to ask Alex if she could help me look into the case.'

'She's a serving officer, Jill. She can't just go digging around in old cases for you just because you want her to.'

'She's my friend,' protested Jill.

Bill finished his plate in silence. It was dark now. Jill pushed her plate back. 'Sorry. It's nothing to do with the food. Not hungry.'

'You know Alex would get into all sorts of shit if someone found she was looking into that stuff for you, Jill?' he said.

Jill scowled. She took the plates to the bowl by the butler

111

sink, scraped her own clean and started to wash them. He took a cloth to dry the dishes.

'If Alex can't help me, you can then,' she said.

He snorted. 'I'm not even a serving officer any more, Jill.'

'Exactly,' she said, handing him a wet plate.

EIGHTEEN

William South and Jill Ferriter talked until late that night.

At around 2 a.m. he made up the bed in the spare room for her. In the morning, when he heard her phone alarm through the wooden walls, he offered her tea. 'No time. Shit. I'm going to be so late for bloody work. And it's Alex's first day back.'

Afterwards, when he'd had breakfast, he walked up to Alex's house and rang the bell. No one answered, but when he stepped back he saw Zoë peering through the curtains of an upstairs window. When she realised he was looking up at her, she stepped back into the darkened room.

'I was thinking of going for a walk,' he called up.

The curtains closed again.

Bill stood by the door and the minutes passed. He rang the bell again. 'Do you want to come?'

The window above opened. 'Don't feel like it,' came a voice.

'I know you don't,' he said. 'But maybe you should.'

It was warm. After a long, windy winter that had frozen the lakes, the headland was alive with the buzz of insects. He walked back up the bank at the back of the house and lay down on the ground, propped up on his elbows, and watched the curtains twitch.

When Zoë realised that he meant it, she came downstairs and stood there with a mug in her hand for a second, then walked barefoot towards him. She hadn't dressed. She was wearing a pair of grey flannel sleeping shorts and a T-shirt that may have once been white; it hung off her bony shoulders.

'Old people always think walking is good for you.'

'I'm not that much older than your mum,' he said.

'Exactly,' said Zoë. 'Old people.' She reached out a hand to him to help him off the pebbles. 'Come on then.'

'Are those your pyjamas?' he asked.

She looked down. 'I'll go change, I suppose,' she said.

They set off with little idea of which way they were heading, and somehow that led them into the sunken woods. A hundred years ago, railway ballast had been dug from this spot, exposing raw soil below. Dense thickets of scrubby trees had sprung up from the thin earth. Paths wound into them now, passing over old lines of railway sleepers that had once held the tracks laid down to haul the stones away.

The entirety of Romney Marsh was a haphazard collaboration between people and nature, and richer for it. Bill loved that about the place. Here, huge numbers of species of moths, bees, sawflies and other bugs fed on the sallows and other plants that had grown on the sparse topsoil exposed by the quarrying.

He had befriended Zoë when she first arrived here, mutely furious at being uprooted from London. While her mother

114

worked, he had let her follow him around, telling her the names of birds. She had been more receptive than he'd expected an awkward teenager to be. At nineteen, she seemed to know almost as much about the natural world around them as he did.

As they emerged into a small clearing, a collie ran up and started sniffing at Zoë. Zoë hissed at the dog.

A horsey woman in Hunter wellies and an green wool gilet arrived and said, 'Don't worry about her, she's just being friendly.'

'She should be on a lead,' Zoë blurted. 'There are ground-nesting birds.'

'And who are you?' The woman sniffed and walked on.

Bill chuckled. Zoë remained stone-faced.

'Don't want to talk about it,' Zoë said, lapsing into silence.

They emerged on the north side of the sunken woods along-side Long Pit, a flooded gravel quarry that could be thick with birds this time of year.

It was hard work tramping the ground alongside the pit. Whereas before she would have paused and examined plants and bugs, the scrapings made by badgers and rabbits, today nothing seemed to interest her.

'Look,' he said, stopping and pointing to a fat bee that was gorging lazily on a white dead-nettle. 'Is that a ruderal bum-blebee?'

She squatted down and looked at it for a second, then walked on.

They were halfway up the eastern side of Long Pit now. She turned east, towards the sea. He followed until, for no apparent reason, she decided she had had enough of walking and sat down on the stones to rest.

He sat beside her. He had known her for almost five years now, watched her growing up. She was a strange girl, uncomfortable in her own skin, often hard to communicate with. He had learned that sometimes you had to give her time.

Zoë spoke eventually. 'It wasn't even a *Bombus ruderatus*,' she said angrily. 'It was a fucking *Bombus hortorum*. It was a male, and ruderal bumblebees have ginger hair on their mandibles, not black.'

She stood and stomped off again and he left her to it, marching through the low gorse towards the road.

'Look out for the ground-nesting birds,' he called after her.

'Fuck off,' she shouted back.

It took twenty minutes for him to catch up with Zoë. She was standing on the road by the Lifeboat Station, still looking furious.

'You were right, obviously,' he said. 'It was just a garden bumblebee.'

She put her head on his shoulder and burst into tears. Bill, who had lived alone all his life, who had never had children, and who could talk to Zoë about birds and bumblebees and wildlife conservation, was lost when she was like this. He patted her shoulder. 'Is it about a boy?' he said.

She cried louder.

'Or a girl? I don't know.'

She kicked him hard in the shin.

'Ow. That really hurt.'

'Don't be a fucking idiot,' she said, through the tears. 'I spent all that time trying to save her life and there was nobody there.'

'How long were you on your own with her?'

116

'It felt like I was with her for an hour. I shouted and shouted but nobody came, so I thought it was all down to me to save her life.'

'And you couldn't?'

Zoë nodded.

'Jesus. Come on. Poor girl. What you need is a cup of tea.'

He set off down towards the lighthouses. When he'd gone a few paces, he turned to check she was following him. After walking out on the rough ground, the flat tarmac was a welcome break. When she came alongside, he said, 'You know that nothing you did would have saved her, don't you?'

Zoë nodded.

'But you tried. And that's an amazing thing. You did your best. I'm so proud of you.'

They had got as far as Prospect Cottage. Tourists were taking selfies standing in front of it.

'You don't understand,' Zoë said angrily.

'I don't understand what?' They stopped and looked at the couple, a man and a woman, holding their camera up against the sun and squinting into the lens.

'I felt like such a fucking idiot,' she said angrily. 'I mean, she was obviously dead, wasn't she? She was cold as a bag of peas. And Mum arrives and I'm still trying to wake her up and then she goes and tells everyone that I moved the body because I'm an idiot.'

Bill looked at her. 'I'm sure she didn't say that.'

'You weren't there.'

'She wouldn't say anything like that.'

'Might as well have done.'

'Come on.' He took her arm. He could feel her trembling. She was such a slight girl it was amazing the wind here didn't blow her away. 'Let's get you home. You need some breakfast.'

They had reached the small roadside sculpture that a local artist had made by planting his old paintbrushes into the soil when she spoke again. 'Something else. Don't tell anyone, promise? Last night I dreamed about her.'

'The dead woman?'

'I was holding her, trying to get her to wake up and she did. She spoke to me.'

Bill turned to her. She stood with arms crossed, scratching her elbows.

'She said, "Next time it will be someone you love."'

Bill didn't know what to say. 'It was just a dream, though.'

She nodded. 'It felt real, though. That's the thing. It felt so real.'

'What do you think she meant? The dream, I mean. What do you think it meant?'

They walked on a little further.

When he had arrived here first, as a young man, a misfit who loved wildlife, there had been a few of the old fishing families still living here; a few still did, though they were getting crowded out by the rich. The old families were not fans of the police and mostly kept their distance from Bill. Sometimes they had cornered him in the pub, accusing him of spying on them. Other times, after a few pints, they told stories about the woman supposed to haunt the old black lighthouse. Some of the people who night-fished on the beach claimed to have been approached by an old man in a hooded fisherman's smock who disappeared

118

when they shone their torches on him. Ghost stories. Bill had taken it all with a pinch of salt.

A group of young men on expensive bicycles went up the road, hands off handlebars, balancing on their saddles, drinking from plastic bottles after a long ride. He said, 'I'll make you porridge if you like. Or toast?'

Zoë made a face and walked on towards the power station. 'I'll just go home,' she said. 'I'm going back to bed. I'm tired.'

'Wait,' he called. 'The woman you dreamed of. Who was she talking about, do you think?'

'Mum, obviously,' said Zoë. 'Only I can't tell her that because she doesn't believe in weird stuff like that.'

NINETEEN

On Tuesday, Jill appeared at Bill's door again, a Lidl shopping bag in one hand. 'Did you hear?'

'What?'

'I've taken a few days' leave,' she said. She explained how she had been taken off the Serious Crime unit because she had not only known the dead woman, but she had slept with the man who was the main suspect in her murder.

'I'm so sorry,' said Bill.

'Upside is, I'm off for a few days.' She handed him the carrier bag.

He looked inside. It seemed to be full of printed paper.

'What is it?'

'You said Alex couldn't do it, so I did. I pulled down records from the Police National Computer on the murders of Wayne Jordan and Mary Spillett. That's them.'

Bill pulled her inside. 'You can't do that,' he scolded her. 'There will be a record of who accessed this.'

'Right now I don't care about that. I have to get this done. And you're going to help me.'

Bill shook his head. 'I'm not going to look into any of this stuff for you. You're a serving detective. You can't do it, any more than Alex can.'

'But you will, won't you?' she said.

'No. You can't just ask me to do something like that.'

But he peered inside the plastic carrier bag again.

There were many more documents than Bill expected. It took him a while to piece the interview transcriptions and incident reports into a coherent narrative, making notes on a yellow A4 pad, putting everything he could find into chronological order.

The earliest was an incident report dated 18 February 1994. That was when a farmer reported finding a Vauxhall Chevette burnt out on a small track on his farm on the north side of the marsh. At first he assumed joyriders, but when he fetched a tractor and chains and was yanking it out of the way, the boot burst open and there, in the boot, was the badly burnt body of a young man.

The related case file later identified the dead man as Wayne Jordan. According to the notes, Jordan was a known drug dealer. The forensic file confirmed that Jordan had been bludgeoned to death with a blunt object, then his body had been set alight.

The second murder had happened at 11.03 a.m. on 3 March 1994. The victim's name was Mary Spillett and she was forty-two years old, the postmistress of the Breznett post office. She had been killed by a single round from a Russian-made Baikal shotgun, which struck her high in the abdomen, lacerating the heart and stomach and piercing the left subclavian artery. The coroner's report concluded that she would have died within a few minutes of the gunshot.

The till roll recorded that there should have been £80.62 in the till, plus a float of £15.50, ten pounds of which was in notes; £1.12 in change was found in the till.

The files included the witness statement of a dog walker who had heard the shooting, and a long, dry description of the content of the CCTV tapes recovered after the incident. The CCTV camera had been positioned inside the front door of the small sub-post office, showing a partial view of the customer area – side on. There was no audio. According to the notes made by some unnamed member of the investigating team, the tape clearly showed a man of Stephen Dowles's height and build entering the frame in a woollen balaclava, removing the gun from a cloth guitar case and pointing it towards the till.

According to the tape's time-code, at 11:02:03 Stephen stepped forward out of shot. When he stepped back he was clutching something, which he put in his pocket. The person who had taken the notes wrote: '*Suspect appears to demand and receive money from M. Spillett?*'

Approximately twenty seconds later, the gunman pulled the trigger. '*Flash visible.*'

Attached separately was a plan of the post office, showing the position in which Mary Spillett's body was found.

When photos of the incident were shared in local newspapers, several people came forward and said they thought the killer resembled the drug user Stephen Dowles. The gun was found at Stephen Dowles's flat in Ashford, as was the balaclava.

A further document in the file noted Dowles's address. *'Unemployed. Known substance abuser.'* Drug paraphernalia was discovered in his bedroom, including pipes that showed residues of cocaine.

A final folder contained colour photographs of the murder scene. Mary Spillett had toppled backwards onto the floor. She had been wearing a bright-blue cardigan, with a red thistle brooch. Lying on her back, blood had flowed quickly from the artery in her chest onto the grey linoleum floor around her. Whether in pain or desperation, she had moved her left arm up and down, making regular semi-circular red marks alongside her. Moon shapes of blood spread out on either side of her. Her eyes were open; her mouth was wide. She looked puzzled.

Dowles went into hiding for a week. Bill remembered it all clearly. When DI Tart found him, living in a derelict property in Ashford, he confessed to the killing. During subsequent questioning, he also confessed to the murder of Wayne Jordan. Two very brutal murders, both in the space of weeks. He admitted to using substantial quantities of coke and meth-amphetamine around the time of the killings. It was all solid police work.

This was the man who said he was Jill's father.

He called Jill up. 'I don't understand what you want me to do?' he said. 'You've seen the reports. It's all there in black and white.'

'No it's not,' said Jill. 'Everything he's done is there, but none of it makes any sense.'

'You at home?'

'Yeah.' Jill lived in a flat in the Panorama Apartments in

Ashford. 'I mean, it's obvious he did it, but there's absolutely no explanation of why it happened. Why did he kill Wayne Jordan? What kind of idiot robs a post office for less than a hundred quid and then murders a woman when he could have walked out of there and got away with it?'

'He was on drugs. People do stupid things.'

'Right. And that's it, is it?' said Jill, ending the call abruptly.

That evening, annoyed at Jill, annoyed at himself for agreeing to help her, he went for a walk along the ridge of shingle that ran above the sea. Some days the sea was full of drama, and you could get lost, staring at it. Other days it was flat, and nothing moved in or above it. Today was one of those days.

As he was returning, he spotted Curly's Ford Ranger parked on the beach. Curly kept a fishing boat on the beach. His family had lived here for generations, but like so many of the fishing families, they'd sold up long before these wooden huts started selling for half a million and more. Now he lived in a terraced house in Littlestone.

Curly was loading engine parts into the rear of the truck.

'Need a hand?'

'Nah,' he said. 'You'll only get your hands dirty. Fuel injector's gone,' he said.

Curly never seemed to go out on the boat any more; he just spent his days tinkering with it.

'Tell me,' said Bill. 'Do you remember Stephen Dowles?'

'Why do you ask?'

'No reason.'

'Couldn't forget that fucker,' said Curly. 'Hope he rots in hell.'

'What about Wayne Jordan?'

124

'Poor old Wayne. Crazy what happened to him. Yeah. I knew him. Don't ask me how, though.'

Bill peered into his eyes. 'You used to buy drugs off him, didn't you?'

Curly made a zipping motion across his mouth. 'He was one of Bobby White's boys. Remember him?'

The name bubbled back into his head. Bobby White. Local drug dealer. 'Yes. I remember now.'

'Scariest fucker on the south coast, Bobby White.' He smiled thinly. 'You never caught him, did you?'

'I was just a local bobby, Curly. I was too busy helping old folk across the road.'

Curly laughed.

Bill returned home in darkness to discover he had left the lamp on outside his door. He was annoyed at himself. He just wanted to be left alone. Below the lamp, a moth was crawling on the glass. When he picked it up and cradled it, smearing brown scales onto his hands, he saw that it had a broken wing, presumably from flying into the bulb, which was his fault. Gently he laid it back down onto the grass, where it ran in circles beneath the electric light.

TWENTY

The next morning, Bill South made up his mind and got on his Kawasaki motorbike and rode out to Ashford.

The road had barely changed since he was last here thirty years ago. Only the weeds between the paving stones were a little bigger than he remembered. He pulled the motorbike onto its stand outside a house with a sign in the window that read *Refugees are welcome here*. The estate, on the far side of Ashford, had been built in the 1960s. Sixty years on, some had been left as red brick, others rendered and painted to add some individuality.

Wayne Jordan's mum was in her seventies now, but looked younger. She had dyed black hair and wore jeans, a multicolour knitted cardigan and a green jewel in her nose. 'I don't know if you remember me,' said Bill.

'Bill South. You were the one came to tell me Wayne had passed,' she answered without pausing for thought, looking past him at the motorbike. 'And then you came to tell me who had killed him. Can't you lot afford cars any more?'

'I'm not a copper these days, Katie. Unofficial business.'

126

'What kind of unofficial business?' She frowned at him.

'Better we talk inside, Katie.'

She hesitated, then opened the door wide. 'In you come then, Bill, if you must,' she said. 'You'll have to be quick, though, I was just heading out. It's about Stephen Dowles, I expect?'

'How do you figure that?' asked Bill, stepping into a crowded hallway.

'I had a letter last week saying he was up on parole,' she said. 'I guess they were warning me the papers would be coming round to stir it up again.'

It figured. However brutal Stephen Dowles's murders had been, he would have served his tariff by now. He would be out soon. And as Jill had said, if the papers discovered that Dowles had a daughter in the same police force that put him away, Jill would be in the glaring light of it all again, and so would Katie. 'And how do you feel about that? About him getting out?'

'Is that what you came to ask me?'

'Pretty much.'

'You want me to let you know if I'm going to go and burn his house down or something?'

She put the kettle on and shouted at a cat to get off the kitchen table. On her fridge were pictures of a younger woman and her children. 'Are you?' he asked.

'As far as I'm concerned, he's nothing at all to do with me. It's up to him what he does. I don't feel anything either way. I can't spare the energy to hate him any more, to be honest. I expect you'd like sugar?'

He nodded at the photograph. 'Grandkids?'

'Three,' Katie answered. 'You?'

'Never married,' said Bill.

She paused to gaze at the pictures. 'Bloody love them. I look after them for their mum three times a week up in Rochester. Plus, two days working at the food bank up Repton Avenue. I'm busier than I ever was in my life, and it's exhausting.' She gave a little laugh, though she didn't look exhausted at all.

'So you don't feel bitterness towards Dowles then? Or blame?'

'Bitter? It's not that. It's a big hole in my heart; a hole the size of a house. Always will be. And *blame* is such a stupid word. I don't have to like Stephen Dowles, or what he did, and I wish to Christ every single day he hadn't done it, but I'm not one of those people who doesn't see the world for what it is. Stephen Dowles did an awful, awful thing. But I see people like him round here every day, young stupid men, getting caught up in all sorts of shittery. And my Wayne was a lovely lad, but he was no angel either, was he, Bill?'

'He didn't deserve to die, Katie.'

'Course he bloody didn't,' she said tetchily. 'None of them did. But he was selling drugs, wasn't he, my boy? Not just weed, either. People had miserable lives because of all that, and he was part of it. It was like a fire burned through here and it's still raging. Haven't you noticed? And you lot have done nothing but made it worse. If I was to start blaming anyone, why not the plod? You certainly didn't help none.'

Not many in this part of town ever had anything good to say about the police. Bill was used to it. 'Dowles was off his face, Katie. That wasn't anything to do with us. I was wondering, did you ever see them together, Wayne and Stephen?'

'Why d'you want to know that?'

128

'Curious, I suppose.'

She shook her head. 'Honest to God, I'd forgotten Stevie existed until you and the family liaison came around to tell me he'd been arrested for the murder of my son.'

'They knew each other then?'

'Of course they knew each other. The drug scene is a little club, or at least it was back then. He just wasn't anyone big in Wayne's life. They were both into their music and their drugs. Everyone round here was. I just never understood what poor Wayne had done to piss Stephen off that much to make him want to do what he did.'

'It could have been nothing at all, given the drugs Stephen was taking in those days,' said Bill.

'Maybe so.' Katie pursed her lips.

'If he does get out and the press come knocking on your door, what are you going to tell them, then?'

'I don't see it's any of your business, but I'll tell them to fuck off. Last time around they called me Drug Mum, remember? On account of I had a couple of convictions for weed that they should have never known about in the first place, only one of your lot told them – thanks a lorryload. I only let you in here because you were the one who came to tell me about how he died and I appreciated that at the time. You were kind to me. You stayed. You put your arms around me when I cried. You didn't treat me like scum, which is what I got from the rest of you lot.'

'I'm sorry for that,' said Bill. 'Genuinely.'

'Yeah, well,' she said. 'Water under the bridge. Not really, though.'

'What about a young woman called Sandra Ferriter?' Sandra. Jill's mother.

She paused, thinking for a second. 'Oh yeah. Sandra. Wayne knew her. He used to hang around with some bad ones. I heard after she was a prostitute. She died too, didn't she, poor girl?'

'Yes, she did.'

'It was like a bloody tornado coming through here, except nobody noticed because the buildings were all still standing. First it was all innocent, everyone raving and taking E. Next thing, everyone had a habit. And I tell you what, it's getting like that again now, and worse, and nobody gives a shit. As far as the government goes, it's good riddance. Let 'em all kill themselves.' She took a breath, held it for a moment, and then let it out again. 'Right. I'm off now. You've had your tea,' she said.

He stood. As he walked through the front door she told him, 'As far as I'm concerned, let him out. Let him get a job somewhere and disappear into the background like the sad old git he probably is now. He did what he did and nothing is going to put that right. But I don't want to have to think about him any more, OK? So I don't want to see you round here, ever again. Fuck off, OK?'

'Wait,' he said, before she closed the door on him. Something had dawned on him. He pointed to a house beyond the T-junction. 'Isn't that where the Whites used to live?'

'That's right.'

The White family. The two eldest brothers, Jake and Bobby White, had been small-time gangsters around that time. Jake had been busted and imprisoned, was diagnosed with testicular cancer and died in his early twenties in the prison hospital, but

130

to the frustration of all the coppers who knew he was up to no good, they had never managed to arrest Bobby.

'Was your lad friends with Bobby and Jake?'

'Same school, so yeah.'

'Are they still there?'

'God, no. The family moved out years ago,' said Katie Jordan. 'Bobby left years ago. I heard he got fed up with the attention from you lot. Are you done here? Only, like I said, I need to go.'

'Bet you were happy to see him go.'

She looked at him disdainfully from her doorstep. 'You guys know nothing. Worst thing that ever happened, round these parts. After the White family left, that was when this place really started to fall apart. Bobby White looked out for us. Bobby White had standards. Nobody round here messed with him. Since Bobby went, it's back to how it was when Wayne died – as far as the kids go, at least.' She glanced around at the anonymous houses. 'Looks nice round here, doesn't it? Only, all you have to do is scratch the surface. County lines round here is insane. Bobby White would never have allowed that to happen. Now fuck off, Bill,' she said, and closed the door on him.

TWENTY-ONE

Thursday morning, the company in Rye wanted Bill to come out to count some bats. 'Sorry,' said Bill, talking on the phone. 'Can't do it. Busy this week . . . What? Oh, just this and that.'

In the morning, Bill took the Kawaskai out again, this time in the other direction, towards Sussex. The journey took him an hour. When he got to the semi in Pevensey Bay, Figgy's wife, Jenn, opened the door and leaned forward to be kissed.

He had known Jenn thirty years and she still looked glamorous – in a punky kind of way. She wore leather trousers and had shiny bleached hair, though she must be well into her sixties now. 'Still living in a shed in Dungeness and gawping at birds?' she asked.

'Nice to see you too.'

'Haven't seen you since God knows when. Figgy's just where you left him last,' Jean said.

Bill hadn't been to visit since before lockdown, but it was a fair guess where he would be. He spent most of his life in the conservatory at the back of the house.

Figgy had been in Kent CID in the 1990s. He'd retired here with Jenn almost twenty years ago, and had the stroke almost immediately afterwards. Some people don't have any luck.

In the extension at the back, Figgy was watching daytime TV. There was an oxygen cylinder and a mask next to him just in case. He switched the TV off when Bill came in.

'Fucking hell. I thought you were dead.'

'Yeah. Same. How's your world, Figgy?' Bill asked.

This place really was Figgy's world. After the stroke, he'd started building railway layouts, gradually filling the conservatory with tracks and mountains. The layout he had created ran around the whole room, leaving space only for a small table and chairs.

'Not done much recently. Just bits and pieces.'

It was an artwork. His experience as a copper, dealing with the everyday catastrophes and pratfalls of ordinary life, had seeped into the model. In a pretty English village at the far end of the layout, a half-timbered house was on fire, a child waiting for rescue at the window. A man who had been repairing a railway station roof was clinging to guttering by his fingertips, his ladder lying flat on the ground beneath him. On a bridge crossing over a river, a minivan had struck another car head on and a dead man, not a seatbelt wearer, had been flung through the windscreen, and his body was lying flat on the bonnet of an Escort, arms stretched in front of him by the force of the collision. The river below was an incredible piece of work. It looked as if there was real water in the river bed, frozen into place. Bill marvelled at the rocks beneath the surface of the water, the tiny pale crests of the waves.

Bill pointed. 'Is that new?'

'Did it a couple of years ago. Epoxy resin. Some other gunk on top to make the ripples. It would take me half a day to tell you and I doubt you'd be interested anyway. Jenn?' he shouted. 'You got those photos of the layout that were in that magazine?'

She didn't answer.

'They sent a photographer. Took all sorts of shots. Came out nice. Sad, isn't it? Me spending all this time on that.'

'Tragic,' said Bill.

On the river, a brightly painted boat was about to tip over a weir, a man at its rear, desperately struggling with the tiller. 'That's supposed to be Jenn's brother. He's a nut about boats.'

'Did you make him too?'

'Nah. Bought him. Bought a few more people and stuck them around the place.' He pointed to a tiny man in a mac who was flashing a queue of nuns at a bus stop.

'Not very appropriate, Figgy,' Bill said.

'Neither's that, then.'

He pointed to a bungalow.

'What?'

'Look inside. I'll show you.' Figgy flicked a tiny switch some-where, and lights came on all over the layout. The burning house began to flicker. He pointed to the other end of the village, towards the window of a bungalow. Inside – lit by a miniature electric lamp – a tiny couple were having model sex, the woman leaning over the man, her arms against the headboard.

Bill squinted at them. 'Pervert.'

'I have to get my kicks where I can these days, Bill, and there's not many of them, I tell you. There's a company in Germany

134

makes the figures – painted and everything. Losing interest in it all now, though, to be honest.'

He switched the lights back off.

Jenn arrived with tea. 'Did he just show you the shaggers in the bungalow?'

'Yes.'

'All the fun he gets these days.' She sat next to Figgy. 'So what did you really come for, Bill? I'm guessing it wasn't to witness his tragically small sex life.'

'Size isn't everything,' muttered Figgy.

Dutifully, Bill laughed. He liked Figgy and Jenn. He should have tried harder to see more of them. Then he said, 'Actually, I came about Stephen Dowles.'

'Oh. That fucker,' Figgy said, glancing at Jenn.

Jenn tutted. It wasn't the language she disapproved of.

'You worked on the Wayne Jordan murder, didn't you, Figgy?'

Figgy picked up a pair of glasses that were next to his cup of tea, put them on and craned forward to examine Bill. 'Why you interested? You're not back on the job, are you?'

'Something just came up, that's all.'

Figgy tilted his head back to examine Bill through his specs. 'You haven't been here for years, Bill. How come the first time I see you in all this time is because you want to ask me about Stephen bloody Dowles?'

'What I wanted to know was, was Stephen Dowles always in the frame for Wayne Jordan's murder?'

'Well, that's nice. No *How are you doing, Figgy?*'

'How are you doing, Figgy?'

'Not so bad, actually.'

Jenn scowled. 'He gets depressed – don't you, Figgy?'

'Living with you, yeah.'

She punched him hard.

'Seriously,' said Figgy. 'What you on about, Bill, coming here and asking that?'

'Was he always one of your suspects?'

'Be nice, Figgy,' Jenn said quietly.

'Honest? No. We never even heard of Stephen Dowles till he was named for the murder of the woman in the post office. What's going on, Bill? Why are you digging up this old stuff?'

'Did the team have anyone else on their list?'

'Why?' There was a note of hostility in his former colleague's voice.

'Just bear with me, Figgy. Wayne Jordan was a dealer. You must have had some kind of intelligence about who his likely killers were?'

Figgy thought about this for a minute. 'Let me get this right. Are you trying to prove that Stephen Dowles didn't do it?'

'I'm just looking into it, like I said.'

'Who for?'

'I can't tell you that.' Figgy had been a cop. If he didn't know Jill, he would have known her mother.

'Because he did it. For a fact. He was a cold killer, Bill. I watched the videotape from the post office. You seen that?'

'No.'

Figgy lapsed into silence.

'Biscuit?' Jenn held out a tin. Bill took one and chewed on it. 'Is that all you came about?' she demanded. 'To ask him about something that happened thirty years back?'

Bill shifted in his chair. 'I'm sorry I haven't been here more often. I should have. You're right.'

'Go on then,' said Figgy. 'Tell me what you're on about.'

Bill took a breath and started again. 'There were around three, four weeks between the murder of Wayne Jordan and Stephen Dowles coming through with a confession. Don't tell me that in all that time you didn't have any suspects.'

'Course we did, Bill.'

'Who were they, then?'

'Why? Tell me why you want to know and I'll tell you.'

'I can't tell you that, Figgy. I just want to know how things played out.'

Figgy scowled. 'They played out fine. We got the man who killed both of them.'

'OK, so tell me. What harm can it do?'

Figgy chewed on the inside of his cheek for a while before he spoke. 'I'm not proud of a lot of the stuff we did, Billy. It didn't make things better. Looking back at my whole career in CID, I sometimes wonder what we were up to. By the time I quit, things were worse than they were when I started. What the hell did we achieve? Well, one of the few things I am proud of is helping to put away Stephen Dowles. But the truth was, until Stephen Dowles came into focus, all of us wanted it to be Bobby White.'

'Bobby White?'

'Alleged drug dealer,' Figgy said sourly.

Bill thought of standing on Katie Jordan's doorstep yesterday, looking out across the junction to the house where the White family had lived. 'Why him?'

137

Figgy made a face. 'Because he knew Wayne. Because it felt like something he would do, that's all. Because we really, really wanted it to be him, because if it was, then we'd have had something to pin on him. Sometimes that's all you have to go on and it's not always right. And it turned out we weren't right. We had fallen into the rabbit hole.'

'I'll leave you two boys to it,' said Jenn, standing. 'Don't let him eat the biscuits, Bill. He's not allowed, on account of the diabetes.'

She left the conservatory, closing the door behind her.

'But you thought it could have been Bobby White, right?' He remembered what Wayne Jordan's mother had said: *Bobby White. He looked out for us.*

TWENTY-TWO

Bill remembered the ravers arriving on Dungeness one hot summer weekend in 1992, big old Scammell lorries full of dread-locked white kids turning up, pitching wagons on the shingle, setting up generators and dancing for days at a time.

Day and night, the pulsing sound of their music drifted across the marshes. It was impossible to stop. By the time locals were aware of what was going on, there were too many cars and trucks to start turning them back. All they could do was wait until the rave had exhausted itself and then move them on.

Drug gangs had been an urban phenomenon. People expected them in Manchester and London, but not here, and suddenly they were everywhere, building a new economy on MDMA before they moved up to cocaine and heroin. Other gang leaders came and went, killed in fights or sent to prison. A few seemed untouchable.

Figgy flicked the switch and the fire in the house started burning again.

'So the first suspect was Bobby White?'

139

'Stupid. We just wanted him so badly. Ironic thing is that we made the gangs what they were. I think about this a lot. I only realised this too late, but everything we tried to do to crack down on drugs gangs back then was a mistake. We got everything wrong. I did that job for ten years, and in all that time we only made all that better, stronger, richer.'

The burning house started to give off real smoke now. Wisps curled upwards slowly. 'Is that real?' Bill pointed.

'Special effect. Good, isn't it? Got a little device in the chimney.'

'Sorry. I thought for a moment . . .'

'That it was properly going up in flames?' Figgy laughed.

'Worried how quick I could get you out of here with all this crap in the way,' said Bill.

'Love to see the coroner's report on that. Man killed by model railway.' Figgy wheezed with laughter for a while and took a suck from the cylinder by his chair. When he'd recovered, he said, 'The thing about drug strategy back then was they just blamed the gangs. If we stamped out the gangs, they thought everything would be better. Doesn't work like that, though, does it? Because people love drugs. Because everything we did to try and stop them just made the gangs better, more vicious. If we put in snitches, they upped the violence so that people were good and scared, too frightened to rat. If we arrested their bagmen, they found younger kids who they knew we couldn't touch because they were juveniles. If we got headlines putting Gang A behind bars, that just meant that Gang B had more customers and they could get bigger, stronger, more evil, more violent. And so after a few years we ended up with guys like Bobby White rolling around in his big black Mercedes, because they were smarter and quicker at knowing all the angles. And more violent. Hundred per cent we made him that way.'

'So you reckoned Bobby White for the killing of Wayne Jordan.'

'I wished it was him, put it that way. It would have made sense. And because if it was him, we'd have finally had something on him. Because people like that got away with it. Back then, Bobby White was just coming up in the world, but he was already Teflon. Wayne Jordan was just a kid who ends up in a burnt-out car boot. Looks obvious, doesn't it. Only it wasn't him.'

'Because Stephen Dowles confesses?'

'And because it turned out Bobby White wasn't even in Kent when Wayne Jordan was killed. He was in Paris proposing to his girlfriend, Mandy. When we went round to his house, they showed us all the photos. Champagne, flowers, the works.'

'At the time, what did you think?'

'Lucky bugger, that's what I thought. I still do. Last thing I heard, he was living in Florida.'

Jenn saw him to the door. 'How did he look to you, Bill?'

'Good. Good,' said Bill.

Jenn looked sceptical. 'Do you miss it, Bill?'

He knew exactly what she meant; 'it' was the job. 'God, no,' he said.

'You're a rubbish liar all round, Bill South,' she said. It was true, he did miss it, he realised as she closed the door on him and he turned away. Not so much companionship exactly, just a sense of being so connected to another world beyond his door, however dark it sometimes was.

★

141

Bill rode hunching low in the saddle, buffeted by the rising wind. The sun was low by the time he made it back to Dungeness. He parked the motorbike outside his house and chained it up, but instead of going inside he walked on down the track towards the cottages.

Zoë was lying on her back on the shingle behind the houses, wrapped in a blanket.

'What the hell are you up to?' asked Bill.

'Eta Aquariid meteor showers,' she answered.

He looked around. 'It's not even dark yet.'

She shrugged. 'Waiting,' she said.

'Your mum in?'

'No. She went swimming except I asked her not to so she probably will anyway.'

'Swimming?'

'With the women in Hythe. The ones who were friends of the dead woman.' She spoke in a low voice. 'The one who was murdered.'

'It was a dream. You know that.' Bill lay down beside her and looked up at the deep-blue evening sky, the wisps of cirrus clouds pinking in the setting sun. There was a front on the way. The rain would be coming soon. They'd be lucky to see the meteor shower before the clouds came.

'Yeah. I know it was just a dream, Bill. That doesn't mean it's not real.'

'Have you had any other dreams about her?'

'Uh-uh.' She shook her head. 'Nothing.'

'That's good then.'

142

Zoë sat up. 'No it's not. I want to dream about her. I want her to talk to me.'

Bill didn't know what to say to her. Though he had many times wished they did, dead people didn't talk to the living.

'I'm scared of the sea now,' said Zoë. 'I don't even want to look at it any more.'

'That's sad,' he said.

'Yes. It is.'

'I'm scared of the sea too. Always have been,' said Bill.

'You got a boat though. So you can't be that scared.'

'Yeah I am,' he answered. 'I don't tell people this, but I can't even swim. The trick is not falling in.'

'You're kidding me?'

'Never learned. Nobody taught us when we were kids. Nothing wrong with being scared of the sea. I mean, who wouldn't be?'

'I can't imagine not being able to swim. Didn't you ever want to learn?'

'Yeah. I did want to. I just never did. And now I'm too scared to start.'

Sitting up too, he heard the sound of a car approaching. When Alex opened the Saab's door, the girl ran over and threw her arms around her mother.

'What's that for?' Alex demanded.

'Did you go swimming?'

'You asked me not to. So I didn't,' Alex answered. Bill watched the skinny girl clinging on to her mother, as if still afraid something terrible might happen to her.

TWENTY-THREE

In the morning, Bill rode the back lanes, enjoying the fresh-
ness of the day, winding along the roads, slowing for the sharp
bends and speeding out of them, and letting the journey clear
his head. The routes around here were as old as the marshes.
They had been built hundreds of years ago on the banks raised
by farmers to drain the land. Many an inexperienced driver had
been caught out by the sudden ninety-degree turns and ended
up with a car, nose first, in a ditch.

Brenzett was a small village in the middle of the flat marsh.
The post office was no longer there by the roundabout. It had
closed down years ago. The building had been converted into a
private house now, recognisable only from the red postbox built
into the side wall.

Bill hauled the heavy bike onto its stand and approached the
house. He pushed open the gate and rang the doorbell but no
one answered, so, guessing the place was unoccupied, he peered
into one of the windows. The venetian blinds that hung inside
were half shut.

'Can I help you?' Bill turned to see a woman with a buggy, standing at the gate. She was in her forties, he guessed, old to be a mother, or young to be a grandmother.

'This your house?'

'Who wants to know?'

He stood back. 'I was trying to remember what this place looked like when it was a post office.'

The woman blinked, looked him up and down; she wore a faux fur coat, leggings and trainers. Bill looked down at the infant in the buggy holding a packet of Monster Munch. The child stared back, sombre. The woman gave a knowing half-smile. 'It's about the murder, is it?'

That took Bill by surprise. 'How did you know?'

The woman sighed, turned her back and unbuckled the boy in the buggy. 'Another one, Milo.'

'Ah. You get a lot of people coming here, asking about the murder?'

The woman straightened, lifting the boy out of the pushchair. 'Ridiculous thing was we hadn't heard anything about there being a killing here until after we'd bought the place. They'll tell you whether a place has subsidence or damp but nobody lets you know that people were shot and left to bleed to death in your house.'

'Sorry.' Bill tried to look it.

'What are you? We had a podcaster here last week. True crime. No, thank you very much.'

'No. I'm not a podcaster.'

'You're not one of them ghost hunters?' She held the child on her hip.

'Me?'

'We had some round a while ago, trying to detect her ghost. I was still pregnant with you, wasn't I?' she said to the boy. 'They brought all this equipment with them, old-fashioned tape recorders and things that looked like bits from old radios, and kept hushing us all the time. I was laughing so much it hurt.' She put her key in the door. 'So what are you, then?'

'I should go.'

'No you don't. You have to tell me why you were nosing round the place first.'

He sighed. 'When the murder happened, I was a local copper. Just personal interest, that's all.'

She grinned at him. 'I should have guessed. Something about you.' The woman held open the door and nodded inside. 'I'm Liz,' she said. 'Come on in.'

Bill followed her inside, looking around as she passed across the threshold into a large living room. 'Shoes,' she said brusquely.

He unzipped his motorcycle boots and walked into the living room, wishing he had put on more respectable socks.

Inside, there was no sign of the place ever having been a post office. Whoever Liz was, she kept her house perfectly. The interior was carefully decorated in blues and pinks. The curtains were ruched pink with blue tie-backs. Giant ceramic baby-blue candlesticks stood in one corner. Spiral filament bulbs hung on blue and pink cords from the ceiling. Where the post office counter must have once been, there was a modern white table covered in pink place mats and pink napkins, as if permanently ready for a dinner party.

'You've done a nice job with the place,' he said politely.

'Thank you,' said Liz. She looked around the room, as if surprised by it herself. 'I get a lot of ideas from magazines. So many bloody magazines.'

Above the mantelpiece was a huge mirror framed in pink ceramic roses. She took off the boy's coat, sat him down on the immaculate white carpet and looked at Bill, examining him. 'Thing is, I don't think you've been entirely honest with me.'

'About the decor?'

Liz laughed. It was a good, generous laugh. 'Whoever you are, you're obviously not here on official business. What's the real reason you've come?'

Bill said, 'As I said, curiosity.'

She tutted. 'Before you go any further, full disclosure. I used to be a CSI in London before I finally got pregnant. My husband's an ex-copper. I'm not a civilian. I know your job almost as well as you do. If someone like you is poking around there's got to be a reason, even if it's not an official one. I'm more bothered by why you're doing this now than the idea of someone being murdered in this house.'

'Ah,' said Bill.

'There is something, then?'

'Well . . .'

'Sit down, I'll put the kettle on, and why don't you explain it all to me.' Liz took a couple of wooden toys – a yellow crane and a red car – and placed them next to the boy, who picked up the crane and put it straight into his mouth. Liz put the kettle on, then stood in the kitchen door, still in her big fur coat, while it roared. 'My husband got a job at the power station as head of

147

their security, working alongside the Civil Nuclear Constabulary. It was a chance for us to move out of London. Now he's there all the bloody time he loves it so much, while I'm stuck here at home.'

He looked around the neat room.

'So, yes, I'm on to you. What are you really doing here?'

Liz arrived back in the room with a tray with two cups and a plate of chocolate chip cookies, then returned to the kitchen to bring back a bottle of warm milk for the child.

'OK,' said Bill. 'It sounds very much like Stephen Dowles is getting out soon. He's the man who—'

'I know exactly who Stephen Dowles is.'

'I wanted to remind myself of what he'd done.'

The boy grizzled until Liz raised the teat to his mouth. She leaned forward and took a biscuit. 'Interesting. It's curiosity, then? Did you ever meet him?'

'I did. Just the once.'

'What was he like? I mean, really?'

Bill looked around the living room. Everything was neat and orderly. Everything looked clean, so clean. He tried to imagine Alex living like this. What kind of mother were you to have a toddler and a perfect white carpet without a single stain on it? There were no smudges on the glass table on which she placed her cup either.

'Ordinary. Very ordinary.'

'So why are you bothered?' Liz asked.

He looked at her for a while. 'Can I trust you?'

'I'd say, yes you can, obviously. You have to make that call.'

'OK then. Confidentially, it turns out that, from prison, he's been claiming to be the dad of someone I know. We're all worried that when he gets out, he'll wreck her life. Plus, if the press get on to it, that he's her father . . .' He looked at Liz.

'Wow. That's weird. Go on.'

'This girl – this young woman – she's had a pretty shitty life, growing up, but she's really made something of herself. If she lets him back into her life, that's her call, not ours. All we can do for her is find out as much about him as we can.'

Baby nestled in her arms, Liz looked a perfect image of contented womanhood, but Bill sensed something wrong in the room. He was trying to put his finger on it.

'What are you hoping to find?'

'She needs to know everything. She needs to know exactly who her father is – if he is her dad.'

She seemed to consider this for a while. 'I always thought the whole thing was interesting,' she said.

'What do you mean?'

The baby's eyes were starting to close. 'I looked into it too,' said Liz quietly. 'I would, wouldn't I, in my line of business. I looked up all the clippings. Professional interest, you might say, like yours is. He was a drug user, drug dealer.'

'That's right.'

'Not a big fish. Minor dealing offences. Not a whiff of violent crime to that point. Nothing with weapons. Never done for anything like that.'

'No,' agreed Bill.

'One day he just gets into a violent argument with a drug dealer, beats him to death. A few weeks later he just rocks up to

149

a post office with a shotgun and kills someone for no apparent reason. Doesn't make any sense to me.' Gingerly, she disentangled a hand from the dozing child and pointed to the ceiling by the front door. 'There was a CCTV camera right there when it happened,' she said. 'Have you had a chance to look at the videotape?'

'No.'

'Apparently she did nothing at all to provoke him.'

'That's right.'

'You got to admit, it's weird. He's a drug user. He's desperate. He's got the money. Why didn't he just leg it?'

'People with guns in their hands do funny things,' said Bill. He would know that, better than anyone.

'So if you haven't seen the videotape, have you looked at the description of it?'

'Why?'

She laid the sleeping boy carefully on the couch, picked up a pillow and wedged it next to him, then she stood. 'When I remodelled this living room, the plaster had to come down from the ceiling. I found the old CCTV cable up there. You can see the exact position of where the camera would have been.' She walked towards the front door and pointed upwards. 'Exactly there. I'm pretty sure from the transcript that the camera must have been focused here.' She moved to the middle of the room, a metre and a half in front of the front door. 'Anyone standing here would have been standing at the post office till. It would give you a good look at the side of their head. You couldn't see the door, and you couldn't see the till, so all we can see is this area where I'm standing. According to the transcript, then, Stephen Dowles stood about' – she took a step backwards – 'here.'

'So you never actually see him fire the gun?'

'You saw him holding it, which is probably good enough. You see the muzzle flash. He pulled the trigger, for sure.'

He didn't understand what she was getting at. 'So what's the problem?'

'What the CCTV doesn't show. What else happened. It was only a partial view.'

The baby stirred on the sofa, made a little whimpering noise.

'How long were you a CSI?'

'Seven years.'

'Liked it?'

'Yeah. Bloody loved it.'

'You haven't left the job at all, have you?' Bill understood her now. The baby was perfectly looked after. The room was clean and decorated. Every single thing was colour-coordinated and planned. Every bit of dust had been banished from the room and it was driving Liz, a former CSI, completely nuts.

'I thought that was why you were here,' she said eventually, a slightly puzzled look on her face. 'That you thought there was something off about the murder too.'

'What do you mean, off?'

'Why did he do it? He could have got away with the money. There was no reason at all to pull the trigger. Everything was OK. He had nothing to worry about. So why?'

Outside, he got on his motorbike, but didn't start the engine for a minute or two. Until he had spoken to Liz, he hadn't realised that he agreed with what she had said. There was something off about the account of the Mary Spillett murder, but he wasn't at all sure what it was either.

TWENTY-FOUR

Bill knocked on Katie Jordan's door for the second time that week. 'Thought I told you to bog off.'

'One question,' he said, standing his ground. 'Did you know Bobby White's wife?'

A young girl appeared at the doorway and took hold of Katie's hand. Katie's granddaughter, he guessed; a girl who would have been Wayne Jordan's niece, had he lived. 'Did I know his wife? Why do you want to know?'

The little girl tugged at Katie's hand, urging her to come back inside.

'I'm just trying to piece a few things together.'

'Let it lie, Bill. Just let it lie, God's sake.'

The girl started to whine.

'Please. Just tell me anything you remember about her.'

Katie sighed. 'As far as I know, Bobby White never married. He had a girl for a while. I never saw them together, but then you never saw him anyway. Only, she wasn't never his wife. They got engaged but they never got married. Mandy was a pretty little thing. Worked at the dentist's on Faversham Road.'

Bill turned and watched as a man rode past on a BMX bike that looked too small for him. 'What happened to him and Mandy?'

'I don't know, do I? It didn't work out, I suppose.'

The man braked, stared at Bill, then rode on.

'When did you last see Bobby?'

'God. Not for ever. He was a bit of a ninja. Kept in the shadows. You'd see his car come around sometimes. Big old black Merc. Bloody classic motor. You'd hear about him often enough though. Anyone who messed with him would end up in the William Harvey. Not ideal, but at least you knew where you stood when he was around.' The girl was bored, tugging at Katie's hand.

'When did he up sticks then?'

'End of the nineties he left here, that's all I know. He's been gone a long time now, more's the pity.'

The silent girl beside her glared at Bill. 'So Bobby just gave up.'

'You get older. You move on. I heard he passed on the business to his second-in-command – remember a guy called Don Swallow? Then all the East European gangs came in and it went to hell.'

Bill did. Swallow was a huge guy with ginger hair who, if Bill remembered rightly, ended up inside for money laundering and fraud.

'You ever see Mandy?'

'Mandy French, I think she was. Funny you should say

that. I saw her at a petrol station a few months back, way up in Rochester. It's where this girl's mummy lives – isn't it, darling?' Shy, the girl buried her face into Katie's waist. 'I was picking her up from there, maybe January, February time. My tank was low so I went to fill up and when I went to pay, there she was in the queue, right in front of me. Her hair was a different colour and she was wearing this big donkey jacket thing, not glamorous Mandy French at all, not like she used to be, but I'd know her anywhere. She paid, turned round, walked right past me like she didn't recognise me at all.' Katie made a face like she'd just swallowed something unpleasant. 'I used to be pretty friendly with her. It's one of the things that happens when your son gets murdered. People you used to know just stop talking to you. They cross to the other side of the street.'

'I'm sorry,' said Bill.

'Yeah. Well. Some of them probably stopped talking to me because of the way your lot described Wayne – as some kind of lowlife. Others stop because they're just embarrassed. They don't know what to say to you so they stop meeting your eye. I don't know which Mandy was, but I haven't spoken to her since God knows when.'

In the empty street, the man on the BMX bike was cycling back the other way now, past Katie's house for a second time.

'Get lost now, Bill. Don't come round here no more. I don't like you no more, if I'm being honest.'

She bent down, lifted the girl into her arms. He stood on her doorstep as she closed the door on him and heard her slip the chain on.

Strapping his helmet back on, he noticed the man on the bike had stopped at the corner, and was leaning against the lamp post, one lanky leg still on the pedal.

He rode his motorbike back to Dungeness the slow way, over the marshes, which were suddenly green. New reeds poked above the water in the ditches. Swallows dipped low over fat lambs.

When he got home, Jill's car was outside his cabin, parked diagonally across the front of his house. When he went to put his key in the front door, he found it was already unlocked.

'I let myself in,' said Jill, looking up from the screen of her phone.

He stood in the doorway, furious.

'You keep the key under a stone by that bird bath,' said Jill. 'Alex told me once.' Before he could object, she said, 'I brought dinner. Have you found anything?'

He ignored the question and unzipped his jacket and hung it on a hook by the door.

'Eat about half an hour?' she asked. When he didn't answer, she added, 'I was thinking we could put a table out the back. Watch the sunset.'

'I prefer to eat inside,' he said.

She shrugged. 'OK.' In the kitchen, she started unpacking ready meals from an M&S carrier bag. She looked around the kitchen, puzzled. 'Where's your microwave?'

He ignored the question.

'OK. I'll just put them in the oven then.' She opened the oven door and then squatted down in front of it, trying to puzzle it out.

'You need a match,' he said. 'To light it. In the drawer by the sink.'

She raised her eyebrows, stood, and set about spooning out the curry dishes she had brought into ovenproof bowls. He disappeared into his bedroom to change his clothes and when he re-emerged the cabin was full of the rich smell of chicken jalfrezi.

They sat opposite each other at the small table and ate in silence. The food was surprisingly good and he hadn't realised how hungry he had been. He finished the bowl she had put in front of him, wiping it clean with the last of the naan. When he was done, she picked up the bowls and took them back to the kitchen and returned to sit opposite him.

'I don't know much more than when I started,' he said eventually. 'But I think if I keep looking, there's something there.'

'What kind of thing?'

'I'm really not sure. I'm trying to track down a woman called Mandy French. She'd be about the same age as your mother.'

'Is she important?'

'I don't know.'

She said, 'Have you tried social media?'

'It's not really my specialist subject,' he said.

'I didn't think so. Come on. Where's your computer?'

He kept the computer on a table in his bedroom. She sat in the old wooden dining chair in front of it and he leaned across her to start it. 'Had it a while, this thing?' she asked. He heard it whirring as it came to life. 'How do you spell her name?'

He wrote it on a bit of paper for her. 'She used to work at a dental practice, if that's any use.'

'OK. Leave me now. I cooked. You do the washing-up,' she said.

Ten minutes later, she called him back. 'She's in the General Dental Council's database of registered practitioners.' She pointed to the screen. Amanda Louise French.

'Where does she work now?'

'She doesn't. That's the problem. Nothing comes up.'

'Maybe she's married and changed her name?'

'Maybe. But we've got her full name and that's a start. I can't find any Facebook profile. She doesn't seem to have one, but then neither do you. Weirdo. Is the washing-up finished?'

'Not quite.' Jill Ferriter did not seem to like working with someone looking over her shoulder, so he retreated to the kitchen again, and when he'd finished the washing-up he put the kettle on for tea.

'You can come back now,' called Jill. When he returned to the bedroom, the screen of his computer was filled with a fuzzy picture of a driving licence.

'What is it?'

'Read the name.'

He leaned closer. 'Amanda Louise French.' The photograph on the licence showed a woman in her forties, with dark permed hair. Whoever had posted the photograph had obscured the address and the licence number. 'Mandy French?'

'Somebody found the driving licence in a purse that had been chucked away at the Esplanade in Rochester, down by the river,' Jill explained. 'They posted it on a Facebook group, Rochester Community Friends, asking if anyone knew her. You can't see the address though, because the woman who posted it blanked it out.'

He peered at the page. The message read: *If you recognise this woman, get in touch.*

'Look,' said Jill, scrolling down. 'There's a reply from a woman called Krakow Dawn. *I know Mandy. Msg me your number and I'll get her to call u.*'

'A Polish woman?'

'Not sure. Crack of Dawn? She went to school in Leeds.' Jill peered at the woman's profile on the screen. 'She owns a really ugly dog and lives in Rochester, Kent.'

'That's Mandy's driving licence,' he said. 'It's her photo on it. It has to be.' Katie Jordan had spotted Mandy in Rochester too. Now here was a woman on Facebook – Krakow Dawn – who lived in the same town, who had recognised Mandy's photo from the driving licence. 'Can you get in touch with her?'

Jill nodded. 'I already messaged Krakow Dawn. And she answered. Look.' She pressed the keyboard to switch to Messenger. Krakow Dawn had replied: *Who wants to know?*

TWENTY-FIVE

'*Who wants to know?* So what shall I tell her?'

Bill read the question, thought for a while. 'Just tell her the truth. Say, *My friend Bill has been trying to track her down to ask her about something that happened thirty years ago.*'

Jill tapped the reply into Messenger. 'Will Amanda French know who you are?' she asked Bill.

'No. But it might get her attention.'

'Who is she anyway?' Jill turned away from the screen. 'And what does that have to do with my dad?'

Bill sat down on his bed. 'I don't know yet.'

Jill raised her eyebrows. The computer bonged and Jill turned back round to face it. 'Bollocks,' she said. 'Krakow Dawn just blocked me.'

'Blocked you?'

'It means I can't send her messages any more.'

'She didn't like you asking after Mandy?'

'Looks like,' answered Jill. She switched back to the original post and leaned a little closer to the screen. 'What happened thirty years ago, Bill?'

'I'm not a hundred per cent sure, but I'm starting to think Mandy French told a big fat lie about something important. What next?'

She pointed to the date of the original post on the Rochester Community Friends Facebook group. 'February the twelfth.' Picking up her phone from the small table, she called a number. 'Charlie? Are you in the office still? Can you do me a favour?'

'What are you doing?' demanded Bill.

'Hold on, Charlie.' Jill put her phone on mute. 'Well, I can't ask Alex to do this, can I?' She unmuted again. 'Yes. I know I'm on leave. Listen. It's complicated, Charlie. A favour. That's all. Can you check on the PNC and find out whether a woman called Amanda Louise French reported a lost or stolen purse on or before the twelfth of February? Thanks, Charlie. You're an angel.'

She put the phone back on mute again.

'Young man?' said Bill.

'New guy on Serious Crime. A DC. Name is Charlie. Young. Keen.' She switched the phone back on. 'What? No record? Shit. Thanks all the same.' She ended the call.

'And he fancies you?' asked Bill.

She made a face. Shook her head. 'No. No.' Then she frowned. 'I don't think so, at least.'

Bill smiled. 'He's only doing something that's not strictly by the book because he respects you as a colleague.'

'Shut up, Bill. It's not like that,' she said, though she didn't sound entirely convinced herself. 'Shit. Another idea. Quiet.'

161

She picked up her phone again. 'Charlie? Me again. Was there any other property reported missing or stolen around that date?'

She listened for a second, then waved her hand at Bill, her hand writing an imaginary note. Bill opened the drawer and pulled out a pencil and notebook, then watched her scribbling in it.

'Great. Any arrests?' asked Jill.

Her tongue protruded slightly from the side of her mouth as she concentrated on writing, turning a page and writing more. 'Thanks, Charlie. That's brilliant. I owe you one.' It was Charlie's turn to talk again. Bill watched as Jill listened. A small frown appeared on her face. 'No. It wouldn't be weird. Let me get back to you on that.' She ended the call and looked at the screen for a second.

'Was that him asking you out on a date?'

She frowned. 'Actually, yes he did.'

Bill laughed.

'Don't look so smug. I'm doing all this for you. Listen. No purse reported stolen by Amanda French.'

'Disappointing.'

'But, here's a thing. There *were* several bag snatches two days earlier. A juvenile called' – she paused to read her notes – 'Mohammed Rafeaa was arrested. His mum turned him in. First offence. Currently on bail. According to the notes, Mohammed works at a place called Lucky Star Amusements in Rochester.' She tore off the page and handed it to him. 'You will tell me what all this is about, won't you, Bill?'

'As soon as I'm sure. I promise,' he said. 'Are you going to go on a date with him – the copper who you just spoke to?'

'I've just asked him to do something that is borderline illegal in passing me information that has no relation to any active investigation. Kind of ought to go on a date at least once, wouldn't you say?'

'I think so,' said Bill.

'Funny thing though,' she said. 'He asked if I minded him bringing his brother too.'

It took Bill an hour to make it up to Rochester on Saturday. The roads were busy. Like so many north Kent towns, Rochester had seen grander days. Ancient narrow red-brick streets overhung by precarious Tudor buildings and crowded with ancient weather-boarding were surrounded by dusty new roads, car washes and cheap bingo halls. Lucky Star Amusements was on the far side of the bridge, across the Medway. From the front, it looked like a tiny arcade; only when Bill stepped inside did he realise that the premises stretched back from the street into a cavernous hall, filled with blinking gambling machines.

Near the front, a man in a blue shirt had taken the front off an old Pac-Man machine and was tinkering with something inside.

'I'm looking for Mohammed,' Bill said.

The man looked him up and down. 'Why?'

'It's a private matter.'

'Don't know him,' the man said.

'I think you do.' Bill nodded slowly. 'Mohammed Rafeaa.'

'Police?'

'No.' A woman in a grey raincoat and headscarf came in and walked to a machine that issued change, fed in a note and then waited as coins chugged out of it.

'What then?' From the way he behaved, Bill guessed this man was the manager.

'It's a private matter.'

'Privately, I can tell you to fuck off then,' said the man, still examining the inside of the machine 'Is he in trouble again?'

'Nothing like that.'

The manager watched as the woman moved on to a game called Jackpot Party, which bleeped as she fed coins into it. 'He's not a bad boy,' the man said. 'He was hanging around with the wrong sort, trying to impress them. He's learned his lesson.'

So he knew about the arrest for bag theft. 'I'm glad to hear it,' said Bill. 'Will he be here later on?'

'You're not a policeman. So why do you want to talk to him?'

Bill weighed the man up. 'About a bag he stole. One that wasn't reported to the police.'

The man was holding a screwdriver in his hand. He seemed to be examining it carefully. 'What about it?'

'That's a private matter between myself and Mohammed.'

The man sniffed, turned his back and started screwing up the front of the machine he had been working on. 'If you want information, go talk to the police,' he said. 'I don't want you in my premises.'

'They can't help me,' Bill said.

'That's not my problem,' the man said. 'Leave the boy alone. He's learned his lesson.'

Bill reached in his pocket, pulled out a wallet, walked to a fruit machine and fed in a ten-pound note before the manager could ask him to leave. The machine chirped back at him as it swallowed his money.

Bill had not played slot machines since he was a kid. They were different then. These ones didn't have actual reels in them. The whole thing was just a screen; the reels were virtual. It confused him. He looked around. The manager was watching him warily, so he turned back to the machine to try and figure it out. He pressed the red button with the heel of his hand. The screen reels whirred as they spun, then clicked into place. Lights flashed. A circular electronic tune played. There was nothing on his WIN line.

He pressed the button again and the same thing happened, but he carried on. A couple of times he won his bet back. A couple of times he won free spins. The ten-pound note gave him twenty minutes of entertainment before it was all gone. By now the manager had gone to sit on a stool near the door, but was watching him carefully. Bill figured that as long as he was spending money, the man would tolerate his presence. He dug in his wallet and pulled out another note.

As he fed it into the machine, three boys came in, one with a thin moustache that failed to cover a line of spots on his upper lip, one with a Pink Floyd T-shirt, and a third with a pair of purple trainers. They crowded silently round a machine called Quantum Roulette. The manager ignored them.

Bill carried on playing at his slot machine, more slowly now, watching them out of the side of his eye. One of the boys banged the roulette machine in frustration. After a couple of minutes the lights flashed on his own machine and Bill realised he had four melons lined up on the screen. The screen flashed £5! *Double your money!* at him. Instead of gambling it again, Bill pressed the CASH OUT button and instead of money, a paper chit jerked slowly out of a slot below him.

165

He went back to the manager and held up the piece of paper. 'What do I do with this?'

The manager jerked his head towards yet another machine.

While Bill was waiting for his payout, he said, 'I really think you should call Mohammed for me. Tell him I want to meet him here.'

'Fuck off out of it,' said the manager. 'Mohammed's a good lad, whatever he done. He doesn't need any more trouble.'

Bill lingered by his stool.

'Go on then. Get out of here.'

'Those three lads.' Bill nodded towards the boys playing roulette. 'I suspect they are underage.'

The man looked, shrugged. 'Don't look it to me.'

Bill pulled out his phone and took a photograph of the three boys.

'What you doing?'

Bill lowered his voice. 'I appreciate the way you're looking after your staff. I'm sure Mohammed is a good lad. I don't wish him harm any more than you do. But I'm an ex-copper. I can see what you're doing here is not strictly legal. I've reason to believe those youngsters are underage and if you don't call up Mohammed and ask him to come down here, I'm going to share this photograph with some former colleagues of mine and they will ask you why you didn't ID them.'

The man grumbled for a while, but he retreated into an office by the entrance door and returned in under a minute. 'He'll be here this evening at eight. You can talk to him, but I'm going to be there with him. No funny business.'

'Thank you,' said Bill.

The three lads carried on playing, undisturbed.

'It was some other lads put him up to it, you know,' said the manager. 'Like an initiation thing. He had to nick credit cards from a bunch of people and take them back to the gang. Stupid fucking idiot. He didn't even get the money.'

'I heard his mum turned him in.'

'She's my sister. Mo is my nephew. Now piss off and come back at eight. And if you try anything at all I will fuck you up, whoever you are.'

Bill walked back across the bridge, into the old high street, and browsed in a second-hand bookshop for a while. He was on the other side of the road, having a coffee, when his phone rang. It was Jill. She sounded rattled.

'He emailed me again,' she said. 'My dad. Stephen Dowles.'

'What did he say?'

Bill's phone vibrated as he held it to his ear. 'Read it for yourself. I just forwarded it.'

He lowered the device and looked at the message on the screen.

Ur friend has been asking about me u best tell him to back off.

TWENTY-SIX

It was getting dark by the time Mohammed came through the back door to the arcade. 'Hey, Uncle.'

'This is him,' said the manager. 'Show him some respect.'

Mohammed eyed Bill. He was nineteen, and walked with a swagger he couldn't really pull off. He wore a small black woollen cap and a pale sweater that looked too big on him.

'My name is Bill South,' said Bill. 'I'm just looking for some information that has to do with whatever you were doing back in February, when you robbed those people. I'm not going to share anything you say with anyone.'

The boy gave the tiniest of nods.

'Back in February, you stole some wallets and bags.'

The boy nodded again.

'And he knows he was an idiot – don't you, Mo?' his uncle said.

'Yeah,' Mo muttered. 'I got caught up in some stupidity.'

'According to the charge sheet, you stole two bags off women.'

The boy looked suitably ashamed. He looked down at his feet. 'I was coerced into it,' he said.

'But I think you might have also stolen a third one that was never reported.'

The boy looked up and frowned.

'A woman's purse was found, empty apart from a driving licence.' Bill took his phone from his jacket pocket and scrolled until he found the photo from Facebook of Amanda French's driving licence. 'Do you recognise this?'

The boy remained tight-lipped.

The manager sighed. 'Come on, Mo. Tell the man.'

Mo nodded. 'Yeah. That was the first one.'

'You stole this woman's purse as well?'

'It had to be three, otherwise they were going to beat me. That was it. I had to nick three lots of cards. Then they'd let me off.'

'Let you off what?'

Mohammed looked miserable, like he wanted the ceiling to cave in on top of him.

A drunk man in a baseball jacket came in, carrying a plastic bag.

'You,' the manager called out. 'You're banned. Get out.'

The intruder hesitated by the door, swaying slightly.

'Out or I call the police.'

When he was gone, the manager said, 'Right. It's private now. Tell him, Mo.'

Mo shook his head. 'Can't.'

The manager sighed, and said, 'It was blackmail. Some girl from round here pretends she fancies boys. Sends them sex messages. You know what it's like. Gets the boys to send videos of themselves doing . . . things to themselves.'

Mo's eyes were fixed on his trainers.

'Mo fell for it. Next thing, they're threatening to show the video to all their mates, to their family. Then it become a game to see how far they can push the poor lads in return for them not posting it on Reddit. It's like a big joke to them.'

Mo sniffed. Turned his head away.

'Tell me about that first woman you robbed, Mohammed,' said Bill. 'Do you remember her?'

There was no answer.

'Was it a handbag? A backpack? Or just a purse?'

The boy said, 'I don't remember nothing.'

The manager took a sip from his tea, looked at Bill and said, 'Sorry, mate. I did as you asked. If he says he can't remember, he can't remember. Now, are we done?'

Mo mumbled something, but Bill couldn't make it out. The witless noise of the slot machines around them drowned him out. He leaned in. 'What?'

'It was a shoulder bag.'

'Do you remember her?'

Mo nodded. 'Dark hair. Bit like Mum.'

'Medium height? Good-looking?' asked the manager.

'Suppose,' said Mo. 'She was pretty angry. Called me all sorts of shit when I was running off with it.'

'Have you seen her again?'

Mohammed shook his head.

'Where did you steal this?'

'Car park at Iceland. She was waiting for an Uber.'

The uncle shook his head. 'Sometimes I can't believe I'm related to you, Mo.'

'What else do you remember about her?' Bill demanded.

170

'Nothing. I swear.' The boy radiated pure misery. 'That's everything, Uncle, swear to God.'

'OK?' The manager glared at Bill. 'Bugger off now.'

'You sure there's nothing?'

'You heard him, didn't you? Come on. What do you want? Blood?'

'Apart from the key,' said Mo, looking up.

'The key?'

'I just remembered.' Mo giggled. 'It was funny.'

'Nothing about this is funny,' grumbled his uncle.

'What about the key?'

Mo seemed to have perked up a little. He grinned. 'The lads who forced me to do this shit. I had to meet them down by the river to hand them what I'd got.'

'The Esplanade?' Bill guessed. That was where someone had found Amanda French's discarded driving licence and posted it on Facebook.

'That's it. Anyway, they only wanted the cards. They chucked everything else into the river to get rid of it. It's muddy there so everything just gets sucked into the mud and no one's ever going to find it for a hundred years. Only, this woman had a key in her bag and when they chucked it, it floated. The key didn't sink. It bobbed straight back up to the surface and went floating up the river.'

'It had a floating key ring of some kind?'

'Must've.'

Bill grinned. 'Good lad,' he said, and strode to the door, glad to be out of the darkened room and its flashing lights. He got on his motorbike and put his helmet back on.

Until Jill Ferriter had asked him to find out about the man who claimed to be her father, he hadn't realised how much he had missed being a police officer. Bill knew exactly what a floating key ring meant. He lived on a shoreline dotted with boats.

Mandy French lived on a boat.

TWENTY-SEVEN

The north Kent coast was dotted with little quays and marinas, but many of them lay above wide mudflats. The tides here made a lot of the shoreline unsuitable for moorings, especially if you wanted to live aboard. Jill had said that the woman who called herself Krakow Dawn lived in Rochester. She had said she knew Mandy French, so the odds were that Mandy lived somewhere round here too, and the nearest marina with electrical hook-ups for boats was a few miles out of town on the south side of the Hoo Peninsula, facing the old town across the Medway.

He woke on Sunday morning, and cooked kippers in a pan. Life was good.

In the afternoon he rode out to Hoo. Like Romney Marsh, Hoo was a rich flatland, full of wildlife – as a young man he used to come here to watch the marsh harriers on the eastern side at Damhead Creek. Port Werburgh was a collection of static homes, a smattering of industrial warehouses and a few jetties that poked haphazardly into the wide head of the River Medway.

The jetties were crammed full of converted boats and barges, around thirty in total, in various states of disrepair. Bill dismounted and removed his helmet. The tide was low and the sunshine warmed the mud, filling the air with a scent of rot. Each vessel moored here had its own profile, its own eccentricities. At the end of the old harbour arm, a disused red lightship was tied up, rust colouring the paint of its latticed glass. A few boats had hoisted flags, which fluttered in a brief gust. A wind turbine mounted on the curved cabin roof of a freshly painted houseboat burst into life and then ground to a halt again after only a few revolutions. Around the pontoons, old Thames barges that people had dreamed of bringing back to life lay rotting, claimed by water, ribs covered in bright green weed.

The boats were quiet. There seemed to be few people around, but he could hear the faint sound of music coming from somewhere.

Each jetty had a white metal gate marked *Private*, but the gates were low enough for Bill to climb over. He descended onto one of the walkways and made his way along it until he found the source of the music. At the far end, a yacht was moored just off the jetty. Bill guessed its draught was too deep for it to come any closer. A young man with tanned skin was standing on the deck, adjusting the stays of the boat.

Bill called out, 'Hello?'

The man turned and squinted at him.

'Can you help me? I'm looking for a woman who might live here. Mandy French.'

The man shook his head. 'Wouldn't know. I just moored up here last night. Try asking Dizzy Rascal.'

Bill must have looked puzzled. 'Over there.' The man pointed. 'Dizzy Rascal.' Moored on the opposite side of the next jetty was an old square industrial barge, a large flat-bottomed steel hull onto which a very rectangular weatherboarded house had been built. The name, carefully painted in fairground-style capitals on the rear of the flat metal, was *Dizzy Rascal*.

Bill made his way round, onto the next planked walkway, and when he knocked, the man who emerged from the door of the houseboat had a scraggly grey beard and an olive army cap. 'I'm looking for a woman called Mandy French,' Bill repeated.

The man stood on *Dizzy Racal*'s rear deck and looked him up and down, squinting from under the brim of his cap. 'Mandy who?'

'Mandy French.'

The man had a thin half-smoked roll-up in his hand. He paused long enough before saying 'Never heard of her' for Bill to suspect that he had, but Bill just nodded and said, 'Thank you for your time.'

Bill walked on to the end of the jetty, then turned and strolled back again to the shore, and back onto the next jetty along. Nobody seemed to be home. When he turned again, he was aware of *Dizzy Rascal*'s owner watching him.

A second time he returned to the shore. This time he stood a little while casting his eye over the moorings, then got back on his motorbike. He started the engine. Only then did *Dizzy Rascal*'s owner go back inside his boat. He rode slowly down the narrow track away from the moorings. At the edge of the mess of buildings was a yard that belonging a scrap metal merchant. The sign at the gate read: *Cash Payments – You Must Have ID*. He rode in through the gate.

A man in blue overalls was dragging an old copper boiler across the yard. He looked up as Bill switched off his engine.

'What time do you close up?' asked Bill.

'Five,' said the man. Bill guessed Turkish or Kurdish.

Bill reached into his trouser pocket and pulled out one of the ten-pound notes he'd won. 'Do you have any old overalls I can borrow? Like maybe the ones you're wearing.'

The man looked him up and down. 'No.'

Bill pulled out the second note. 'What if I buy them?' Then a third.

'I have just your size,' said the man.

'Will you look after my bike for me?'

'If you're not back by five, we'll scrap it,' said the man.

Bill ambled back to a static caravan that had been turned into a small diner for residents of the caravan park, ordered tea to take away and used their bathroom to change into the overalls. Two tractors used for hauling boats were rusting on the hard standing. He positioned himself behind the bigger of the two, took out a pair of binoculars and waited.

As he drank the tea, people came and went. A woman returned with children; they boarded one of the bigger boats. A lone woman on a bike arrived, pushed the bike through the gate and tied it onto the side of her boat. Next, an oldish couple turned up carrying a mattress, with which they struggled down one of the jetties. Another couple, in their forties, drove up in a Kia and boarded a beautifully painted narrowboat.

The wind came up and the afternoon began to turn chillier. The wind turbine that had struggled to turn before now began to whizz around. Small white wavelets formed on the rising grey water of the estuary.

Bill never minded staying still and watching. Above the estuary, lapwings curved and flapped in the air, their calls whistling above the hum of generators and TVs. A Deliveroo bike arrived with food for the bigger boat, the one with the children.

When lights came on in a few of the boats, Bill realised it was already after seven and hoped the guy from the metal yard had been joking. And then he saw the man in the olive cap emerge from the *Dizzy Rascal* and look around before heading down towards the shoreline. He turned and opened the gate to the next jetty along, then disappeared into one of the smaller boats.

It was the one the woman on the bicycle had disappeared into.

Bill had spent years of his life in cold fields with a pair of binoculars. Patiently watching the world from a distance was what he was best at.

After around a quarter of an hour, the man returned to his boat.

When he was sure he wasn't being watched, Bill climbed over the white gate and walked along the pontoon until he reached the boat the man in the cap had visited. It was a small, old wooden motorsailer called *Venus*.

Through a small oval window in the cockpit door, he could see a light on inside. He crouched down and listened. Above the noise of the boats gently bobbing against their fenders and the gentle creak of ropes came the sound of a woman crying.

TWENTY-EIGHT

'Mandy,' Bill said, loud enough for her to hear.

The crying inside the boat stopped.

'Mandy, I need a word with you.'

There was no answer from inside the motorsailer.

'I need to talk to you about something from a long time ago. It's something to do with a friend of mine.'

Evening estuary light was the best. The sun on mud and water. The absurd greens and reds. Maybe he should try living on a boat sometime.

'I can wait. I'm not going anywhere,' said Bill.

He sat down on the jetty, dropped his legs over the side and lay back, looking up at the stars emerging from the blue. The evening air was chilly.

'This friend of mine,' said Bill out loud. 'She's trying to find out about her dad. She's never met him, you know how it is? She needs to know what he's like. I'm just trying to help her.'

The boats bumped gently against each other and the jetties, a few steel shrouds tinked gently against aluminium masts, but apart from that it was quiet. The woman in the boat was listening to him. He was pretty sure of it.

'I had the luxury of knowing my dad,' said Bill. 'If you can call it a luxury. My dad was a mean bastard who used his fists on my mum and me.' Bill was silent for a long while. The boat seemed to creak. He wondered if it was the woman inside moving, so she could hear better. 'But this girl, Jill – well, she's not a girl, she's half your age, probably – her dad was a bit like mine. A proper scoundrel. Violent too. But still, she wants to get to know him.'

Somewhere a little way off in the darkness, curlews were making that bubbling sound that always made him feel sad.

'At first I thought she was an idiot for wanting to know him. Leave well alone, you know what I mean?'

He waited, as if for a response, but there wasn't one.

'Because why do you want someone like that in your life? I spent my life trying to get as far away from my dad as possible, even after he was dead.'

He had started by trying to lure her out, but once he had begun talking, it was hard to stop.

'I don't have kids. After what my father was, I didn't want to do that all over. I regret it now. I think I could have done it better than him.' He laughed. 'Anybody could, if I'm honest. But the point is that I knew my dad, and I know who I am because of it. I knew that I never wanted to be like him. And so . . .'

He sighed, sat up and noticed that the lights had been switched off in the motor cruiser. Perhaps she hadn't been listening at all. He was about to stand when he realised something else. The

180

door from the cockpit to the main cabin was now open – not by much, but just a little. She had opened it so she could hear him perhaps, he decided.

'And so,' he said, raising his voice just to make sure. 'And so I thought this girl – woman – probably deserves a chance to know her dad, however much of a shit he really is.'

It was the top of the tide now, the water black beneath his feet. A gust of wind passed through the moorings and the place seemed to come alive, boats knocking together, straining at their lines. A loose tarp flapped loudly and then it was quiet again.

'I figure anyone can get caught up in things. It happened to me. When I was younger, I did things I was ashamed of. I served time. I think everyone needs a second chance and I'm lucky. I got one. My friends – my real friends – they stuck by me. So I thought maybe her dad deserves a second chance, despite what he did. So I told her I'd find out a little about this man.'

The wind had come up still more. Though Bill loved the beauty of a flat landscape, it did nothing to stop the wind. A blue EU flag that someone was flying from their stays started flapping hard. He realised he had been sitting still for a long time now. Even in the dungarees, he was starting to feel the chill. It was going to be a long and cold ride home. He would have to get moving soon.

As the motorsailer moved on the water, the door opened a little further, then swung back again.

To his right, on the furthest pontoon, Bill could just make out a dark figure checking mooring lines to their yacht. High tide had slackened the ropes and their boat was jerking against them.

'So I should get to the point. Her father was a man called Stephen Dowles. Stevie Dowles. He was a bit of a villain back in the day. Back when you were going out with Bobby White.'

Nobody moved in the motor cruiser. The door swung slowly open again.

'Stevie Dowles was convicted of killing a man named Wayne Jordan. Does that ring any bells? I've been taking a wild guess that Wayne was working for Bobby at the time, shifting drugs. Back then, the police assumed that Bobby was involved in Wayne's murder, but it turned out that Bobby was in Paris with you that day. Or so you told the police. I've been thinking about that a lot. It's what I want to talk to you about, because you were Bobby White's alibi. But I don't think you were in Paris at all that day, were you?'

The boards he was sitting on floated above the water, rising and falling with the tide. As the wind whipped up small waves on the Medway, he felt the pontoon shifting under him.

'I don't know what Bobby White was up to thirty years ago, but I think it has something to do with what happened to Stephen Dowles. And I think you can help me. All I want is a chat, Mandy.'

He sighed.

'All I want is a chance to set the record straight. All I want is for this girl to know exactly who her dad was so she can know what kind of person she is too. She wants to love herself. She wants love from the people around her. It's what all of us want, really.'

The boat in front of him rolled more sharply, and the door swung again, this time closing with a clack. If anyone asked him, the wind stinging his eyes would explain the tears on his cheeks, he thought, wondering if he had been talking to himself all this time.

'Mandy?'

He looked over to the boat moored on the far jetty, the one called *Dizzy Rascal*. All that was visible now was its silhouette, and smoke, darker than the evening sky, drifting from its silver flue. There was something familiar about the boat, though also unfamiliar too. He was sure he had seen it before, but at the same time the boat was different from what he had seen. It was as if he had dreamed it. He shook his head.

'Mandy?'

And then everything stopped.

The cold he felt, when he came to, was fierce. It made his body hurt inside and out.

In a fraction of a second, he understood that he was underwater. Terror took hold, yet he was lucid. Time slowed. The back of his head stung and he understood clearly that someone must have snuck up on him and hit him from behind, that he had fallen into the Medway and that he was going to die.

In panic, he sucked air, but his lungs took in icy water.

If he could swim, his chances might have been better. If he had not been wearing boots for his motorcycle, he might have had a chance. If these overalls he had borrowed were not waterlogged, he could have raised an arm above the surface of the water, but the waves were too far above him now and the darkness was pulling him down.

The mud held his feet, like hands on his boots, pulling them down, making escape from the river impossible. Death was much simpler than he imagined it would be.

Sailors claimed that drowning in seawater was an easier death than in fresh water. Perhaps they were right. He stopped struggling.

In the tiny window of time before he lost consciousness completely his mind was full, as if it were taking this last second or so for a full accounting.

His mother was young again, plump and funny, defiant and fresh, cigarette in hand. He was at Hooker's Pits, watching a black-winged stilt wading on its overlong red legs like some absurd puppet. His friend Bob was beside him, incandescent with happiness at seeing such a rarity. He was meeting DS Cupidi for the first time and stepping into her rubbish-strewn car and she was asking him whether he preferred to be called Bill or Will and he was answering curtly, 'William.'

There was late evening sunshine over Dungeness, catching the white flowers and making them glow and he was leaning over them, explaining to Zoë that this was Nottingham catchfly – and how at night its petals open and release a pungent sweet scent to attract moths, and Zoë, wonderful mad girl, insisting they stay up to watch them open.

All of these things and more seemed to be taking place at once, and yet each millisecond was rich with detail. There was more he could have done and women he could have loved, but in the last few years he had found a kind of happiness at least and that was a great surprise to him.

And then he was gone.

PART THREE

PART THREE

TWENTY-NINE

A police car would have blue lights that might make her journey quicker. She drove as fast as the Saab would take her, Zoë pale in the seat beside her.

On the M20, a Polish refrigerated lorry pulled out in front of her without signalling. She slammed on the brakes, waited for it to inch its way past another lorry, then changed down and sped past it.

'I dreamed it, Mum. I dreamed it all,' said Zoë. 'I dreamed he drowned.'

It took her forty minutes to reach the small marina. Police cars were gathered in the lane near an industrial cabin that seemed to be used as a diner.

Alex abandoned her car and trotted past the parked cars in the dark, Zoë at her side, making their way towards the lights ahead and a thin line of police tape.

'Can't go this way now. You live on one of the boats?' A constable had stepped out of the darkness.

'I'm a police officer,' she said, though in her hurry she had left her shoulder bag and warrant card in the car and had nothing on her to prove it. 'Where is Detective Constable Jill Ferriter?'

'Who?'

Alex attempted patience. 'A man was pulled from the water here, I understand.'

The constable nodded. 'In a bad way. Carted off in the heli-copter. They say he probably didn't make it.'

'Oh. He was dead?'

'Were you a friend of his? You best speak to—'

'Were?' Zoë replied, pale.

Alex's phone rang. She turned away from the copper. 'Jill?'

'Where are you?' Jill asked.

'I'm here. Where's Bill? Where are you?'

'They airlifted him to Queen Mary's Hospital in Sidcup. He was unconscious when they dragged him from the water.'

'The policeman outside said he was dead.'

Looking past the constable, she could see moored boats. From some, lights shone.

'They opened up a cafe for us. Come and join us. If you're by the boats, it's just on the other side of the cordon.'

The cafe was brightly lit. A young woman in jeans was serving tea and coffee to a young officer.

Jill was sitting in one of the cafe chairs, talking to an older man in an olive-green cap, but stood up as Alex walked in and threw her arms around both of them. 'Oh my God,' she said. 'I'm so glad to see you.' All three of them hugged for a while as everyone else in the cafe looked on.

'You his friends?' asked the woman running the cafe eventually.

Alex nodded.

'I'm so sorry,' she said.

Alex pulled Jill into a corner. 'What was he even doing here?'

Jill looked nervous. 'I don't know. I mean. I do know, but I don't know exactly.'

Alex peered at her. 'What do you mean, Jill?'

'I asked him to do something for me. To look into something.'

Alex was thrown. 'What thing? Why didn't you ask me?'

Jill tugged her down towards a waiting chair. They sat together while Zoë watched. 'Because we weren't allowed to talk to each other, for one.'

Alex picked up on the awkwardness in her voice. She understood now. 'And two was because what you asked him to do was something I wouldn't have been allowed to do even if I'd wanted to?'

Jill still wasn't meeting her eyes. 'Kind of,' she said quietly. 'I'm sorry.'

Alex took Jill's hand. 'Oh, Jill. What the hell has been doing on?'

The woman running the cafe put two teas – sage-green cups and saucers – on the table. 'On the house,' she said. 'Put sugar in. It's good for shock.' There were chocolate Bourbons on the side.

Jill leaned forward. 'I can't tell you, Alex. Not yet. And certainly not here.' Jill scanned the room. She raised her voice again. 'This guy here says he must have fallen in.' She pointed towards the man in the olive cap.

'That's right,' said the man.

Alex said, 'Did you know he couldn't swim?'

191

'Oh. Christ, Alex.'

Alex pulled out a chair for the man Jill had pointed out and asked him, 'Did you recognise him – the man who fell in?'

The man shook his head. 'No. Never seen him round here before in my life – and I know pretty much everyone round here. Shouldn't have been where he was, that's for sure. Private property, around here.'

Alex asked, 'Who was it pulled him out?'

'Me, mostly,' said the man. 'Some of the other guys. One guy knew CPR.'

'We put the defibrillator on him,' said the woman who ran the cafe. 'There's one in the campsite. We did our best, I promise. All of us.'

'We're very grateful to you for helping him. He was a good friend of ours,' said Alex. 'But you have no idea at all what he was doing around here?'

'Like I said,' said the man. 'No idea.'

'We should get to the hospital,' said Jill quietly.

Alex pulled the car keys out of her bag, then hesitated. 'Where did he fall in?'

'Off one of the pontoons,' said the woman behind the counter. 'That's where they pulled him out, at least.'

Alex stood. 'I'll just go and take a look.'

'Wait for me,' Jill said.

Alex, Jill and Zoë made their way to the moorings. The boats were alive, all in motion. There were three pontoons. The middle pontoon was still dotted with wet footprints. Alex switched on the torch on her phone and stepped over the white gate. 'Just wait here a moment, Zoë.'

Jill followed her. 'So?' said Alex, now they were alone. 'What the hell was he doing here, Jill?'

Jill didn't answer. Halfway along the pontoon, the jetty was awash with water. 'Reckon they pulled him out here,' suggested Jill. 'Look.'

The wettest boards were on the right side, which would suggest that was where his unconscious body had been pulled out, where someone had performed CPR on him, trying to keep him alive.

'Anyone here?' called Alex, hoping to rouse someone on the boats.

No one answered. The boats all seemed unoccupied.

There were cleats every couple of metres on each side of the pontoon. In the dark it might be easy for someone inexperienced to trip on one and fall, she supposed.

'Can I help you, ladies?' There was a sudden light in their faces.

'Who's that?' demanded Alex.

He lowered the torch briefly and Alex saw it was the man in the olive cap, the one they had been speaking to in the cafe. He had followed them. He raised the torch again, dazzling them. Alex raised an arm to shade her eyes.

'Where exactly was he when you pulled him out?'

'Just where you were standing.'

'See?' said Jill.

Alex looked down at the patch of dark water between the closely packed boats.

'Anything else you want to know?' he asked.

'And where were you when it happened?'

The man said, 'Why?'

'I'm just trying to work out what happened,' said Alex.

'I was in my boat.'

'Which is where?'

The man pointed the torch to the pontoon to the west of them, shining it on what looked like a caravan floating on water. Its name was painted in bright colours.

'*Dizzy Rascal?*'

'That's her. *Dizzy* because she's flat-bottomed. Hard to steer. Tends to go round in circles.'

'Thanks for your help, Mr . . .'

The man shut off the torch. 'You're welcome.'

Alex spent some time looking at the wet footprints, trying to imagine how the disastrous evening had unfolded. She looked down at the wet marks leading along the jetty. A long wet line, marked with occasional footprints, led all the way along to the end of the boards, stopping where there was no boat moored.

Right at the end, a little way off from the end of the jetty, there was a big white sailing yacht, an expensive-looking one, a dim light showing in the window.

'Come on. We need to go,' said Zoë.

Alex stepped over the gate, but lingered a little while, looking at the two other jetties until her daughter pulled her away.

THIRTY

Bill's chest was on fire. His throat was agony. His mouth was bruised, as if someone had punched him in the face. When he tried to move, he found there were tubes all over him.

He turned his head slightly to the right. There was a corridor. People moving in it.

He tried turning his head to the other side and there was a woman asleep in a chair. Drool had dropped down her chin, making a dark mark on her lime shirt.

'Hello?' said a voice.

Someone was standing on the other side of him.

'How are you doing?' He moved his head slowly to the right again.

'You were in an accident.' A man in blue stood with a board in his hand.

'On my motorbike?' he tried to say, but his throat was too dry and nothing emerged.

'Bit sore?'

Bill nodded.

'Can you tell me your name?'

'William,' he mouthed.

'Great.'

The man reached down and took his hand. 'Can you squeeze my hand?'

Bill squeezed.

'Pretty bloody good,' he said. 'Do you know what year it is?'

Bill opened his mouth, then frowned. There was nothing there. The man looked at him for a little while longer, then said, 'No?' He made a note on his board. 'Don't worry. It'll come to you.'

'How old are you?' The man kept asking stupid questions.

'Twenty?' suggested Bill. That didn't sound quite right though.

'He's awake?' The woman's voice now.

He turned his head slowly the other way. The woman was grinning at him like an idiot. 'Bill!' She was very pretty. Fair-haired, with blue eyes.

The man spoke again. 'Do you remember what happened?'

Bill mumbled, 'Motorbike accident?'

'No. It wasn't a motorbike accident,' said the man waiting with the board. 'Nothing?'

Bill frowned. He had no idea at all what he was doing here.

The man made another note in his pad, then gently moved his head across. 'Do you remember who this woman is?'

Bill struggled to think.

'What is her name?'

He closed his eyes and tried to remember if he knew her.

And then there were more people whom he knew coming into the room. The older woman . . . tall, slightly clumsy. There was

196

something vaguely familiar about her, but he couldn't remember exactly who she was or how he might have known her or whether she simply looked like someone he had once known.

And then a girl beside her. A teenager who looked like she was undernourished, as if you could so easily pick her up with one hand. He peered into her face as if trying to understand why that face made emotions bubble in his chest, then felt embarrassed and ashamed at the way she stared back at him with such horror.

He must look a total mess. Something awful must have happened.

'Bill. Oh, Bill,' said the young one. 'What happened to his face?'

'It's just bruising. It happens when they're trying to force tubes into his throat and lungs,' someone answered.

'Jesus Christ,' said the tall woman. 'Poor Bill.'

They were all looking at him, shocked, concerned, anxious. He had no idea who any of them were or what he was doing here.

A doctor of some kind was talking now. 'Apparently, he must have slipped in the dark and then hit the back of his head when he fell in the water. And the water was cold, which slowed his body down enough.'

He wondered who they were talking about. It was hard to concentrate.

'We don't know how long his heart had stopped for. It may have been for some time. He's very lucky indeed to be alive at all. It's too early to tell what kind of damage that's caused to his brain function. I'm sorry.'

'But he will get better, won't he?' asked the skinny girl.

Backing out of the room, the doctor said, 'We very much hope so,' in a way that suggested that she thought it was very unlikely.

'So,' said the tall woman to the pretty one. 'I think it's time you told me what Bill was really doing at the marina.'

The pretty one lowered her voice so he could hardly hear her. 'It's about my father,' she said.

The older one sounded confused. 'Your father? You don't have a father.'

'Apparently I do. He's not a good man. Let's put it this way . . . He did a lot of bad things.'

'And Bill was helping you try to find him?'

Bill had no idea what they were talking about.

'No. Not him. I know where he is. He's in prison. He was trying to find . . . other people. Listen. It's best if you don't know. Trust me.'

Bill lapsed back into unconsciousness. Time passed. Things bleeped. He drifted in and out of sleep. When he woke – it felt like hours later – the same three women were still at his bedside, talking among themselves like he wasn't there.

'You know Rose?' He recognised the teenager's voice.

'The swimmer?'

'She told me she tried to commit suicide.'

'When?'

'She lost her job in London and tried to harm herself. That's why she knew Mimi. Mimi had been looking after her. Rose had taken pills. I think that's why she took Mimi's death so badly.'

Bill understood nothing. He didn't recognise the names they were saying. He didn't understand what they were doing here.

Perhaps they were in the wrong room. They must have mistaken him for someone else. The youngest one sounded so sad. He wanted to reach out to her but he was just too exhausted.

'I think the other swimmers are worried she's going to try again now Mimi's gone. What should I do?'

'Be her friend, of course, if you feel you can be.'

He peered through his half-open eyelids. The girl nodded, wiped her nose on the sleeve of her cardigan.

'You like her?'

'She's just got depression. Victor says he's visiting her to make sure she's OK.'

'Which one's he?'

'Isobel's husband. He's really nice. He's been looking out for her.'

The older woman said, 'Funny. I thought he was a bit of an arsehole.'

'You think everyone's an arsehole, Mum. Apart from Bill.' The girl dropped her voice. 'Is he really going to be OK? Or is he just going to be like this?'

They thought he was asleep. And then he was – and their voices stopped making any sense at all.

THIRTY-ONE

'I'm so sorry,' said Toby McAdam the next morning at the office. 'I know you two were close. It must be a blow.'

Alex had driven home into the dawn with Zoë sleeping beside her. Jill had stayed at the hospital. She told them she would stay on as long as she could; she had nothing else to do, she said. Jill had refused to tell her who or what Bill had been looking for at the marina. 'You have to trust me, Alex,' she had said as Bill drifted in and out of consciousness. 'Bill was doing this for me because he's not in the police. Don't ask me any more.'

'Is there any hope he'll recover?' McAdam asked.

'They don't know yet.' She was standing in front of his desk, a coffee in her hand.

'What a terrible thing to happen. Tripping in the dark in a place like that. What a night. First Charlie getting firebombed and then this. You must be exhausted.' McAdam looked tired too. 'Some of the lads are doing a collection for Bill,' he said. 'People here seem to have liked him a lot.'

Alex nodded. 'But he'll hate the idea of people collecting money for him.' She shifted on her feet. 'That attack on Charlie Reed . . .'

'Yes?' He looked up at her.

'I wonder if it was my fault. The covert team . . . Had they had many responses from his profile on the dating app?

McAdam shuffled through the papers on his desk and pulled out a print-off of an email. 'Quite a few.'

'Anyone who responds to the advert gets a message from the covert team saying that it's not a genuine listing, right? We tell any woman who responds that we posted the profile because we're looking for a man called Malcolm. What if one of the women who answered it told Malcolm about the listing – that the police were looking for him? What did the women get as a reply?'

McAdam flicked through the papers on his desk and pulled out sheet. She lifted it and read the agreed response. *'Apologies for contacting you in this manner. This is not a genuine profile. I am a police officer trying to track down an individual who was active on this network until recently under the username Malcolm who we believe may be a witness in an investigation. He is approximately 5' 10" with fair hair and blue eyes. If you think you know him, or have conversed with him on this app, we would very much like to hear back from you. If you wish to speak directly to an officer, please call the following number.'*

'So – because the covert team were using Charlie's profile – they might have assumed it was Charlie himself who was looking for Malcolm. Maybe they thought it was something personal. A vendetta?'

201

'Unfortunately, that's a possibility.'

'In that case, I have a potential lead,' Alex said.

While they were getting the paperwork ready for a raid on the Johncocks' house, she took the anonymised responses back to her desk and read through them.

Fuck off!@! You are kidding me? No can't msg him has he deleted his profile??

No. Sorry dont hv deets for Malcolm he never told me. Cant help. Cute profile tho!!! Xxx

Aw! Disappointed, but I'd be very happy to investigate you any time. Xx

They hadn't made it clear in the agreed response that the person who was responding to the messages wasn't the good-looking young man in the photographs. There were others, too.

*Malcolm is a c**t.*

OMG. Yes!! I dated Malcolm for a while. Not seen him for weeks. Is he OK????

And this one:

Is he the one who got my BF pregnant and then fucked off??

Alex had asked for uniformed officers to be present when she returned to the Johncock brothers' house at number 105 the following day. Like Malcolm, they were builders.

When Alex arrived, the van was parked in the paved area outside 105. The curtains to the living room – which had been open when Alex was there the previous morning – were drawn. Looking along the road, she saw that the police car had parked about twenty metres further down, far enough away not to be conspicuous. Alex grew up next to them and got out. There were two officers inside, a man and a woman. Alex knocked on the window.

'Have you had a chance to look around?' she asked.

'Only just got here,' said the constable at the wheel – the woman. 'The other car is round the back on Somerset Road.'

'Have they eyes on the back of the house?'

'You think they're going to try and skip?' She spoke into her lapel. 'Delta Four Nine. Have you eyes on the back of the house?'

There was a crackle on the radio. 'Can't see it from our car. There's other houses in the way.'

Alex checked the map on her phone. 'Isn't there an alleyway between the houses or something?'

'Did you hear that, Delta Four Nine? There is an alleyway between the houses.'

The two officers got out of the car, tugged their tactical vests down and followed Alex to the house. She stood behind them as they switched on their body cams, then, when they looked round to check, she gave them the nod. It was the man who went to the door. He pressed the bell, but it was a cheap one and no light came on, so assuming it wasn't working, he banged on the door with the side of his fist.

'I thought I saw the curtains twitch,' said the woman officer.

Alex had been looking at the door and hadn't noticed it.

The man banged on the door again. 'We are police officers. Please open the door.'

Alex stepped back onto the pavement to get a better look at

the whole house. Beyond the possible twitch of the curtain, there were no other clues to anyone else being inside.

'There was definitely someone,' said the woman. She talked into her radio. 'Delta Four Nine. Anything happening at the back of the house?'

The radio crackled back. 'Moving in to check.'

Several houses away was the alleyway she had spotted on Sunday. She left the two officers to their job and set off towards it, first walking, then at a trot. The first short alley met another longer one that ran the length of the backs of all the houses. As she reached it, she looked left and right. To the left, another uniformed officer was making his way towards her. To the right, twenty or thirty metres away, it opened up onto the next street.

'Anything?' she called to the policeman.

'Nah.' He called up the officers at the front. 'Delta Four One. What's happening?'

'Nobody's answering,' came the woman officer's voice. 'Think they are still inside.'

'OK.'

Alex and the officer approached. 'Any idea which house it is?' he asked.

'Don't you know?'

'Only just arrived here,' he said.

'Shit,' muttered Alex. 'We should have scouted this first.'

They were walking up an alley with old brick walls on both sides, punctuated by garden gates. The air smelt of foxes and dog shit. Alex could see the tops of the houses over the wall and was trying to figure out which one belonged to the Johncocks.

She took out her phone and checked. The blue dot was an unreliable indication of their location, but it suggested they were still a couple of doors south of number 105. 'Come on,' she said, beckoning the officer forwards.

The next gate but one was open. She peered in. An old bike frame rusted on what had once been a lawn. Behind it were piles of scaffolding boards and clamps. An old oil barrel had been turned into an incinerator. A couple of nylon folding garden chairs sat next to it. There was an empty tin of Polish lager sitting on what was left of the grass. 'This is it,' she said, going in.

'Hello?' she called.

'Delta Four One,' said the copper. 'We're at the rear of the property now. Rear door is open.'

The house had a side return. Halfway down, a door opened into the kitchen.

'Hello? I am a police officer,' Alex called into the open doorway. 'If there's anyone there, I would appreciate it if you came to the door.'

She paused. The house seemed silent. The officer was at her side now. 'OK. I'm just going to step inside,' Alex said loudly.

She had expected the kitchen to have the same scruffiness as the living room but it was tidy. A couple of dishes and mugs sat in a drying rack. On the table was a packet of Bran Flakes, top neatly closed. 'Is there anyone here?'

Nobody answered. 'Shit,' she muttered. She had a bad feeling about this.

The officer had his baton at the ready. He stepped ahead of her into the hallway. 'Hello?' Stopped and listened.

She went with him into the living room and drew the curtains.

Light flooded into the darkened room. The resiny smell of cannabis permeated everything. The builders' merchants catalogues she had seen the previous morning still lay on the floor. The officer opened the front door and uniformed coppers barged into the building.

Taking a pair of nitrile gloves from her bag, she tugged them on and lifted the catalogue off the floor. There was a postal label on the cover addressed to Martin Johncock. They were in the right house, at least.

'Upstairs is clear,' someone shouted.

The officer sighed. 'Bollocks,' He turned to her. 'Sorry, Sarge. Totally my fault. I should have spotted them. They must have legged it fast as soon as they saw us park up.'

The back door had been open. So had the gate.

'Four Nine,' he was saying into the radio. 'Maybe take the car and have a look round. It looks like they saw us coming and made a break for it out the back.'

Alex returned to the hallway and headed up the stairs, followed by the officer who was recording her movements. If she did find anything incriminating, a defence lawyer would inevitably attempt to argue that police had entered the house illegally; worse, that police had planted evidence.

There were three bedrooms on the next floor. One brother appeared to be tidier than the other. One had made his bed, pulling a blue duvet up to the pillows; the other's had a pile of discarded clothes lying on the floor and the fitted bottom sheet had come loose from one corner of the mattress. 'Bag up their trainers,' she said. 'We need to compare them to the footprints at the scene of crime.'

She left them to it. The third bedroom had a desk in it, on which sat a computer and a pile of invoices.

She peered at the paperwork. The Johncocks seemed to run a building business of some kind, but from looking around, there didn't seem to be much else in their lives. The other officers were already trooping out of the house to look for the missing suspects.

'OK. Let's go,' she called, and turned to go down the stairs. The constable followed her down, carrying a clear plastic bag with two pairs of shoes in it. Walking to the back door, she stopped. Instead of leaving, she raised her finger to her lips, and pointed to the officer's radio. She drew a finger across her throat.

For a second, he looked confused, then he raised his eyebrows. She pointed at the ceiling above them and this time he understood and switched off his police radio and slowly lowered the bag of shoes to the floor. 'Waste of bloody time,' she said loudly, and closed the back door, remaining in the kitchen.

The two of them stood for a while, listening.

An electric clock ticked quietly. A tap dripped into a stainless steel sink.

She shrugged and had put her gloved hand back on the door handle to leave when they both heard it. From upstairs, the sound of scuffling feet and laughter.

THIRTY-TWO

There were four police officers waiting at the bottom of the stairs when the Johncock brothers appeared at the top and their smiles and laughter disappeared. 'Shit,' one said.

'Come down here and don't make a big fuss,' said one of the uniformed officers. 'We just want a chat.'

The brothers were big, muscular boys in their early forties, but saw they were outnumbered. At the bottom of the stairs, the officers led them out to the cars, leaving Alex alone in the house.

The boys had been hiding behind the wardrobe. The wardrobe contained a rail of coats and jackets, and behind them a set of sliding doors. 'Just like Narnia,' one of the coppers said. 'Only with drugs.'

A metre of the room had been turned into a small hydroponic cannabis farm. Four giant green cannabis plants prospered under artificial light. A fifth had been harvested and hung upside down, drying on the wall. The brothers had opened the back gate and the kitchen door to make it look like they'd done a runner, and hidden in here.

Alex looked around the space. The cannabis was illegal, but it didn't seem to be a major operation. From the smell of the living room, the brothers smoked most of it themselves.

She went out of the back door and looked around, peering into the rusting oil barrel that had been used as an incinerator. There was a thick layer of ash at the bottom. A garden fork was propped against the garden wall. Lifting it, she poked it into the barrel and saw dull embers come to life. The incinerator had been lit in the last couple of days. She was pretty sure that forensics would find the remains of trainers and clothes in it.

Next to the front door, propped on the same side as the hinge, was a big wooden pickaxe handle. They might not have that much weed, but they had enough to make them paranoid.

Alex stopped off at Guy and Charlie's house before she headed back to the station. 'You're still here then,' she said when Charlie answered the door. 'I thought they were going to rehouse you?'

'Nowhere suitable so far,' answered Charlie. 'You got the Johncocks, then? About time.'

'Sorry to hear about your friend,' said Guy.

'You heard?'

'McAdam told me you were upset,' said Charlie.

When she went back outside, there were two new police cars parked outside the Johncocks' house. A forensics team had arrived and a second crew were due to arrive later in the day to collect the cannabis plants. Getting into the car, she spied the next-door neighbour who had tipped her off about the Johncock brothers looking at her through a gap in the nets. He smiled at her, gave her the thumbs up. She nodded back at him.

Ethan Johncock was the younger of the two brothers by a couple of years. The uniformed police had taken both of them to Maidstone because the interview room at Ashford wasn't in a fit state to be used.

Alex sat across the table from Ethan and his lawyer, a personable young woman Alex had met a few times. She was representing both of them and had just sat through a mostly identical interview with Ethan's brother, Martin.

'To start with, the cannabis,' said Alex.

'Personal use,' said Ethan with a small smile.

Alex made a show of writing this in her notebook. 'Personal use,' she repeated.

'Exactly.' Both of the brothers were stocky; both had dark thinning hair, shaven close. Ethan was less plump than his brother, and when he smiled, small creases on the side of his mouth and around his eyes deepened, giving him a roguish charm that he seemed to be well aware he possessed.

'Just the odd bit of puff,' he said.

The first interview was always straightforward. You let the suspect say whatever they wanted to say. You simply watched them for any cracks. 'OK. Now. Where were you and your brother at around two a.m on Saturday night?'

Charlie and Guy's house had been firebombed at around two. Ethan took no time at all to answer. 'At home, watching telly.'

'What was on television?'

'Can't remember. I was a bit stoned,' said Ethan, smiling

210

again. 'A little memory loss, you know? Probably something on Netflix.'

Again, she very deliberately made a note, though everything was being videoed and recorded. His brother had said they probably watched *Match of the Day* on iPlayer. Other than that, there was nothing much between the accounts so far.

'OK,' she said. 'Any reason why you hid in the back of your wardrobe when we came to call this morning, Ethan?'

'We weren't hiding. We were up there watering the plants.'

She looked up. 'And you didn't hear us knocking?'

He shrugged.

'You usually leave the back door wide open?'

He nodded. 'It's a very nice neighbourhood.' He turned to his lawyer and smirked. The lawyer ignored him. This too was almost exactly what his brother had just said thirty minutes earlier. They had been kept in separate cells and hadn't had a chance to confer. They were annoying, but neither of them was thick.

'Even though you keep a pick handle by the front door?'

'Habit,' said Ethan. 'Where we grew up wasn't so nice.'

She got out her phone, opened her photos and selected one. 'Can you identify this?'

Ethan leaned forward and peered at the photo, then looked at his counsel for a fraction of a second. 'It's a petrol can.'

'Can you explain why you had it in the back of your van?'

Ethan answered with a shrug. 'Because it has petrol in it. In case the van breaks down.'

'There was barely any petrol in it,' she said.

'We must have broken down, then,' said Ethan.

'Did you use the petrol in the can to set light to Guy and Charlie Reed's car and to the front door of their house?'

Ethan's face tightened just a little, but he shook his head calmly enough.

'Can you say that aloud please, for the record?'

'No. Didn't.'

'Thank you.' Alex paused for a while, smiled at Ethan. 'What about your brother? Did he use the petrol in that can to endanger the lives of Police Constable Charles Reed and his disabled brother?'

'No.'

'And you're sure of that because . . . ?'

'Because I was watching TV with him all night.'

More notes. 'Right. Remind me again what you watched?'

'Can't remember.'

'Did you hear any commotion in the street outside some time after midnight, before, say, two in the morning?'

'Had the telly on.'

'Of course you did.' She had asked the same questions of his brother, hoping they would invent different stories. 'I noticed you had a bit of a bonfire recently, didn't you?'

Ethan put his palms on the table in front of him and circled them, like a bored child in class. 'What do you mean, bonfire?'

'In your back garden. In the incinerator.'

Again, the little smile. 'Yeah. Warm in the day, but still quite chilly of an evening, isn't it? Quite nice, smoking a bit of puff outside, having a beer.'

'What did you burn?'

'You know. Bits and pieces. There's always a few bits of scrap timber lying about the place.'

'Shoes? Clothes, anything like that?'

'Maybe. We're builders. You know how they treat builders any time you go to the local tip? Shocker, isn't it? They want to charge us a fortune, these days. And we wouldn't want to go fly-tipping, would we? We're law-abiding citizens, if you don't count the marijuana. We burn all sorts.'

She closed her notebook and looked straight at him. 'One last question. And this is very important. Have you ever worked with a carpenter called Malcolm?'

This time, a little flicker of the eyes before Ethan shook his head. 'No.'

'Really?' She sounded deliberately sceptical. 'Not on any building site you've been on? A chippy of some kind.'

'Definitely.'

'You're absolutely sure of that?'

'Well. I don't know.' He wavered. 'Common name, isn't it? Might have.'

'Not particularly common, no,' contradicted Alex. 'Not these days. I think you'd probably remember, if you had.'

Ethan looked unbothered by the exchange. 'Not that I recall. No. Don't remember.'

'That's a shame.' Alex sat watching him for a while. 'And what about Mimi Greene?'

'Who?'

His brother had looked equally perplexed. 'Malcolm's ex-girlfriend, Mimi Greene. The one who's dead. Whose death we are investigating. Which is why we want to get in touch with Malcolm.'

She could hear Ethan's breath quicken, just as his brother's had. The solicitor turned to look at her client.

'Right,' Alex said eventually with an even smile. 'That will be all for now. I'm sure we'll have more questions for you tomorrow once the forensics are done with your house. Thank you.'

'Well?' asked McAdam. It was past 9 p.m. when she made it back to Ashford to pick up her car, but when she went to the office to pick up her keys, McAdam was still at his desk.

Alex slung her bag onto a chair. 'Did you watch it?'

'Yes, but you were in the room with them. What did you make of them?'

She had been thinking about it in the car all the way from Maidstone. 'When I said the name Malcolm, both of them recognised it, I'm positive. They were expecting the question and were prepared to deflect it. But when I said Mimi Greene, they both looked thrown. The younger one looked scared, I'd say. I don't think they knew about Mimi.'

'Scared?'

'I get the feeling that neither of them knew there was a potential murder involved. They thought they were just protecting their mate's back.'

'They commit arson on the house of a police officer and a disabled man and they're not worried about that?'

'They think they've got away with that. There was no CCTV. Bet you there's no match on the footprints on any of the shoes we bagged either. They burned the clothes they wore and the shoes too. But they were a bit shocked to find out they were

214

helping a man who we're looking for in a murder enquiry. Let's give them a little while to think a bit harder about that.'

Outside, she called Zoë. 'I'm sorry,' she said. 'I'll be late home.'

'So will I,' said Zoë. 'I'm with Rose.'

'Rose?'

'I told her what happened to Bill. She offered to give me a lift to the hospital this evening. I'm up there now. With her.'

'Oh,' said Alex. 'That's very kind of her. So she's feeling better?'

'She's still very sad about Mimi. We both are.'

'How is Bill?'

'He looks so bad. He's sleeping a lot.'

'No change?'

'They've moved him off intensive care and put him in a ward. That's got to be good, hasn't it?'

'So you'll get a lift home then?'

Alex could hear the voices in the background. She pictured Zoë sitting in the hospital corridor outside a busy ward.

'I was thinking, Mum. Do you think Bill would mind if I stayed at his house, to look after it until he comes back? I asked him, but he doesn't really understand what I'm talking about.'

'I'm sure he'd appreciate that,' said Alex. 'Pick me out some clothes for him and I'll take them up to the hospital for when he comes out.'

'What if he doesn't?'

Alex wanted very much to tell her everything would be OK but all she could say was, 'I don't know, my love.'

She ended the call. She should be glad at least that Zoë had found new friends.

215

THIRTY-THREE

The chubby consultant said, 'You're a pretty lucky man.'

Bill spoke slowly, quietly. It was still an effort to use his lungs. 'Lucky is the last thing I feel.'

The consultant giggled like a small child. Bill was awake now and had managed to sit up, though it had been painful. The drugs that had made him so vague were wearing off but though the fog was clearing, the pain was worse. The pain seemed easier than the constant panic at feeling so lost.

The consultant had thin, almost non-existent eyebrows, fuzzy white hair and big dark eyes. He reminded Bill of a baby barn owl. 'It's great that people know CPR these days,' the consultant was saying, 'but the truth is most people don't come back. You are one of the few who make it. The fact that you were fit probably helped, as did the temperature of the water you fell into, but it can be a tough journey to recovery. No wife? No relations?'

'No.'

'I thought you had a daughter. The young girl who comes to visit?'

'I don't think so.' Bill closed his eyes and tried hard to think of the girl's name. 'She was here?'

'She came with another young woman. I saw them in here just an hour ago. You've had a lot of visitors. A lot of people want to know that you're getting better.'

'Am I getting better?'

'Of course you are,' said the consultant.

'What about my memory?'

'Mmm.' The noise that the consultant made was not reassuring.

'I can't remember things. I don't mean just about the accident. All sorts of things have disappeared. People come to visit me and I can't remember who they are. I don't remember their names. I'm missing chunks of my life.'

'Yes,' said the consultant, still smiling.

'I know that there's something really important that I have to do . . . I just can't remember what.'

'And this makes you anxious?'

'Anxious? No. Scared. I'm scared about something and I don't know what it is.'

The consultant smiled and nodded. 'This is not unusual. You have been through something terrible. You were a hair's breadth from death and you came back. It's traumatic. It is perfectly normal to be frightened.'

Bill tried to smile back. Nothing felt perfectly normal at all.

When the round-faced man had gone, he lay back down and tried to remember the girl's name but it was not there. He felt that if he could find this piece of the puzzle, other things would fall into place. Instead, he had a memory of a boat heading for a weir, dragged along by the current. He wondered if that was how he had drowned. There was something unreal about the scene. Something that did not fit.

The world was wrong but he had no idea of how to fix it.

Bill woke a little later in semi-darkness, his throat dry.

He turned his head slowly to the right. There was a small bedside locker there. On top of it was a kind of drinking cup that looked like it was meant for an infant. His right hand had some device attached to his finger, so with his left he reached out slowly towards it and lifted it to his dry lips and drank, and was grateful to the lukewarm water for coating his throat. As he lifted the beaker away, water spilled onto his pyjamas.

Annoyed at his own clumsiness, he replaced the cup on the locker top and looked down at his pyjamas. They weren't his pyjamas at all.

The water had matted the pyjama top to his chest. Feeling it cooling his skin, he had a sudden memory of water and his chest tightened.

He breathed.

Someone hurried down the corridor outside. A phone rang somewhere.

When someone close by began coughing, he woke again and realised he must have at least dozed for a while. There was a man in the bed next to him, he realised, and wondered how long he had been there. He tried to sit up.

A large nurse arrived and started checking his blood pressure. 'Was there a woman here?' he asked.

'Three women,' she said. 'You're a lucky fellow.'

'Three women?'

'One of them was here all day. Then the girl came. She just went a little while ago with her friend. All the ladies love you, Bill.'

He struggled to think who they might be and what they meant to him. 'What time is it?' he asked.

She checked her watch. 'Just coming up to ten.'

'In the morning?'

'No. It's night now,' she said. 'Are you feeling rough?'

'Mouth's sore.'

She leaned over him and examined his bruised lips. 'I'll see if we can get you some cream for that.'

'Fell off a motorbike,' he said. 'I think I did.'

'Is that how you ended up in the water?'

'Water?' He was puzzled.

'Yes. You drowned, pretty much.'

'Drowned? I can't swim.'

She looked at him, concern on her face. 'You were very lucky indeed. Apparently, you were unconscious for some time. They had to restart your heart.'

He sat up slowly and noticed that the locker next to him had a drawer, but the drawer was half open. Curious, he peered inside. There was a wallet in there, with credit cards and receipts – still damp. It smelt dank and mouldy but it also felt familiar in his hands. There were house keys too, and the keys to a Kawasaki motorbike.

He struggled to remember the incident. He saw himself below the water surface, arms raised, but wasn't sure whether that was just some nightmare he'd had.

The inability to remember anything more specific terrified him. He was wide awake now, looking round for any clues to his circumstances. The nurse said he had almost drowned.

What unsettled him more was that he knew he had something urgent to say – to tell someone. Something extremely important; something that he had discovered or something only he understood. He had the feeling that a great deal depended on it. It scared him that he had no idea what that thing was, or whom he had wanted to tell it to.

The feeling of not knowing was like being in water with nothing beneath him.

THIRTY-FOUR

Alex spent the night alone in the house. She woke early, sunlight seeping through the curtains, and then she remembered Bill lying in a hospital bed, miles away. She messaged Zoë a bright **Good morning xx**, but there was no reply from her.

When she drove down the track she had been meaning to stop at Bill's cottage to say hello to her, but as she approached she saw that there was a blue Volkswagen Beetle parked outside. There was a flower sticker on the petrol cap.

She drove on. It must be Rose's car, she realised.

The covert team came back with the details of two witnesses who had been in contact with Malcolm on Hinge and were willing to be interviewed. The first was called Amber; she lived near Maidstone and worked at the shopping mall. Amber had agreed to go to headquarters there for a formal interview later in the week, but things were moving fast. At her desk, Alex tried her phone number.

Amber took a cigarette break. 'Definitely something to do with building,' she agreed. 'Dated him twice and first time he had all this dust in his hair when he turned up at the restaurant. He said he was working on a site in Dover somewhere. Two dates and then he just disappeared. Ghosted me completely. All they have to do is say that you're not their type.'

'Did you have a phone number for him?'

'As it happens, I did. First few days we messaged on it. Then when he didn't answer I called him on it and he never picked up. 'I tried again just now. What a dick.'

'Can we have the number?'

'Yeah. I'll text it to you now, if you like. I'm not sure which one of these it is, but he's one of them.'

Amber sent three contacts through. When Alex opened them, she saw that all of them were named Knob.

'Sorry. I'm not sure which of those he was.'

'I take it Knob wasn't his last name, then?' said Alex.

'All my exes are called Knob. I don't delete their numbers, I just rename them.'

'Was he ever violent to you, Amber?'

She sounded a little shocked by the question.

'No. Never. He wasn't like that at all.'

'Did he have a temper?'

'No. He was always sweet and polite. Didn't even swear much, to be honest.'

The second woman worked for a digital advertising agency in Canterbury. Alex drove out to a tiny office in the centre of Canterbury that afternoon. They were on the first floor of a small weatherboarded garage that had been converted into workspaces. Rochelle, a pretty young woman with a black hairband and big dark eyes, said, 'I have to say the sex was amazing.'

Rochelle laughed. It was a good, throaty, dirty laugh. 'And he was great at the talk too. Smooth, you know. I have a tiny flat in Royal Parade. We hooked up in January, like I said, and by February he had brought a bag of pants and socks round to mine. I said, "What's all that? You moving in on me?" He just laughed.'

'He lived with you?'

'I wouldn't say lived. Up until the end of March he was at mine most nights. Then he started saying he was working late or going out for a drink with his pals. I knew then he was dating other women. One time he had these scratches down his back. He said it was a work thing. Fell down onto a pile of timber.' Rochelle's smile was rueful. 'Pile of timber with fingernails.'

The room was full of computer screens, but nobody seemed to be working on them.

'Did you mind?'

'Easy come, easy go. I'm not looking for a life partner. I don't want all that, but I never trust a man who doesn't leave his phone on the table when he goes for a piss.'

'What do you mean?'

'Well, it's obvious, isn't it? He doesn't want you to see some message from another woman coming up on the lock screen. He always kept his phone close.'

'Really?'

'Yeah. And he changed numbers too. All the bloody time. I must have had three different numbers for him. "Lost my phone," he'd say.'

'You didn't believe him?'

'Course not. I wasn't born yesterday. If you lose your phone you can still keep your number, can't you? He was a slippery boy, but I'm attracted to that sort.' Again, she laughed. 'What's this about? The police who contacted me wouldn't say, but it must be something serious. Is he in trouble?'

Alex ignored the question. 'Did he ever talk about friends . . . relations?'

Rochelle grinned. 'That was it. It was like a policy. Right at the beginning, he said, "It's you I'm going out with, not your sister, not your mum, not your pals." He kind of cut me off the moment I talked about them. Whenever I asked about his family, he just brushed it off. And you know very well that a man like that is not going to stick around.'

'So he was practised at hiding who he really was?'

'That's it a hundred per cent. I think it was kind of a tic. Almost like he'd been doing it so long he couldn't help it.'

'What about his surname?'

'Kember!' She grinned triumphantly.

'Malcolm Kember?'

'He was cagey about that, too. I noticed he didn't ever carry a wallet. No credit cards. Paid for everything on his phone. I asked him what his last name was on our first date and he told me it was Smith.'

'So how did you find out it was Kember?'

'Fuck you, Mr Kember!' she said.

'What?'

'It was back in February when the weather was really cold and disgusting. I said, "I don't want to go to work. Let's just spend the day in bed." This is my business, so I can work when I like. But around eleven in the morning he had a call come through from someone he was supposed to be working for. Some builder, I think. He was angry because Malcolm hadn't showed up. Malcolm made a few excuses but the guy just said, "Fuck you, Mr Kember." So I said, "What happened to Smith?" Malcolm just laughed it off.'

'Malcolm Kember?'

'Yeah.'

In some ways, Rochelle seemed to be like another Mimi. A woman with their own flat, successful, witty, not really minding that Malcolm was a rake.

'He likes independent women,' decided Alex. It was a pattern. 'Women who didn't see him as a long-term partner.'

'I don't think you'd ever accuse him of feminism,' said Rochelle.

Alex asked the same questions she had asked Amber. 'Was he ever angry with you? Did he ever threaten you in any way?'

The smile left her face. 'Has he done something bad?'

'I think so,' said Alex.

Rochelle looked shocked. 'Can you tell me what he did?'

'No. I'm afraid I can't. I promise, we will tell you when we can. But if he ever gets in touch with you, stay well out of his way. And let us know, right?'

Rochelle went quiet for a while. 'I've always thought I was a good judge of character. You have to be when you run a small business. He never did anything bad to me beyond lie about who he slept with, but maybe deep down, you don't ever know people. I find that quite a scary thought,' she said.

'Isn't it?' Alex answered.

★

225

She parked up on a lay-by on the way back to Ashford and called Zoë.

She didn't pick up, so Alex left a message. 'I'm going to be working late this evening. Should be back around nine. Will you be OK to cook yourself something at Bill's?'

The car was buffeted by the wake of a passing lorry.

'Nothing dangerous,' she added. 'Don't worry.' And then wished she hadn't added that last reassurance, because Zoë would always assume the opposite of whatever she said.

THIRTY-FIVE

When Bill woke next, there was another woman by his bed. He was pretty sure he hadn't seen this one before since he'd been here. She looked in her sixties, but she had bleached hair and leather trousers on.

'Morning, Bill,' she said.

He blinked at her, trying to place her. 'I'm sorry. I don't know who you are. I'm having a lot of trouble with my memory.'

'Poor old Bill,' she said. 'Looks like someone gave you a right going-over.'

Bill took a breath. He tried to sit up, but it hurt to do so. 'Who are you, exactly?'

'Sorry. I can't hear you too well, Bill. Can you speak up?'

He tried, but he seemed too short of breath.

'I brought you that,' she said. She pointed to a huge basket of fruit wrapped in cellophane that was now sitting on the bedside table next to him. 'Don't expect you can eat a lot of it right now, but give it to the nurses and they'll tuck you up all nice, know what I mean, Bill?'

227

A nurse pulled back the curtains that were around his bed. He seemed to be in a ward with lots of other men. Bill had never liked hospitals, he knew that about himself at least. Across the room, a family was visiting a man whose leg was in some kind of sling. A young boy, bored, turned and stared at Bill. Bill stuck his tongue out at him. The boy smiled back.

'How is Mr South this morning?' the nurse asked his visitor.

'I don't know. I don't think he understands me. He just mumbles stuff.'

A nurse had recently given him some pills, which had been painful to swallow. He had told Bill they would make him feel drowsy.

'How. Are. You. Bill?' the woman who had brought the fruit mouthed, voice loud, like she was talking to a geriatric. She leaned over him and put her lips on his forehead. 'Poor Bill.'

He spoke as clearly as his swollen mouth allowed. 'I don't remember anything.'

She leaned close and he repeated himself. 'He said he doesn't remember anything,' she told the nurse.

'Poor love. That must be scary for you.'

He nodded.

'Looks like he's forgotten everything,' said the woman to the nurse.

'He was unconscious for a long time,' said the nurse. 'It can cause lasting damage, I'm afraid.'

The woman stroked his forehead. 'And you don't remember why you were up the marina? What you were doing there? Who you spoke to?'

'What marina?' he asked, puzzled by the question.

'Poor old bugger,' she said to the nurse. 'Probably for the best, though, in the circumstances. You don't have any idea, do you?'

From nowhere, a picture of a tiny house came to him. Inside the window, two tiny model people were having sex. It was so strange, but also so vivid. He was not sure where it had appeared from.

The woman looked at Bill with a sympathetic smile. Something was very wrong. He struggled to work out what it was and why this woman thought that it was for the best.

He struggled to stay awake, but the medication he had taken was making him drowsy and it was impossible. When he woke the woman had gone and he wondered if he'd dreamed her. But when he looked to his left there was an enormous basket of fruit sitting on his locker.

THIRTY-SIX

The light was on in Bill's cabin so Alex stopped outside it.

Zoë was alone inside, lying on the floor, Bill's books around her. There was a bowl of something half eaten next to her on the floor. 'So. How was Rose?'

'Good,' said Zoë, eyes firmly on a book about insects. It had great big photos of them on every right-hand page.

'It's always possible Bill may never fully recover. You do understand that, don't you?'

'Yes he will,' said Zoë, not looking up from the book.

'Are you staying here again tonight?' asked Alex.

'Yes,' said her daughter. 'I don't want his house to be empty.'

Second interview was when you went in harder. You gathered as much information as you could to try and chip away at what they'd said first time around. Alex parked in the car park behind the HQ and made her way into the building. A constable was waiting on a chair outside Interview Room 3. He jumped up when she arrived.

'Sorry,' she said. 'I'm a little late. Anybody found a Malcolm Kember yet?'

'Not a peep. Apparently no one with that name.'

'Shit,' she said. Perhaps Rochelle had been wrong about it. 'Anything from the door-to-doors?'

She had been hoping that someone local might have been able to contradict Ethan's statement that he hadn't left the house after midnight, but no one had noticed him and there was no available CCTV.

'And digital forensics couldn't find a contact for anyone called Malcolm in his phone, either. But there's this.' He handed her an envelope.

She opened it, read, nodded, smiled at the constable. 'Oh, this is good.'

'Isn't it?'

'Shall we?' she said, opening the door. Inside, Ethan sat, looking tired. The Johncock brothers had spent the night in custody.

She did the preliminaries for the video record, then launched straight into it, peering down at the transcript of their first interview. 'You said you didn't know a man called Malcolm.'

'Yeah.'

'Sure of that?'

Again. 'Yeah.'

'Because we are looking for him in relation to the recent murder of a woman. Were you aware of that when you torched Detective Constable Charles Reed's car on Saturday night, that Malcolm was connected to a very nasty killing?'

'Jesus, no,' Ethan said emphatically. 'Swear to God.'

Alex looked up from her notes. 'You weren't aware of it when you torched his car?'

'No. I mean. I didn't set fire to it. I didn't know about this bloke Malcolm being wanted for murder.'

'So you did know Malcolm?'

'No. No I didn't.'

'You knew it was Charlie Reed's car though, didn't you?'

'Course not. I didn't do it.'

'Come on. Charlie Reed reported your van for not being taxed. You're pretending you weren't well aware he lived across the road from you?'

'No comment,' said Ethan.

Alex smiled back at him. 'Just to be clear. You claim you didn't know it was Charlie Reed's car. You don't know Malcolm. You weren't aware of anyone called Malcolm being linked to the murder of a young woman.'

'No. I was not. All of it.' He crossed his arms in front of him.

Alex took a few seconds before asking the next question, waiting for the silence to fill the room before saying, 'Have you been on any dating sites recently, Ethan?'

'What?'

'Have you?'

He smirked, turned to his lawyer. 'Not a crime, is it?'

'Far from it,' said Alex. 'Have you?'

'Maybe,' he said.

She opened up the envelope. 'Our digital forensics team have made an initial report on your phone. Apparently the lock screen code is 1111.'

Ethan laughed. 'Nothing to hide, have I? What were you looking for? Contact details for Malcolm?'

'Yes, actually. But we didn't find any so far.'

'I said, didn't I?'

'But we did find that you joined Hinge. On Saturday.'

He tightened his folded arms. Sniffed. 'So?'

'Coincidence?'

'Don't know what you mean.'

'Why does your Hinge profile say you're a woman, Ethan? A woman named Eve.'

Ethan coloured. 'I've got my own, you know, kinks.'

'Heterosexual woman seeking heterosexual man.'

'Funny. That's all. Entertainment.'

Alex leaned back on her chair, tilting the front legs off the floor. 'Here's what I think happened, Ethan. I don't think you're a bad man. Growing a bit of weed isn't the worst crime. But protecting your friend Malcolm is a stupid idea. I think Malcolm – or someone who knew Malcolm – told you that there was a guy on Hinge asking questions about him, and so you got yourself a Hinge profile because you wanted to take a look and find out who was trying to get at your pal. And when you did, you found the profile of this guy who already shopped you for out-of-date Vehicle Road Tax – and you figure out it's him who was asking questions about Malcolm – *heterosexual man seeking heterosexual woman.*'

Ethan's face tightened.

'And you decided to send him a message.'

He sniffed. Unfolded his arms. Put his palms on the table.

'You're in quite a lot of trouble, Ethan. Vandalising a car

233

isn't exactly the worst crime in the world, but an arson attack on a home – the home of a wheelchair user – is. And aiding and abetting a suspected killer is not great. Perverting the course of justice, as your lawyer here will tell you, is a very serious charge that can and will end up putting you in prison for a very long time. Continuing to lie will not work in your favour. So tell me again. What happened on Saturday night?'

Ethan was scratching the back of his left hand with his right. He looked up. Turned to his lawyer. 'Yeah. OK.'

'OK what?' asked Alex.

He ignored her, and addressed his lawyer instead. 'I think you and I need to talk.'

'Ten minutes?' said Alex, ending the recording.

It took two before Alex was beckoned back into the room.

'I did it,' said Ethan, when she had restarted the recording.

'You did what?'

He laid his palms flat on the table in front of him. 'I set Charlie's car on fire. I broke his petrol cap open and put a rag in, then set light to it. It was a stupid thing to do. Then I put another rag through the front door. It only had a bit of petrol on it, that one, just to give them a scare, just a little dribble really. I'm sorry.'

'Why did you do it, Ethan?'

'I heard he was doing this sneaky thing of looking for Malcolm.' He raised his palms off the table. 'A woman I know who does internet dating got a message from the feds about Malcolm. She called me and told me Malcolm might want to know, because she didn't have a way of contacting him. So I joined up and that's when I saw that it was PC plod around the corner.

But I swear I didn't know Malcolm had anything to do with any murder. If I had, I would not have done this.' He looked at his lawyer for reassurance. 'Honest to God. And I never meant to hurt the copper either, even if he is a bit of a dick.'

Alex had probably thought the same herself, for a while. 'Thank you. So when did you last speak to Malcolm directly?'

'Not for two or three weeks. Longer probably. He keeps himself to himself, you know?'

Alex looked up at the camera, then down at Ethan again. 'So why did you think the police were after Malcolm?'

Ethan went quiet.

'You must have some idea. After all, it was a pretty elaborate operation we had there, using Charlie to contact women who might have gone out with Malcolm.'

Ethan looked away from Alex, away from his lawyer, stared straight at a blank wall. 'Thing is, people like you are always after something on people like us. Some small thing we get wrong.' There was a contained anger in his voice.

'Like driving an untaxed vehicle?'

'Yeah, actually. That.'

'So you are saying you believed the Kent Police were after Malcolm for some minor regulations infringement, or tax issue?'

'What's so funny about that?' said Ethan.

Alex took a spiral-bound notebook from her shoulder bag, flicked through it until she found a blank page and pushed it towards him. 'Write me down his full name and his contact details.'

He left the pen on the table.

'His real name's Tom Kember. The Malcolm thing is just a joke. A nickname.'

That's why they couldn't find him. Malcolm wasn't his real name. Kember was, though.

'When we first worked with him, Malcolm was eighteen. He was new to the area, looking for work. We just knew him as Tom back then. He was pretty hopeless at the start. No experience at all, but he picked it all up pretty fast. Quiet, though. Didn't use bad language. Just kept his head down and got on with it. Nice lad. Never swore or nothing.'

'How did he come by the nickname?'

'It was kind of like his own alias. Another identity.'

'What do you mean?'

'We used to go out as a gang, me, my brother and Malcolm. We were working on this office block in Faversham, and Tom – he was just Tom then – cut his thumb pretty bad on an aluminium window frame so the boss drove him to Accident and Emergency. A day later he called up and said, "Think your mate Malcolm has left his bag behind." I said, "We don't know anyone called Malcolm." The boss said, "Yes you do. That bloke I took to hospital yesterday. His driving licence is right here in the bag." So we swung by to pick it up and there it was, proper-looking driving licence, photo of Tom, but the name's Malcolm.'

'Malcolm Kember?' repeated Alex, looking up at the camera.

'No. Something else. Don't remember what. This was a few years back. Proper James Bond, though. Licence was a fake he'd made up, he said, when we showed it to him, just in case he got caught speeding or something . . . I don't know. It was just funny. He said he could get them made up for us too, if we wanted.'

'And you believed him when he said it was fake?'

Ethan looked puzzled by the question. 'It's what he said.'

'But it looked real to you?'

'But you can get anything made up now, if you want. So we started calling him Malcolm after that, because it was funny.'

'Malcolm was funny?'

'Course it is. Funny name, isn't it, Malcolm? He was a bit annoyed with us at first, but he sucked it up after a bit. So that's what we called him. Malcolm.'

Her phone rang the minute she walked out of the interview room. 'Got him,' said DI McAdam. 'Tom Kember. Thirty-two. Builder. Address: Slylane House, Appledore Road, TN30.'

'On my way.' Alex pumped a fist into the air from the thrill, and then felt guilty for the momentary joy.

THIRTY-SEVEN

It was an old white farmhouse. At the rear was an assortment of wooden outhouses, clad in white clapboard. They looked like they'd been built to let to holidaymakers, but now the place looked unloved. Old agricultural equipment clogged the space in front of the small chalets. There was a pile of lumber in what had once been a farmyard and Alex spotted a large wooden workbench in one of the sheds, with a pile of wooden window frames leaning against a wall behind it.

'Definitely the place,' Alex said to the sergeant accompanying her. The sergeant had arrived with two uniformed officers.

'Help you?'

She turned to see a wide man with a flabby face holding a bull terrier of some kind on a lead. Bad skin as a teenager had left scars pocked on his cheeks. Definitely not Malcolm.

She pulled her ID from her shoulder bag. 'We're looking for Tom Kember. He lives here?'

'On and off. He rents one of the bungalows off me. Your name is?'

'Detective Sergeant Alexandra Cupidi. And you?'

'Smith,' he said.

'What do you mean, on and off?'

'I mean when he's not staying with one of his young ladies.'

'Is he here now?'

'Haven't seen him for a few days, to be honest. I expect some lucky girl is getting the full advantage of his boyish charm.'

'What do you mean by that?'

'I'm used to him disappearing for a few weeks. He loves them for a while, then he moves on.'

Alex looked around her. An old maroon Jaguar was parked at the rear of the house. It looked like it hadn't gone anywhere in years. Green mould clouded its windows and moss sprouted on the sills. 'You said you hadn't seen him for a few days. So when was he last here?'

'I don't know. A week ago?'

A week ago would have been just after the killing of Mimi Greene. 'Can you be more exact?'

Amused, the man scratched the side of his head. 'Weekend before last, maybe.'

On or around the time that Mimi Greene was killed. 'How was he?'

'How was he?'

'Was he acting differently at all? Did you notice anything in particular about his behaviour?'

'He keeps himself to himself, mostly. Pays the rent and gets on with it. I mind my own business.'

'Was he nervous? Happy?'

The man was deliberately vague. 'Don't really know.'

It was exasperating. 'We need to see his room.'

The man folded his arms. His dog sat down and started licking its genitals. 'What's he done? Supposed to have done, anyway.'

'His room,' she repeated.

'Where's your warrant?'

Alex looked him in the eye. 'We can come back with one. It'll take a day or two. However, we're in pursuit of Mr Kember in relation to a serious crime, which would allow us to enter without one. But this is your property presumably. You can make things simple for us and just let us in, if you like.'

'How serious?' Smith said, more interested.

'Just about as serious as it gets.'

'That's such a shame,' said Smith. 'He was very good with his rent.'

'Let me guess,' said Alex. 'He paid in cash?'

'Lovely crisp notes,' Smith said.

Alex paused. 'Did he ever bring any of his girlfriends here?'

'No. He was worried I'd steal them off him, I expect. This way, then.'

He led Alex towards the rear of the yard, then through an arched door in the wall to where the cabins were. 'This is his one.' And he unlocked the door.

They stepped into a small, sparse living room, whose tongue-and-groove panelled walls and wood floor made it resemble a sauna, were it not for the fact that it had what looked like a 97-inch TV taking up most of one wall. There was a huge, plump armchair facing it, and, sitting on the kitchen counter, the kind of coffee machine that was covered in dials, handles and silver pipes.

She pulled a pair of blue gloves from her bag. 'Likes his luxuries, then?'

'Some things yes, some things no. He drives a 1993 Ford Orion. A pile of crap.'

She moved into his bedroom. It was neat. The first thing she found when opening the top drawer of his bedside table was a gold watch. It was a Rolex Yacht-Master, and it was real, too. When she had been an officer in the Met, she had worked on counterfeiting and had learned to tell a fake. She felt the weight of it. 'That's a twenty-grand watch, at least,' she said, holding it up. 'You ever see him wearing it?'

Smith shook his head.

'What kind of chippy goes round wearing a twenty-thousand-pound watch?'

'A successful one, I would say.'

'Wears a Rolex, still drives a 1993 Ford Orion. That's weird. Do you have a contact for him?'

'I have got a number,' he said. He pulled out his phone. Alex copied it down. 'Good luck with it. He never answers. He calls back in a while but he won't if he doesn't recognise your number. I know that for a fact. You want me to give him a bell?'

'We'd obviously be grateful if you didn't, Mr Smith.'

'You can't stop me,' he said.

'Obviously not. But we want to speak to him in relation to an extremely serious crime. I'd have a chat with your lawyer before you attempt to contact Mr Kember, Mr Smith.'

She opened a kitchen cupboard. Bizarrely, there was a pile

241

of vehicle number plates inside. She took them out and photographed them, one by one.

Back at her car, she called McAdam.

'Not here. Hasn't been back here for ten days. He seems to use multiple number plates and stays at multiple addresses, often belonging to his girlfriends.'

Mr Smith was watching her from the window of his white house.

She thought about the difference between the watch and the car. 'He likes to hide,' she said. 'He's been doing it for years. He could afford a flashy car, but he doesn't drive one. Why is that?'

'I can give you a couple of reasons,' said McAdam. 'The photo went out to the press and we've had a lot of women saying they know him. They're as far afield as Buckinghamshire and Dorset. A couple have kids by him. Never paid a cent in maintenance.'

'And all the women I spoke to said he's so nice. What's the other one?'

'I'm not sure. There's something off, and I can't figure out what it is. It's like he appeared here in Kent out of nowhere when he was about eighteen. No trace of him existing before that.'

Alex was trying to think all this new information through. 'So his hiding from us has nothing to do with the murder of Mimi Greene?'

The plain-clothes officers were getting back into their cars.

'Or maybe it just made him think he could get away with it more easily,' said McAdam.

THIRTY-EIGHT

Kent seemed huge. These days, Alex seemed to spend whole days in a car, driving between Dungeness, Maidstone, Ashford and the hospital in Sidcup. Bill was asleep when Alex got there. Jill was already in the room with him, holding his hand.

'He's definitely more alert than he was yesterday,' said Jill.

Alex nodded. 'Who was he looking for there? I think I need to know.'

'You sure?'

'I can't take not knowing. Seeing as we're both here in the same room and we're not even supposed to be, I reckon we're OK.'

Jill took a breath and said, 'I'm pretty sure he was looking for a woman called Mandy French.'

'Why?'

Jill let go of Bill and reached out her hand, laying it on top of Alex's. 'It's because of my dad,' she said. And she told her the little she knew about her father, the two murders in 1994, and the woman Mandy French who Bill thought had told a 'big fat lie' about something, but Jill didn't know what.

243

Alex listened in silence, shocked. 'Jesus Jill,' she said when her friend explained what she knew. 'This man is your dad? This is what you were trying to tell me that day Zoe found the body?'

Jill nodded.

'I'm so sorry.'

'Don't matter.'

'That's a lot to carry.'

Jill grinned. 'Yeah. Right, So anyway. Bill had this thing about Mandy French and he said he needed to talk to her because he thought there was something off with her, but he never got the chance to tell me what.'

'And that took him to the marina?'

'Honestly? I haven't the slightest. Bill was just trying to help because I asked him to. Because I couldn't talk to you. I still can't, really. And even if I had been able to tell you, it's like he said. We're both serving officers. We can't just go digging around because some fucker with a double murder conviction says he's my dad. So he was keeping it all close to his chest.'

'Did something happen to him because of all that, do you think?'

Jill shrugged. 'Don't know. The consultant says it was an accident. If this was my fault, I don't know what I'm going to do.'

Bill lay propped up by the bed. His beard had grown, thought Alex. Grey and black stubble covered his chin. He needed a shave. Even in the days when he had been drinking too much, he had always shaved in the morning. They sat for half an hour, but he didn't stir.

'You look tired,' said Jill.

'Thanks. You're no picture either.'

244

'I know I shouldn't ask, I know I'm not supposed to know anything about it, but seeing as I just told you all this stuff, are you any closer to finding Mimi's killer?'

'Maybe. The man you slept with. His name wasn't Malcolm, you know?'

'Wow. He lied. Quelle surprise.'

'Yes. I don't get it, though. He's out there, but he's hiding, but he's been hiding for ages, before any of this ever happened. He tricked a load of women. He hides behind this name, Malcolm, so they can never trace him. He's done it loads, one after the other. He'll have one on the go, then he starts chasing after the next behind her back.'

'Monkey branching. That's what he was doing with me and Mimi.'

'God.' Alex grinned at her friend. 'Your generation even has a name for it, obviously.'

'It's like a monkey swinging from trees, not letting go of one branch until he's grabbed the next one. It's like a narcissistic personality disorder, going from one relationship to the next. As soon as you have one, you start the next.'

'You say everything's a narcissistic personality disorder.'

'It's an actual thing,' protested Jill.

Alex checked the time on her phone. She should try and get home, get some sleep. She stood, leaned forward over Bill. 'I want you back, Bill. I love you.'

His eyes remained shut, his breathing steady.

They were just getting up to head back to their cars when Alex got a message on her phone. She looked up. 'Holy shit!' She grabbed Jill's arm. 'There's a fire at the boatyard.'

245

They ran down the stairs, not waiting for the lift, and jumped into Alex's car together. In half an hour they were back at Hoo.

The air was full of the sharp tang of soot and chemicals.

Firefighters were still walking in full breathing apparatus.

'What happened?' Jill asked a police officer who was marking out a cordon.

'One of the boats caught fire. Spread pretty quickly. Seven boats wrecked. Hell of an insurance claim.'

'Anybody hurt?'

'Doesn't appear to be, but they're still checking the hull of the first boat to go up.'

Emergency lights had been trained on the worst of it. Boats they had walked past on Sunday night were no more than black, steaming ribs of wood. Nearby, a white fibreglass sailing boat had lost most of its cabin and upper deck.

'There was a wind, see,' said the copper. 'Blew the fire from one boat to the next. Gas bottles on board and everything. Flames shot way up into the sky, they're telling me.'

Part of the jetty had simply disintegrated. There was a black gap two metres across, close to where Bill had gone into the water.

It was carnage.

Some boats had moved away, mooring on their anchors a little way off. Alex recognised the white yacht that had been at the end of the jetty, lit by the gleam of work lights off the water.

'Your friend,' the copper asked Alex. 'How's he doing?

'You were here on Sunday?'

'Yep. I recognised you.'

'Not so good,' said Alex.

'But he's getting better,' added Jill.

'Good. Good,' said the man. 'Strange times, hey?'

Alex was watching a man stepping down from the white yacht into a rubber dinghy. He started an outboard motor and was at the end of the third jetty in a couple of seconds. 'Excuse me. There's a man I need to talk to.'

'Wait for me,' said Jill, following her.

The man was just finishing tying up when Alex reached him. He wore pale shorts and a loose shirt. 'Hell of a mess,' she said.

He looked up from the water. 'You got that right.'

From the dinghy below, he held out his hand to her. Alex grasped it and pulled him up. 'Two incidents in less than a week,' she said. 'That's a little more than bad luck.'

'Bloody right. This place is . . . weird. We're pulling anchor and moving on first thing tomorrow. Don't like it here one little bit,' he said.

'It was you who pulled the man from the water on Sunday night, wasn't it?' said Alex.

He frowned. 'How did you know that?'

'You came over and tied up to the end of that jetty to pull him out.' She pointed to where she'd seen the trail of wet footsteps on Sunday night. They had led to the end of the jetty where this man had just moored his little dinghy. The man in the olive cap had not told the whole truth about what had happened, which made Alex curious. 'He was our friend. So thank you.'

The man looked a little embarrassed.

'Look. I'm a police officer. I need to talk to you.'

'You're police?'

'I just want to get some facts straight. A man was almost killed on Sunday night.'

'He's still alive then?' the man said. 'I didn't know if he was going to pull through.'

'Yes. We just came from the hospital.'

'He's going to be OK,' said Jill. Jill seemed more certain of it than she was, thought Alex.

'That's good.'

'So can we talk?' asked Alex. The man seemed hesitant. From his tan, Alex guessed he lived aboard the yacht. People on the move like him were always suspicious of police. 'I just need to understand what our friend was doing here.'

'Same,' said Jill.

The man made up his mind. 'Not here. This place is too bloody strange. Give me two minutes. I have to pick up a package.' He left them waiting by the dinghy.

Firefighters had focused lights on the ribs of the boat that seemed to have started the fire. A man in diving gear was sitting on the edge of a fibreglass boat nearby.

Within a minute, the man was back with some post in his hand. 'Get in,' he said. 'It'll be more private on our boat.'

He stepped in first, then guided Alex down into the boat. It wobbled as she sat on the edge. 'Oh shit,' said Jill as the boat moved underneath her. With practised ease, the man yanked the toggle on the engine and started it, and guided them across to the rear of the yacht.

'I have some people with me,' he called into the cockpit.

A woman's voice came from inside the boat. 'Who?'

'Some friends of the man who was in the water.'

Alex said, 'I just want to ask you both a couple of questions.'

'Why?'

'Because we're trying to find out what Bill was doing here in the first place.'

The man pulled open the hatch. 'Come in quick,' the woman shouted. 'The wind is blowing my cards everywhere.'

The cabin was orderly but lived-in. A pot of something sat on a small cooker. A shelf of well-thumbed books was held in place by a multicoloured bungee cord. Photographs had been tacked to the cabin wall. The couple standing on the roof of their boat, in a delicious palm-fringed bay. A picture of her at the helm, squinting into a snow flurry.

'What did you want to ask?' The woman swept her arm across the table, gathering up the game of cards she had been playing.

'So. What happened on Sunday night?'

'It was horrible,' he said. 'I learned CPR. I just never had to do it before.'

'I know.' Alex remembered the first time she had done it – the shock of breaking an old man's ribs as she pressed down on him. If someone's heart had stopped, chances of it doing any good were minuscule. 'How did you find him?'

'We were having a bite to eat in here when I heard a splash – weren't we? I know the noise of someone falling in the water.'

The woman was shuffling the cards. 'It's never a good sound.'

'I was cooking, so I was nearest the hatch. Jumped into the dinghy and was over here in a second. Poor guy was right under the water. Only way to get him out was to jump in.'

'Both of us,' said the woman.

'We got his head out and then got rope around his chest and hauled him out so I could do CPR until someone brought the defibrillator.'

It was painful to hear. 'When you went out there, did you see anyone else?'

'Why?' asked the woman.

'Did you?'

The man shook his head. 'Not until we were pulling him out. That's when the guy from that boat *Dizzy Rascal* appeared, which was useful because he was heavy. All that water in his clothes. It took three of us to get him out of the water.'

Jill exchanged a glance with Alex. They were thinking the same thing. Jill was the one who said it. 'Why did he say he was the one who pulled Bill out?'

'What are you talking about?' asked the woman.

'Shock maybe,' said Alex.

'He didn't look shocked.'

'Maybe because he wanted to take all the credit . . .' said Alex.

'. . . or 'cause he didn't want us chatting to these two,' Jill completed the thought.

THIRTY-NINE

Bill woke.

He looked outside. There was a woman's voice in his head. She had said, 'I love you.' She spoke with a tenderness he was unused to. He imagined it was his mother, though, on reflection, it didn't sound like his mother at all.

He couldn't remember her name, but for no reason, he remembered her daughter's. Zoë. The name seemed to float out of the air towards him. The thin girl who had been by his bed. Her name was Zoë, and she loved birds as much as he did.

Excited, he tried to sit up in bed. He wanted to search for a pen to write the name down with. He opened the drawer and felt around, but there was only a wallet and some keys.

'Hello?' he called.

The ward was dark and quiet apart from the sound of coughing.

251

FORTY

The boat they sat inside swung slowly from side to side on its mooring on the outgoing tide. 'Why would the man who owns the boat *Dizzy Rascal* have not wanted us to talk to you two?' Alex wondered aloud in the galley.

'It's a good question,' Jill said.

The woman dealt out a row of cards.

'Do we even have any idea why Bill was here?' asked Jill.

'I'm not sure,' said Alex. 'But I know Bill. He's a careful man. He knows about boats. He's not the kind of man who just falls in the water.'

The man said, 'You think it wasn't an accident?'

'Maybe it wasn't,' Alex replied.

The man looked at the woman. She nodded. 'Tell them.'

'I'd met him earlier. He told me he was looking for someone – a woman.'

Jill leaned forward towards the man. 'What?' she asked cautiously. 'What woman?'

'He rocked up on his motorbike. Asked about some woman.

252

I told him we'd only just moored up. We were strangers here.'

'A woman?'

'A woman who he thought had a boat here, I guess. I told him I didn't know, so I told him to talk to Dizzy Rascal. The guy in that boat was the one who'd told us that this mooring was free for a couple of days, so I figured he would know. There's always somebody moored up who acts like they run the place. That was him.'

The boat rolled a little in the wind. Flotsam bumped the hull.

'Did he ask for her by name?'

'Sorry. Probably. I can't remember.'

'It's extremely important,' said Alex. 'We need to know what he was doing here.'

The man closed his eyes for a second. When he opened them he said, 'I'm sorry. I didn't recognise it and I can't remember it.'

Jill exchanged a glance with Alex. 'Was it Amanda French?' she asked.

The man looked startled. 'Yes. I think it was.'

Alex looked at her, curious. 'The woman he was looking for?'

'Yes. Remember? I told you Bill thought she was something to do with my dad,' said Jill.

'What time was this?' Alex asked.

'I don't know. Two, maybe? Three on Sunday afternoon?'

'And Bill found the man from *Dizzy Rascal* and talked to him?'

'Yeah. They talked. And then your friend got on his motorbike and left.'

'He left?' Alex said.

253

'I saw him go.'

Jill said, 'So what was he doing back here three or four hours later?'

'And where is his motorbike?' added Alex. 'I didn't notice it anywhere.'

The man said, 'I think he must have been working on a boat or something.'

'Yeah. Maybe. That would be Bill,' said Jill.

The rocking of the boat made Alex feel a little queasy.

'Except it was getting dark. Why would you work on a boat at that time of night?' The woman had spoken without looking up from her cards.

'What made you think he was working on a boat?' Alex asked the man.

'He had put on overalls. When he arrived, he was just in trousers and a kind of aviator jacket. When we pulled him out of the water he was wearing overalls. Part of the reason he was so heavy. It was soaked.'

'He had changed clothes?' Jill said. 'That sounds more like he was trying to disappear into the background.'

Alex looked at her watch.

'You're leaving, right?' Jill asked them. 'You don't like it here?'

'It's just an atmosphere,' said the woman. 'And too much bad stuff going on. We were lucky. Our draught is too deep to come in close, so we were safe from the fire, but a few people lost their boats tonight. That's no joke.'

'How does a fire start on a boat?' Alex asked.

'Gas leak, I expect. Happens sometimes,' the woman said. 'A lot of people on boats prefer propane because it works in cold weather. Trouble is, if it gets into your bilges, it builds up. Some little spark can set it off. Automatic bilge pump. Anything. Woof.'

'I hear it was spectacular.'

'Not if you're on another boat. Just plain scary.'

'You better take them back soon,' said the woman. 'Tide's racing. You'll lose the water. You'll be stuck with us for the night if you're not careful.'

The man led them back into the cockpit. Alex looked around. 'Where's *Dizzy Rascal*?' she asked.

The man climbed up onto the top of the cabin and looked around. 'Weird. She was here earlier today.'

'Was she one of the boats that caught fire?'

'No. She was on the far pontoon. She'd have been fine. Maybe like us, he just didn't want to stick around to see what happens next.'

He guided them both back into the little boat and took them across the current, which was running faster now. The crowd around the gap in the jetty seemed to have grown. Someone had run more electrical cables down the ruined jetty. There were even more lights now. An orange RNLI lifeboat was standing a few metres off from the sunken boat, shining its searchlight from the opposite direction.

'Can you find out someone's name from the name of their boat?' asked Jill.

'The man I'd normally ask about that kind of thing is lying in a hospital bed, thirty miles away,' said Alex, looking around. The tide had gone out. The burnt boat looked like an animal carcass, charred ribs curving upwards out of the mud.

FORTY-ONE

When Alex woke early in the morning, needing to pee, she tiptoed past Zoë's room before remembering that she wasn't there. She had stayed at Bill's for a third night. It was almost as if she'd moved out completely.

McAdam had asked everyone in for an early start. When she drove past Bill's place at 7.30, Rose's car was parked outside for a second time. She must have arrived late; Alex hadn't got back from the marina until after ten. She wondered if they were sleeping together. It was Zoë's business if they were. She was an adult – technically, at least. She should be pleased that her daughter had found a friend, she thought, but couldn't help being a little hurt that her daughter told her so little.

Everyone was crammed into the Portakabin for the morning's early meeting. There were people perched on desks, others standing in the narrow space between them. Charlie was back on duty. They nodded at each other. Charlie gave her a thumbs up.

'OK, everyone. So we know that the main suspect in Mimi

Greene's murder is Tom Kember, thirty-two, home address in East Kent, general builder and carpenter by trade. We have no recent sightings of him and though we have a phone number, it's not pinging. He's dumped it or is just keeping it switched off. Our number one priority is to find this man. From talking to former lovers, there is no history of violence. So scenario one: he is just a witness rather than a suspect – but a very slippery one. Scenario two: if he is the man who killed Mimi Greene, he's done something that's out of character. Something that he probably regrets. We have to consider that there's a possibility of self-harm here, and that's why no one has heard from him over the last eleven days.'

'You mean you think he's topped himself?' someone asked.

'It's one possibility. He's used to being the one who abandons women. Mimi Greene rejected him. If he did kill her in a fit of anger at her kicking him out, he may have been remorseful. Someone out there has seen him. Someone knows where he is, or where he's been.'

'A lot of girlfriends,' said someone. 'He loved the ladies. We have contacts from all over the place.'

'Exactly. Can you put all this on a map? We might be able to work out where he likes to go.'

It seemed like they were closing in on Kember. They had put a map up on the wall, with pins marking each of the contacts, from the dating app and from the general public in response to the weekend's news item. All information was useful. It might expose some kind of pattern.

'I should also point out that we are not the only ones who've been trying to track down Malcolm. Several of the respondents are also trying to find him. Two women who got in touch after the public appeal appear to be the mothers of his children. He has three children. The women have been unsuccessfully trying to pursue him for maintenance payments and come up with the same problem. Malcolm doesn't exist. He doesn't answer his phone. He doesn't do anything apart from make profiles on dating apps.'

'Shit,' said Alex. 'That's why he's been hiding all these years,' said Alex. 'He's had plenty of practice. He changes his phone number all the time and never answers anyone unless he recognises their number. It wasn't the Mimi Greene murder that made him go under the radar. He's been like that a long time.'

'It appears so.'

'He doesn't think he owes anyone anything.' Alex was thinking out loud. 'Not even the women whose children he fathered.' Publicly, he was just Malcolm. Jack the Lad in his old Ford Orion. Privately, Tom Kember was someone else completely.

'Someone's bound to have seen him,' said one of the other detectives.

'One of the methods he's been using to avoid detection is using cloned number plates,' continued McAdam. 'The number plates Alex recovered from Slylane House were all cloned, mostly from other Ford Orions. He's been very methodical about how he keeps below the radar. But we have those plates now, and we're closing in on him. His options are becoming more limited by the day.'

'If he's alive,' said someone.

Alex was sure he was. He was a man who felt he was entitled

to everything. People like that didn't ever think they were going to lose.

'Anything else?' McAdam was asking.

'There was a fire last night at Hoo Marina,' said Alex. 'It's the same place former Police Constable William South was when he almost drowned on Sunday night.'

'Was anybody hurt?'

'I don't think so.'

McAdam looked a little puzzled by the interjection.

'It's just . . . What if there's a connection between Bill's accident and the fire?'

McAdam looked at her curiously. 'Like what?'

'Honestly? I haven't the foggiest,' said Alex. She looked around the small room, hoping someone else would pick up on her question, but no one did. The last thing she wanted to let on was that she'd been with Jill last night at the marina, looking around. She tried again. 'It's just weird, isn't it? Two near-fatal accidents in the same location within four days of each other.'

McAdam considered this. 'But nothing specific here?'

'No. Nothing,' said Alex, frustrated at being unable to say what she knew.

'OK. Well. Obviously we'll bear that in mind . . .'

The phone was buzzing in the back pocket of her trousers. She lifted it out and saw Jill's name. Before anyone could see, she replaced it in her pocket. It buzzed again. She was just trying to think of an excuse to leave the room to answer the call when Charlie spoke up.

'Boss!'

The room looked round.

'Just had a message from Constable Ferriter!' Charlie called out. 'Jill Ferriter. She says that Malcolm just called her.'

He lifted up the screen and pointed it towards McAdam.

FORTY-TWO

'Tom Kember contacted you?' McAdam said. 'On your personal phone?'

They had contacted her on Teams. Jill Ferriter was sitting at the dining table of her flat in Ashford. Alex recognised the poster on the wall behind her.

In brightly coloured letters it read:

Live simple.
Dream big.
Love lots.

It was very Jill Ferriter.

'Yes. He called me just now.'

'Send us the number he sent it from.'

'Already did,' she said. 'I sent it to Charlie.'

'How did Kember get your number?' asked Alex.

'He never gave me his number, but I am pretty sure I gave him mine.'

One of the constables was already calling someone to get the number traced.

'What did he say?' demanded Alex.

Everyone was crowding round the screen. 'Funny, really. He was in a total panic. He told me I'd got everything wrong and he never laid a hand on Mimi Greene.'

'So why has he just disappeared?'

'He wouldn't say. He just said it's not him. I said, so he should come in and give us an interview, but he said he wasn't going to do that and then he hung up. That's all.'

'What did he sound like?' she asked.

'Freaking out. He said it wasn't him. He was angry that we were suggesting he'd done it. He said we'd ruined his life.'

Alex and McAdam exchanged a glance. It was hardly unusual for a killer to protest his innocence, but what if they had been chasing the wrong person all this time?

'Can you call him back?' asked McAdam.

'Tried, obviously, but now he's not picking up.'

It would take at least half an hour for the tech team to come back with anything, probably longer.

'I miss you a lot,' said Jill. 'Even you, boss.'

Alex's phone was buzzing again. This time it was Zoë. Her calls were so rare these days, she took it and stepped out of the cabin into the cooler air.

'Hello, love, everything all right?'

'It's Rose,' Zoë said. 'I think I upset her.'

'Oh?'

Alex walked way from the Portakabin to try and get some privacy.

'Thing is, I really like her, and we've been getting along great. I've been talking to her. She's really sad about Mimi still, and she was in a pretty dark place.'

'You're a good person,' said Alex. 'You know that?'

'You know she's gay, right?'

'Well, yes. I guessed.'

'She has multiple issues. And she fell out with this woman in London and it turned into a big situation and that's why she lost her job and ended up down here. And she's been self-harming.'

Part of Alex wanted to end the call and head straight back into the office; the case she had been working on for a week and a half had just burst open. She stayed listening to her daughter.

'I like her too. A lot. Like, really a lot. And she came and stayed over with me at Bill's place on Tuesday and it was nice.'

Charlie stuck his head out of the door of the cabin and looked around. He spotted her and waved. 'I'll be one minute,' Alex shouted.

'What's that?' demanded Zoë.

'Nothing, love. Go on.'

'Then she came again last night without me even asking. She just appeared. And that was good, I suppose, but this morning I asked her if she could give me a little space. I just want to be in Bill's place on my own. He is my friend. She doesn't know him and he's lying there in that hospital—'

'You were in the right,' Alex assured her.

'But I felt she was crowding me and taking everything too fast. So this morning I asked her to give me some space – and she went absolutely mental.'

'What do you mean, mental?'

263

'Crying. Like really crying. Shouting at me and saying I didn't understand her, then saying sorry and, like, really begging me to let her stay. I think I made a mistake by encouraging her or something.'

'No, Zoë. You didn't. You didn't make a mistake.'

Charlie had come out of the office now and was standing close, waiting for her to end her call.

'She's obviously got issues with boundaries, Zoë. The woman in London? The reason she gave up her last job. It's not the first time this has happened.'

She could hear the agitation in her daughter's voice. 'I'm worried she's going to do something stupid. I feel horrible.'

'It's not your fault, Zoë. Tell you what I'll do. I'll call Isobel and ask if she can go round and see her – make sure she's OK. Now stay in the house, and if she comes back, just stay calm and tell her that you're her friend, but she can't stay the night with you.'

Zoë gulped her assent.

'Listen, love. I have to go. There's a situation here. I'll call Isobel as soon as I can.'

She ended the call.

'Boss wants you,' said Charlie.

McAdam was standing in front of the big map. 'Not a surprise, I suppose, but the phone Kember made the call to Constable Ferriter on has been switched off. It was a new number, never activated before. It's only made the one call and that came from somewhere in New Romney.'

He stood and walked towards the map, and picked up another pin. 'Somewhere here,' McAdam said, placing it at the north

264

end of the small village. 'We are going to flood the place with police now.'

'No. Too many roads out of there,' Alex said. 'If he's adept at hiding, he'll know we traced the call. Odds are he just drove there to throw us off the scent and he's gone already. Don't waste officers flooding the place. Save the cavalry for later.'

The room was quiet.

'Sorry. I just meant . . .'

'No. You're probably right.' McAdam gave a small, curt nod.

'Just a few officers, asking around. Shops. Petrol stations. Cafes. Has anyone clocked him? It's near to me. He might know Charlie from the picture on Hinge, but he doesn't know what I look like, does he?'

'What are you going to do?'

'It's a small area. I'll be there in thirty minutes – an hour after he's gone. This is the closest we've been to him all this time . . .'

McAdam looked around the room, as if looking for someone to go with her.

'I'll be fine,' she said. 'Quicker we get there the better.'

FORTY-THREE

He had woken with a start with the girl's name in his head. And then, like a dream that vanished before you had time to tell anyone about it, it had gone. He had been sure he had her name, and now there was just an empty space where it had been.

He was furious at himself for having it so close and then letting go of it. In the bed opposite there was a thin man who kept asking where his wife was. 'Where are my clothes?' he demanded. 'I have to get dressed because my wife is coming to collect me.'

The man in the bed next to him leaned towards him. '*Dementia*,' he mouthed. '*Shouldn't even be in here.*'

'Can I have a pen and paper?' Bill asked the nurse who came to check his blood pressure.

She disappeared and he thought she had forgotten, but she returned an hour later with several sheets of A4 and a Bic biro. He asked the man in the bed next to his if he could borrow one of his magazines.

'Go ahead, mate,' he said.

He propped the paper on the magazine on his knees and tried to think. There was something about the girl's name that was unusual. He was convinced that it was a very short word, but he could not remember what it was, so he tried writing a list of names that it might be.

Over the next twenty minutes, he wrote *Mia, Sky, Una, Eva, May, Ivy,* but it was none of them.

The man next to him had some relations visiting. They had brought books and more puzzle magazines. 'You can keep that one, mate,' he told Bill. 'I've some new ones now.'

When his family left, he said, 'What are you doing? Is it a puzzle?'

He looked at his neighbour and said, 'Girl's name, three letters.'

'Have you tried Pam? Or Dot?' he said. 'Ava, like Ava Gardner?'

He added them to the list. The neighbour settled down and started doing puzzles of his own. 'Bluish white metal, four letters,' he said.

'Zinc,' Bill answered, revelling in the fact that the word had come to him easily. After these days in hospital, it felt like a kind of miracle that his brain could produce a word from nowhere – but the name he was looking for remained elusive.

'Gawd. That gives me a letter Z to start. *Formerly called Rhodesia, eight letters.* It's on the tip of my tongue.'

A trolley came around with lunch. They missed Bill's bed – he still had difficulty eating because of the tubes that had been forced down his throat when he was unconscious, so they were feeding him what they described as 'thin liquids'.

'Begins with Z,' said the man again, putting the magazine aside to make way for the tray of food.

'Zoë,' said Bill out loud.

'That's the name you were saying in your sleep last night,' said the man. 'Zoë. Only three letters. Doesn't fit.'

'As a matter of fact, it does,' Bill said, grinning like an idiot.

FORTY-FOUR

New Romney was mostly a busy main road through a pretty old village. Alex studied the print-out of the phone report. The phone had pinged from the north end of the village. There was not much there, which helped – a large caravan site, three houses and the visitor centre for a small wildlife sanctuary.

She parked outside the caravan site office and pulled out a picture of Tom Kember. The woman behind the counter shook her head. She tried the campsite bar next – a large barn-like space with tables and chairs set regularly around the room. 'If I'd seen him, I'd have recognised him,' said one of the young women who served food there, giggling.

Alex tried the houses next, on the opposite side of the road. Two bungalows were dark. The third was a large farmhouse. A teenage boy came to the door, but he, like everyone else so far, said that he had not seen anyone who looked like the photograph of Tom Kember. She left him and drove the short way to the wildlife visitor centre. It was a big white shed in a scrap of wild land. Zoë used to volunteer here when she was younger and had come home with blistered hands.

Inside, a woman in a gilet sat behind a till. 'No, but I only just clocked on.' She turned to the kitchen behind her. 'Janice? Can you help this lady?'

The next woman, Janice, looked at the photograph on Alex's phone. 'Yeah. He had a scone couple of hours ago. Sat there.' She pointed to a table in the corner, next to a bookshelf.

Alex perked up. 'He did?'

'Yeah. Pretty sure it was him. Nice bloke. Polite. Tipped, which nobody ever does round here.'

'Did you see what kind of car he was driving? Anything like that?'

'What's he done?'

Alex ignored the question. 'Do you remember what he was wearing?'

'Um. T-shirt. Jeans.'

Alex stepped outside with her phone and called McAdam. 'Kember was at the Romney Marsh Visitor Centre two hours ago.' She looked up. There was a security camera in the eaves of the building.

She went back inside. 'Where does the footage for your security camera end up?'

Janice looked blank. 'In the office, I expect. You want me to call someone up?'

Alex ordered coffee and sat, waiting for an administrator to arrive. Before the coffee arrived, her phone rang. It was Zoë again. Alex cursed herself for not having phoned Isobel yet. 'Are you OK?'

'Did you phone her?' was the first thing Zoë gabbled.

'I'm sorry. I haven't had a second, but I'll do it right now.'

'No, don't. Rose called me and apologised. She said she was completely in the wrong. She was really sweet about it. She said she understood about Bill and the cottage and she was sorry she'd been so insensitive, that she had got things completely wrong and that she was really trying to control her behaviour. It was something Mimi had been trying to help her with. We're going to go freshwater swimming this evening.'

'Are you sure that's a good idea?'

'You should have heard her, Mum. She was really sorry. I think it's a good thing. I like her. I just don't like her when she goes mental.'

'That's good,' said Alex. 'I'm glad. Text me, though, won't you?' She ended the call.

A yellow Aygo drove into the car park and a woman in a long grey cardigan got out and looked her up and down. 'Are you the policewoman?' Alex followed the administrator into the office. 'It'll be on the hard drive,' she said. 'Who is it you're looking for?'

'Someone who made a phone call from here at around nine this morning. We need to see if there's CCTV of him arriving.'

'Should be simple then. We've only just opened up and there are generally only one or two visitors at that hour.' The woman took glasses out of a case and put them on, then started up a computer. It only took a few minutes.

'Is that him?' She froze the frame on a man halfway out of a dark car. It was a Ford Orion. And even in grainy black and white it was unmistakably Tom Kember.

'Play it some more,' ordered Alex. The man got out of the car, looking nervous and agitated. He looked around, as if checking to see if anyone was following him, then disappeared into the building. Another car arrived, but the occupant was a dog walker who spent a little time changing her shoes for boots, then headed off towards one of the paths that led away from the car park. According to the time-code, it was twenty minutes before Kember reappeared, got into his car again and drove it away. During those twenty minutes he had phoned Jill.

'Rewind a little,' said Alex. 'Can you get a clear view of the number plate?'

Alex photographed the screen, wrote down the number on a scrap of paper and called it in straight away. 'Can I get an urgent ANPR report on Mike Victor Zero Two Tango Lima Delta?'

Then she called McAdam to let him know that they had a number plate for Kember's car. 'It's another false plate. The car is a Ford Orion. The registration is for a 2002 vehicle though. But it may be enough.'

She ordered another coffee and waited. Her phone went a few minutes later. The false number plate had pinged two cameras on the A259, the first in New Romney itself, the second in Dymchurch, a little way to the north. 'Nothing after that?'

'Nothing. So your vehicle may be parked up at Dymchurch . . .'

'Or, more likely, he may have taken minor roads from there.' Which would definitely be Kember's way. To keep out of sight. 'Can you see anything over the last week?'

'Nothing. No records except today.'

Kember had changed plates today.

'Have you got a map?' she asked the administrator.

272

The woman fetched an Ordnance Survey map from a shelf and laid it out on one of the cafe tables. Alex looked at the roads around Dymchurch. Only three roads headed west into Romney Marsh from Dymchurch. The last place his car had been spotted was at the crossing just by the City of London pub. It was still heading north at that point before it disappeared – and that was after the turnings onto St Mary's Road and Eastbridge Road. So either it had parked somewhere local, or it had turned left and driven up Burmarsh Road.

She traced her finger up the yellow unclassified road, towards the village of Burmarsh. About a mile outside Dymchurch was a blue symbol. A tent and a caravan. 'Do you know this place?'

'The caravan site? Willow View, it's called.'

'Is it just a campsite, or do people live there?'

'There's a whole bunch of static caravans there.' The administrator turned to Janice. 'Isn't that right?'

Janice agreed. 'Some people live there all year round. Middle of bloody nowhere.'

North of Burmarsh, the road split. If he'd taken the Burmarsh Road he could have gone anywhere, but Alex's eyes kept being drawn back to the campsite. It was kind of on the way back to the office, she reasoned. What was the harm in just popping in there on her way?

FORTY-FIVE

Willow View caravan park sat in the flat marsh surrounded by wheat fields and sheep, the dark line of the South Downs rising on the horizon behind it. It was a small family business, not like the bigger, much slicker caravan park Alex had visited an hour or so earlier in Romney. She rolled past the entrance slowly, but decided to drive on a little way. She was in an unmarked car, but anyone looking closely would see it was a police car from the computer next to the dashboard and the matrix display in the rear window, so she parked it a couple of hundred metres up the road and walked back.

The door of the reception hut was locked and there was no one on duty. It wasn't holiday season yet. The static caravans were arranged among trees and hedges. A few looked occupied, but when she knocked on doors, no one answered. The whole place seemed calm and quiet. It took a few minutes to find a small woman sitting on a garden chair. She had wool on her lap and a crochet needle in her hand, and the Sara Cox show was playing on her radio.

'Do you crochet?' the woman asked, pausing her needle, when she realised she was being watched.

The question took Alex aback. She hadn't imagined she looked like the kind of person who would crochet.

'It's very satisfying. Good for the brain. Stops you from going la-la,' the woman said, and went back to working on her square of yellow, black and red wool.

'What is it going to be?' Alex found herself asking.

'A dog blanket. At least, I think so.' The woman giggled and held it up. 'Do you have a dog? No? Me neither.'

'Mind if I ask you something?' Alex stepped forward and showed her a photo of Tom Kember on her phone. 'Have you seen this man?'

The woman peered, then shook her head. 'No. Not seen him. Done something, has he?'

'Yes,' said Alex. 'I think he probably has.'

The woman *tsk*-ed and carried on working the needle.

Alex thanked her and moved on, arms behind her back. When she had first come here to Romney Marsh, the flatness of the land had frightened her. It seemed unnatural to have such a big sky above her. Today, big clouds were building over the Downs. You could see the rain coming from miles away.

She rounded the corner and stopped. There was a black Ford Orion parked next to a pale-green mobile home. There was a green plastic chair outside the door and a paperback book sitting, spine up, on the step. Pulling out her phone, she checked the registration from the shot she'd taken of the CCTV, but it was different. That didn't mean anything.

She stepped forward to knock on the door, then thought

better of it. If it was Kember's car and he'd changed the plates yet again, she should wait for backup. Retracing her steps, she was reaching into her back pocket when she passed the woman with the crochet again.

'Did you see him?' she asked brightly.

'No.'

'Oh. I thought he must have walked right past you.'

'Who?'

'That man you showed me. He was just here.'

Alex pulled out her phone to call McAdam and started jogging back towards the caravan where she had seen the Orion. The man she had been looking for all this time was halfway to it when he heard her and turned.

'Hello, Tom,' she said quietly.

He stared back at her.

'Who are you?' he demanded. His gaze was hostile but he spoke softly.

'My name is Alexandra Cupidi. I'm a police officer. I've been looking for you,' she said.

Kember took a step forward.

'It's about Mimi Greene,' she said.

'I didn't have squat to do with that,' he said. 'You know that just as well as I do.'

'I'm not saying you did. But you might be able to help us find who was responsible.'

He stood there looking at her. 'And what if I don't want to?'

'Then I'll have to arrest you for driving a car with false number plates under the 1994 Vehicle Excise and Registration Act.'

'Right,' he said. 'Of course you will.'

'We can sit and talk, if you like.'

He seemed to be weighing this up for just a second. 'I don't think so,' he said quietly.

She was about to answer when, with no warning, he sprang away from the car and set off sprinting down the path towards the static caravans, spraying stones.

'Tom,' she called after him. 'Don't do this. I hate running after people.' Alex pulled out her phone and dialled, but nothing seemed to be connecting. There was only a single bar. 'Shit,' she said, and set off after him. Jill never approved of the trainers Alex wore to work but they came in useful. She reached the end of the pathway in time to see him vaulting over a wooden gate on the north side of the campsite. He was younger than her, and fast. She launched herself over. By the time she was standing in the green wheat, he was halfway across it, leaving a pathway of crushed stems behind him.

'Don't be stupid, Tom,' she shouted. He kept on running. She sighed, then set off through the field after him.

At the far end of the field lay a water-filled ditch. By the time Alex reached it, Kember was already a small dot halfway across the next field, sheep scattering in front of him.

Ahead was an old barn, its curved metal roof rust red. She dropped down into the wet ditch, stumbling, stinging her hands on the nettles as she slid into the mud, soaking her trainers. 'Ow,' she shouted. 'This is idiotic.'

By the time she had scrambled up the other side of it, he had disappeared. She paused, panting for breath. Then pushed herself up, running towards the barn.

'Tom,' she shouted when she reached a metal gate into the

277

yard he must have disappeared into. She leaned down, breathed hard, then stood again. 'Don't be a dick. I don't think you killed Mimi Greene. But don't you want to help me find whoever did?'

There was no answer. The metal barn sat on the far side of a small yard. To one side of it, an ancient harrow was being claimed by brambles. To the other, another gate led to a lane. She climbed over the metal gate and looked down the lane, but there was no sign of him. He could be far away by now, she thought.

Under the shelter of the barn there was an old white caravan that moss and mould had turned green. Its roof was covered in bird droppings. Even its windows were dark with streaks of green. She peered under it. There was no one there.

At the back of the barn, on the far side of the caravan, there was a small stack of hay bales. Pigeons flapped away noisily as she approached them. Turning around again, she looked back at the caravan and noticed for the first time that its door - hidden from her before - was open.

She looked around, listened for any sign of movement. 'Tom,' she said. 'Come out. The police will be here in a minute anyway.'

She reached for the phone in her back pocket. It wasn't there.

She tapped the other pockets. She had had it only a second ago.

'Oh God,' she groaned. She looked up. Pigeons lined up along the metal roof beams above her, looking down. A male was attempting to mate with a reluctant female, cooing loudly. Cautiously, Alex approached the open door of the caravan. 'Tom? Are you in there? I spoke to a few of your exes. None of them said you were violent. Whatever else you've been up to, I'm not interested in any of that now. I just want to talk about Mimi Greene, because we really need to figure out who killed her. You liked her, didn't you? I think you liked them all, in fact.' Above the noise of the pigeons, she heard something move inside the caravan. 'Tom?'

Again there was a clattering inside the caravan, as if Tom had knocked something over. At least she had ascertained where he was; now she should step away, find somewhere safe and observe him until she could find a way of contacting other officers. There was no point doing this on her own.

As quietly as she could, she took a step backwards and was shocked when the hand came around her mouth and she felt the prod of something sharp in her back.

279

FORTY-SIX

'My my, Mr South,' said the nurse. 'A man this time. I was beginning to think it was only ladies who visited you.'

The man had appeared by his bedside. Fifty-ish, a little beard, dressed in dark glasses, a small olive cap on his head. He leaned over Bill and said, 'You poor bloody thing.'

Bill squinted up at him. 'I know you, don't I? I've been having some trouble with my memory and I can't remember your name, though.'

The man took off his dark glasses. 'Don't worry, Bill. You don't know my name.'

'So who are you?'

'Do you remember coming to talk to me last Sunday?'

He sat up a little more. 'Did I? I'm sorry. I seem to have forgotten a great deal.'

'Let me help you. You were looking for a woman called Mandy.'

The name meant absolutely nothing to him. 'Mandy?'

He sat down on the plastic chair by the bed and said, 'All this,

280

everything that happened to you, it's because of Mandy. And I'm sorry. I just wanted to come and see that you were OK.'

He blinked. 'Mandy?'

'You came looking for her. You came to the marina in Hoo asking for Mandy. Do you know why you were looking for her?'

'I'm sorry. Bits are coming back to me but it still doesn't make any sense.'

'What bits?'

Bill looked around. His neighbour in the next bed was snoring gently to himself. 'How do I know I can trust you?'

The man looked so sad. 'You're right. You can't. I wish I'd trusted you then, though. All this shit would never have happened. Mandy French. Does that mean anything at all?'

Bill looked down. The shirt of his pyjamas was open, showing the paleness of his chest. He reached for the buttons to do them up. 'I'm sorry. No. I'm having trouble remembering all sorts of things.'

He lowered his head a little. 'What about Bobby White, then?'

It was like a distant bell had rung somewhere. 'What?'

'Bobby White.'

The name, spoken a second time, was a little spark. 'Oh Christ. Bobby White . . .'

'Coming to you now?'

Bill's jaw fell open. 'Bobby White,' he said again. The names of known criminals take on their own kind of shape. 'The gang leader.'

'Yes. That Bobby White.'

'And Mandy French was the woman who alibied him for the killing of . . .' He struggled again.

Bill raised his head to look into the visitor's eyes and the man looked right back at him with a sort of fascination, as if he were watching the memories form in Bill's mind. 'The name you're looking for is Wayne Jordan,' he said.

'That's right.' It felt as if dust sheets were being pulled off old tables and chairs, revealing their shape, exposing them to light for the first time in an age. 'And she lied about it, didn't she? She lied about the alibi.'

He looked surprised. 'What makes you think Mandy lied?'

'Because otherwise none of this would be happening, would it? Because Mandy – or someone – wanted to stop me from figuring that out.' He looked around, suddenly worried. He was still weak. He had not just fallen in. Someone had tried to kill him, he realised, because he had been trying to track her down. Mandy herself, maybe. But she had been in the boat, hadn't she? He stared at the man next to him, afraid.

'Is that why you were trying to find her? Why would you care about that? It was so long ago.'

He tried to remember. 'Stephen Dowles,' he said. 'Stevie Dowles.'

'Christ. You know Stevie?' he said. 'Is that why you're doing this?'

This name seemed like a key that unlocked more doors. 'No. I don't know Stephen Dowles. But I know his daughter.'

It was the man's turn to look confused. 'Stevie has a daughter? I didn't know.'

'Why did you come here?' Bill asked.

'Because I'm angry. I thought all this shit was done with

thirty years ago and we could get on with our lives in peace. It turns out I was wrong.'

'We?'

'Mandy. She is my sister. Last night, they tried to kill her. They burned her boat. I don't know what kind of shit you stirred up, but it's not doing anyone any good. Leave it alone, William South.'

Bill looked around the ward. People were snoozing calmly around him. 'I'm sorry.'

'I have to go now. I'm glad you're OK. I just wish you'd never poked your nose in.'

'Well, I'm not bloody OK,' Bill said. 'I was just trying to help a friend.'

'And you need to know that if you know this stuff, you are in danger too, just like we are. Whatever it was you were doing and whoever it was you were doing it for, you need to stop.'

'What happened?'

The man stood. Replaced his dark glasses. 'I took a risk coming here to see you. I can't come again. But you're in danger and I just need to tell you that. I've done it. Now I'm going.'

'Who am I in danger from? It's Bobby White, isn't it?'

A snort. 'Oh Jesus Christ. It's not even funny any more.'

'What?'

'Look after yourself, William South. Keep an eye out.'

'For Bobby White?'

He leaned down towards him. 'I'm going to tell you a secret, William South. Bobby White is gone.'

'He's in Florida?'

He looked surprised. 'Who told you that?'

Bill tried to remember who had told him that. He had no idea at all.

'Listen up, Bill. Some advice. The person you need to be afraid of is much more dangerous than Bobby bloody White. You haven't got a bloody clue, Bill, so stay well out of it. You've already caused enough fuckin' damage.'

And he turned and walked away, pushing past a nurse who was carrying a pile of sheets through the ward.

'Wait. Stop the man,' Bill tried to shout, but his voice was still weak, and in hospitals nobody blinked an eye at a patient acting strangely.

The door at the end of the ward swung and he was gone. Bill sat up in bed, pulled the blood monitor off his finger and stood. Only marching towards the doors did he realise how weak his legs were. Spots formed in his vision. He stopped, breathed and made it to the hallway. At the nurse's station, a man was looking at a computer screen.

'Which way did he go?' Bill demanded.

'Which way did who go?' answered the man, not even bothering to look up.

FORTY-SEVEN

'You're in no fit state.'

But Bill insisted. He knew the law. The nurse huffed and found a ward manager, and the ward manager called the patient advice liaison service, and they came back with a form they insisted he sign before he did anything.

'Well, you can't go like that,' said the nurse when he had signed the form.

He looked down at the striped pyjamas he was wearing.

'There are clothes in your locker. The clothes you were wearing on the day of the accident were ruined, I'm afraid, but one of your friends brought them in for you. The woman.'

'Which woman?'

'You have so many of them,' said the nurse.

'Alex?' The name came to him out of the blue.

'Don't remember her name,' said the nurse. 'Tall one.'

'Alex,' he said again, grateful to have another part of his life returned to him.

Alex had been to his house and brought him a check shirt,

hazel corduroy trousers and a pair of black boots. Perfect. He grinned.

The taxi dropped him back at the boatyard.

The hospital had told him that that was where he had been picked out of the water. The man who had visited had confirmed it. He remembered now. He had gone there to look for Mandy French because she was Bobby White's alibi. If he was going to find her again, he could start here.

The state of the boatyard shocked him though. Everything was different. Part of the jetty had been burned away – the part he had been standing on, he remembered. Mandy's boat had been moored to it. That too had completely disappeared. There was tape closing off a section of the jetty and all the boats that had been moored on it had been moved because it was no longer safe.

He kept back from the water. The darkness of it scared him. He remembered being beneath it now, hands raised upwards, cold water taking him down.

'What happened to the boat?' he asked the woman who ran the cafe. 'I think it belonged to a woman called Mandy French.'

'Oh my giddy uncle,' she exclaimed. 'You're the man who drowned.'

'Sort of,' he said.

'I thought you were done for.' She stepped forward from behind the counter and gave him a hug. 'Her boat caught fire, poor girl. Gas leak, they said. Whole place nearly went up. Nothing happens round here normally and then one day

286

everything goes crazy. Gas bottles exploded. You could see it from Rochester, apparently.'

'She's dead?'

'She wasn't even on board. The others who lost their boats aren't happy she left her cooker on, no doubt.'

He nodded, ordered tea and a slice of millionaire's shortbread, and sat thinking things through, and his heart began to beat a little faster.

'Are you OK?' she asked. 'You look rough.'

'Yes. Well. Sorry. I'm still getting over it.'

'You weren't even supposed to be on those pontoons, specially in the dark.'

He took a bite of his cake and chewed it carefully. It was so sweet it stung his throat.

'Know how I can get in touch with her?' he asked cautiously.

'Why would you want to do that?' She looked suspicious now.

'I was trying to visit her. That's when I fell in.'

'Mandy never likes having visitors. She keeps herself to herself.'

He nodded. 'I understand.'

'Yeah, well. Don't forget your motorbike,' she said.

He looked up at her. 'What about it?'

'You left it up at the scrapyard, didn't you, love?'

He looked at her, puzzled. 'How did you know that?' Now he thought about it, he had noticed a familiar-looking metal recycling yard on the way in, in the taxi. Why had he left his motorbike there?

'Guys were in the next day and we were talking about it. They wanted to know if the guy who they'd fished out of the water was the same one as left the bike up at their yard. Borrowed some dungarees or something too. What the hell were you up to?'

'Dungarees?'

'You know. Overalls. You were pulled out of the water in them.'

He had been looking for Mandy French, but he had been hiding from someone too. That alarmed him. He looked around, trying to piece the events of that day together, unsure if he would recognise the person he had been trying to avoid. He ran his hand up the back of his head. The skin on his skull was broken there, tender.

He stood. 'Aren't you going to finish your tea?' the woman said.

'I have to go,' he said, fishing into his pocket for a tip.

Bill pushed out of the door and down the steps to the lane.

The last thing he heard was the cafe woman saying, 'I don't think he's all there. He left half his cake.'

Cautiously, he made his way to the boatyard and tried to piece the dimly remembered sequence of events together. He had been looking for Mandy French and had thought he'd found her boat. From there, everything was blank.

If somebody had tried to kill him once, he would be in danger again now, as Mandy's brother had said. He scanned the boats and tried to work out what the scene told him. He remembered a white yacht, moored a little way off. That was nowhere to be seen. The rest of the boats were such an eccentric muddle of shapes and colours and designs that it was hard to figure out what he should be looking for.

The man who had come to him in hospital had lived on a

288

strange-looking craft, almost like a caravan fitted onto a barge, he recalled. That came back to him, at least. He scanned the boats. That had gone too, he realised.

Glancing back to make sure he was not being followed, he made his way back up the track, away from the boatyard, past the cafe. He recognised the scrapyard and the man who stood by a pile of washing-machine drums. 'Do you have a motorbike of mine?' he asked.

The man looked up, and then his eyes flicked to the right.

As Bill entered the yard he realised there was someone standing out of sight, just behind the gate, who stepped out. Bill flinched, too weak for a fight, but no blow came. A woman's voice said, 'So why you still looking for me? Don't you ever learn anything?'

FORTY-EIGHT

Alex had been so focused on the person in the caravan she had not noticed anyone moving behind her.

The sharp object – whatever it was – dug into her back. 'Get inside,' ordered a man's voice.

He shoved her forward, towards the open door, the darkness and the stink of mildew. She stepped up through the open door and into a small kitchen, with a table and benches behind it. Looking around, she saw no one at all inside. On the dining table stood a single pigeon, twitching its head at Alex.

'Hello, pigeon,' she said.

There was no one else in the caravan. It must have been the bird that she had heard inside, flapping around, trying to find a way out.

As she turned in the gloom of the caravan, she saw the blade he held in his right hand. A kitchen knife of some kind. The drawer he must have taken it from was still half open.

'Get inside,' said Kember. 'Sit down and shut up.'

'I'm going to do exactly what you say, Tom. So please, just stay calm. I know you don't mean me any harm.'

She backed away, startling the pigeon, which flew up in alarm, flapping at her head and then falling to the floor at her feet between her and Kember.

'Sit down,' he repeated.

She turned and edged slowly towards the table, then lowered herself onto one of the cushioned benches on either side of it and looked around. Kember brushed his fringe out of his eyes with his left hand, still holding the knife in front of him.

'Tell me about Mimi Greene,' she said.

He looked startled.

'She's the reason we've been trying to talk to you, so tell me something about her.'

He had a sweet face. His lips were fuller than Charlie's and his fringe a little lower, and that gave him a roguish look. She could see why all the girls fell for him. 'Well, I'm sorry she's dead,' he said. 'She was a lovely person, but I wish I'd never met her. I had nothing to do with any of that.'

'I realise that now,' said Alex, adjusting to the darkness of the small space. Rather than look at the blade of the knife, she looked straight in his blue eyes. Trapped between them, the pigeon flapped its wings unhappily on the floor.

'So why don't you leave me alone?'

'That's not really how police investigations work, Tom. We need to speak to everyone involved. We need to rule everyone out. And you were involved. When was the last time you saw her?'

'I don't have to say anything, I know that,' he said softly.

291

'I been through all this before with you lot. What's so funny? Why you grinning at me?'

'Because all this is funny. Of course you don't have to say anything, but this is hardly a conventional police interview though, is it? You're holding a knife.'

He looked down at the knife in his hand. 'Because I don't trust you,' he said, his voice soft again.

'Why go to all this trouble, Tom? Why all the hiding? It's pretty elaborate, you have to admit.'

He smiled. 'Yeah. Isn't it? I'm invisible. Could have stayed that way except for Mimi. I feel bad about her. You probably don't believe me, do you?'

'What is it, Tom? If it wasn't us you were hiding from, who is it?'

The smile stayed absolutely fixed. 'Never you mind about that,' he said. 'That's nothing to do with Mimi. That's my own business.'

'You've gone to a lot of trouble to keep yourself hidden. Or someone else has.'

This time, there was the tiniest twitch of his lips.

'OK. So when was the last time you saw Mimi?'

'The night she chucked me out. Swear to God. That was the last time. I had nothing to do with that and don't try and pin any of it on me.'

'The night you had a date with Jill Ferriter?'

The pigeon tried to fly, but the space it was in was too restricted now; all it could do was flap its wings uselessly. 'Nice woman. Very nice-looking. Bit of a drinker, mind you. I didn't know she was a fed. My bad. I'd never have dated her if I'd've known. Not that I got anything against the police,' he said. 'Except you.'

The air inside the caravan was oppressively fetid. 'What did Mimi say? What did she say when she threw you out?'

'She just told me to go. Obviously. Caught me red-handed. Fair play. Not the first time it happened. I'm not naturally monogamous. Men aren't. We're not supposed to be.'

'Says who?'

'It's nature, isn't it?'

'Whereas women . . . ?'

'What are you, a sociologist? Mimi asked me to leave. Said she couldn't stand people who deceived other people. She hated people who pretended to be one thing and then turned out to be liars. She said she had had enough of it.'

'She had your number, then,' said Alex.

But all he said was, 'I have my reasons.'

She breathed as deeply as she dared in the dank air. 'We think Mimi Greene was unlawfully killed, Tom. If it wasn't you—'

'It wasn't.'

'If it wasn't you – and that's just an *if* as far as I'm concerned – do you have any idea who did it?'

'I've been thinking a lot about that, believe it or not,' he said.

'So have we.'

He snorted. 'Well, you've not been much good at it, then.'

'No. I don't suppose we have. We make mistakes, just like you do.'

'Just because I put it about a bit doesn't mean I don't care.'

'Nobody's saying you don't, Tom.'

293

'You want to know what I think? It was one of those swimming fanatics.'

'Because none of them liked you?'

He laughed. 'Who says they didn't?'

Up until now, she thought she had understood something of his charm. There was something about his smug laugh that turned her stomach. 'Oh,' she said. 'Mimi wasn't the only one you tried to sleep with, then.'

He laughed again. 'I could have slept with any of them.'

'You must be irresistible.'

'Yeah. I am,' he said, smiling back at her. 'I know what women want.'

'Mostly I want someone to do the laundry and not to leave toenails in the bath. You do that?'

He laughed. 'You're funny. I'm just saying. If I want to sleep with a woman, I usually can.'

The caravan had never felt more claustrophobic.

'So did you? Sleep with any of the other women?'

'Don't get me wrong. I wouldn't have done that to Mimi.'

Alex said, 'But sleeping with Jill Ferriter is fine.'

'Mimi didn't *know* Jill. That's different.'

'Right. Of course it is.'

'But I could have done. I got enough of a come-on.'

Alex frowned. 'Who from?'

'The one with the Asian name.'

Alex raised her eyebrows. 'Kimaya?'

'They're not angels. Any of them. You take a closer look. You ask who killed Mimi Greene? It wasn't me. It was one of them.

294

Mimi was the only one of them who was sane, if you ask me. Even Mimi was getting creeped out by them.'

Alex's skin prickled. 'What do you mean?'

'Mimi wouldn't tell me what, but I knew that for the last couple of weeks something had been upsetting her about them all. That's why she didn't want to swim with them any more.'

'What?' All of the group had said she was acting differently, and that she was turning up less often. 'She fell out with them?'

'I wouldn't say fell out. Mimi never really fell out with anyone.'

'Except for you.'

He held up his left hand, palm forward. 'We were done anyway. She didn't fall out with them, but maybe someone fell out with her.'

All this wasted time looking for 'Malcolm'.

'Which one?'

'You think you know everything, don't you? You blamed all this on me and you didn't see what was staring you right in the face.'

'What, Tom?'

'I would reckon Rose, wouldn't you?'

The caravan seemed to shrink in size around her. Zoë was planning to meet with Rose this evening.

FORTY-NINE

Mandy French had the round, shiny face of a drinker. She looked worn down.

'Hello, Mandy,' said Bill.

'Heard you nosing round the place again, asking after me,' she said. Her hair was dyed black now and her eyes looked smaller than they had in the driving licence photo he had seen. She wore a demin jacket and a shiny shirt that bulged at the midriff.

'I'm glad to meet you eventually.'

'I wish you'd stayed under the bloody water,' she said quietly. 'I didn't have much, now I got nothing, all thanks to you.'

'I'm sorry about your boat.'

'Good riddance to it. You ever actually tried living on a boat? Everybody thinks it's so romantic. In the summer the place stinks of rotten mud. In the winter it's bloody freezing. It's not exactly where I thought I'd be living in my best years,' she said.

The man in the overalls took some cigarettes out of a pocket, offered one to Bill, then to Mandy. She took one off him, then said, 'Now back off. Private conversation. Comprenez?'

'It wasn't an accident, then, the fire?' said Bill, when the man had stepped away, retreating into his workshop.

Mandy snorted. 'What do you think?'

'Who was responsible, Mandy?'

'You're bad for my health. My life has been hard enough without you coming along and making it worse.' The noise of an angle-grinder came from inside the shed.

'Was it the man from the boat that's called *Dizzy Rascal*?'

She laughed again, blowing out smoke. 'Jesus. You came here messing up my life and you didn't have the first clue, did you?'

'I came to ask you about Bobby White,' said Bill. 'You were engaged to be married to him, weren't you?'

Mandy laughed. 'Oh my God. Hilarious.'

'Why don't you tell me then?'

'You came to my home – to my boat – and started giving me a sob story about your dad, and about this poor girl who just wants to find out who her father was, and you had no idea at all. What about my life? What about everything shit that happened to me? I was going to be something. I had a career. People told me I could have been a model, you know? You take one bloody wrong turn and it all turns to mud. Everyone else round here was paid off – 'cept me.'

'What do you mean, paid off?'

She put the hand without a cigarette next to the side of her mouth and made a zipping motion.

'Please,' said Bill. 'I need to know.'

She stamped out her cigarette and beckoned him with a curled finger. 'Listen to me carefully now. You don't need to know. You really don't. Nobody's life is going to get better for you digging around like this, least of all yours. You're lucky to be alive. So am I, no thanks to you. For both of our sakes, don't ever come near me again, OK? Or I will find someone who will push you right back into the river, and this time I'll make them hold you down, OK?'

Bill raised both hands. 'OK.'

'Go home and don't come back.' She took a step towards the gate, then paused. 'Just one thing. You said that Stevie Dowles had a daughter.'

'Did I?'

'Yeah. You did. What's she like?'

'She's a great girl,' said Bill.

'Well, bully for bloody her,' said Mandy French, and disappeared into the lane outside.

Leaning against the door frame of his workshop, the scrap-metal man removed a pair of safety goggles and let out a long, low whistle. 'I don't think she likes you, friend.'

'You know her?'

He shook his head. Bill walked towards him, legs stiff. He was not used to standing for so long. 'So. Do you have a motorbike of mine?' he asked again, half expecting the man to deny having ever seen it. But the man grinned. 'This way,' he said. Inside the dark shed that smelt of engine oil and metal sat Bill's Kawasaki, his helmet sitting on the pillion. 'I put it out of sight,' the man explained.

Bill remembered offering him money for a pair of overalls. He pulled out his wallet again and offered him twenty pounds for looking after the bike, but the man refused it. 'I'm just so happy you're not dead,' he said.

'Me too.'

Strapping on the helmet, he got on the bike and it started first time. There was something very comforting and familiar about the hum of it. He knew the machine. The muscle memory was there when he twisted his right hand to open the throttle. He would take it slowly on the way home. There was no hurry and he needed to think.

FIFTY

'Talk to me, Tom,' said Alex, more urgently now. 'You have all this figured out. You're good at this stuff.'

'Trying to come on to me too?' Tom laughed. He had opened the kitchen drawer and was rummaging around in it, looking for something. Alex wondered if she could rush him now, but she was stuck with her legs under the small table. It would not be easy to just jump up.

'Please,' said Alex.

'Rose was a les. Did you know that?'

The pigeon seemed to have calmed down. It was just standing there in the middle of the floor as if it had given up and was just happy to die. 'She's gay. Yes, I knew that. How did you find that out? Did you try it on with her too?'

'Bit young for me. She fancied the hell out of Mimi. Know that too?' He stepped back and started pulling out at small drawers.

'No. I didn't.'

'She tried it on with Mimi. Bet you didn't know that, either.'

Even with the door open, the air seemed stiflingly hot. 'No,' Alex said quietly.

Tom pulled a black leather belt from the drawer. It was dotted with white mould. 'And when Mimi said she wasn't interested, Rose went mental. Totally mental. Mimi told me. She says she was scared of what Rose would do.'

'She meant self-harm. Rose hurts herself.'

'Oh yeah. Rose tell you why she left her last job? Same thing happened. Rose had a crush on some co-worker and when the co-worker wasn't interested, Rose went crazy. You spent your whole time looking for me, ruining my life, and you didn't even think any of them might have something to do with it.'

'How do you mean, she went crazy?'

Tom just smiled at her. 'You should be asking her that, you know, not me.'

Zoë was going to meet Rose on her own. 'Look. I need to get out of here,' said Alex.

'Sorry about that. I let you out of here, you're just going to tell your mates I'm here. You're not going anywhere,' said Tom. 'Not for a while at least.' He stepped forward, over the terrified pigeon. 'Stand up,' he ordered.

'Don't do anything stupid, Tom.'

'Stupid? I'm not the one who's wasted all the time looking for the wrong killer,' he said quietly. 'I know a thing or two about bad people, believe me.' He turned the belt into a noose, looping the end through the buckle, and held it in his left hand. Alex looked at the hole made by the belt and tried not to show fear. He held up the knife in the other hand. 'Stand and turn around.'

It was a tight space. Standing meant squashing her thighs

against the top of the small table and then shuffling sideways until she could be upright.

'Now turn your back to me,' he said, holding up the knife. She was ready to kick back at him the moment the belt approached the top of her head, but instead he just said, 'Arms,' and she understood that he meant to tie it behind her, not put it around her neck.

'What if I don't? You going to stab me?'

'You want to find out?'

'Not really.' She placed her hands behind her and immediately the belt tightened on them, then he dragged her backwards down the small corridor between the cooker and the fridge. Holding on to her hands with his left hand on the belt, he nudged the back of her shins.

She fell forward onto her knees. The pigeon, panicking again, tried to fly, wings clattering against her face. She had nothing to fend it away with and could only scrunch her eyes tight and wait for it to stop.

When she opened them again, the pigeon was back on the table, where it had been when she came in.

Tom was behind her, opening drawers again. Still kneeling at the table edge, she tried to stand, lifting one leg, but she was too close to its edge and any movement was awkward in this confined space.

Roughly, he put a hand on her shoulder and forced her back down again. She fell forward, hitting her mouth on the table edge.

'Sorry. Didn't mean to hurt you. But you should have stayed where you were.' He had looped something round her feet now and was tightening that too.

'You have to let me go,' she said. 'I have to get home. It's important. I think my daughter is in real danger, Tom. She needs me.'

'I don't believe anything you say.' Tom gave the belt another yank. She was trussed now, unable to move her arms or her legs.

'She's with Rose. She's with Rose. Don't you understand?'

He stopped. 'Well, you should have thought about that earlier, shouldn't you? You're the one got it all backwards. All I wanted was to be left alone.'

He took hold of her feet, dragging her down the corridor on her knees, then lifted them so that her torso fell forward onto the dirty floor.

'Now open your mouth.'

'Please, Tom. At least tell someone I'm here. Phone Jill again.'

'You'll be fine. I won't hurt you. I just need you to let me get well away from here.' He was holding an old blue fibre cloth he had found in the sink. Putting the knife down, he rolled it into a ball. 'Open,' he said.

He reached out and squeezed the bridge of her nose. Forced to open her mouth, he stuffed the cloth inside, pushing it behind her teeth with his fingers. Then he was tying an old tea towel around her chin to hold it in.

The cloth was dusty and dry. It stuck to her gums and tongue and tasted of cheap washing-up liquid and dust.

She heard him leave, closing the door behind him.

'Help,' she tried to shout.

In frustration, Alex kicked her legs at the fridge door.

PART FOUR

PART FOUR

FIFTY-ONE

There was something wrong with Bill's house, but at first, pulling the motorbike up onto its stand, Bill couldn't work out what it was.

The curtains were closed, for starters. He would have left them open.

He walked round the house once. Hanging up on the wire that he had strung from the back corner of his house to a metal pole a few metres away was a pair of women's knickers. He frowned.

He opened the door and looked to his left. There were unwashed bowls in the kitchen sink. He recognised a pair of Zoë's trainers in the middle of the living-room floor, beside piles of books.

'Hello?'

He opened the bedroom door. His bed was unmade. In his absence, Zoë had obviously stayed over.

He put the kettle on and made himself tea, but when he went to the fridge there was only a carton of oat milk and a plastic half-litre of milk that had turned. He had been away days, he realised.

His mobile phone had been trashed by water, but his old land-line handset was on his desk in the living room. In the drawer was his old address book. He called Alex's number, but it went straight to voicemail.

Next, he found Figgy's number and called it. It was always Jenn who answered.

'It's Bill,' he said.

'Bill? I wasn't expecting you to call. Are you in the hospital still?'

'I checked myself out,' said Bill. 'Could I have a word with Figgy?'

There was a hesitation in Jenn's voice. 'He's not here. He's at the clinic. He has an appointment. Tell me what you want to ask him. I can pass it on.'

'I wanted to tell him something. I was looking for Mandy French. That's what I was doing at the boatyard. I don't think I fell in. I think someone attacked me while I was there.'

'Your memory is back,' said Jenn. 'That's a bloody miracle. They said you might never recover.'

Bill fingered a pencil on his desk. 'You were at the hospital. I remember now. You brought me fruit.'

'I came two days after you almost drowned. The doctor said you might not recover. You're proving them wrong. Go, Bill! That's wonderful.'

'Couldn't stand being there any more. Back home I'm more myself, you know? Someone else came to see me at the hospital. He said some funny stuff about Bobby White. I wanted to run it past Figgy. Will you tell Figgy to call me?'

'Course I will, Bill. Tell me, you remember anything else?'

'Some.' He was going to say more, but it was not clear in his head yet. He needed to think it through. It would help if he could talk to Figgy. 'I have to go, Jenn.'

He tried Alex's number again, but she was still not picking up.

He sat in the living room staring out at the flatland behind him as the sun made its way down in the west and the shadow of his cabin grew longer, turning green gorse bushes black.

Zoë didn't come back. That irritated him. She had left his house untidy. Her pants were still on the wire outside.

He put on a coat and locked the door, then walked the track to the house where Zoë lived with her mother. He approached as he usually did from the back door, walking round the end of the terrace first.

He rang the bell, stood and waited, but no lights came on. There was no one home. He leaned forward and peered into the kitchen window. The place seemed to be deserted. Neither of them was there.

Disconcerted, he walked back down the single-track road, grateful at least to have the dome of stars over his head. He had hated the hospital. He was not used to buildings as big and solid as that. By the time he got home, he realised how exhausted he was, but something was still eating at him. He got unsteadily onto his motorbike again; pulling its weight back off the stand, he almost toppled over. He was still weaker than he thought.

Curly's house was easy to recognise; it was the one with the tattered Union Jack flying from the flagpole in the middle of his garden. Curly opened the door to his terraced house and blinked into the darkness. 'Bloody hell, Bill. I heard you were in hospital. What are you doing here, this time of day?'

'They let me out.'

'I heard you lost it.'

'I think I may have,' said Bill.

Curly made his way to the kitchen at the back of the house and put the kettle on. 'You never come round this way, so I'm guessing this isn't social.'

'Tell me about Bobby White,' said Bill.

'Good riddance to him. Scary bastard.'

'Did you ever meet him?'

Curly kept his tea bags in a tin coronation caddy. 'Me? I was never involved in anything that serious, Bill. You know that.'

'That's not what I asked.'

'I know. Scared of him, though. Scared of his rep. Remember Skin-the-Cat?'

'Now you're going back a while.' Bill remembered Skin-the-Cat was the nickname of a local dealer who had begun to cook meth out of a caravan on the beach. 'When was that? 97? 98?'

'About then, yeah. Remember how he ended up?'

'In hospital, wasn't it? That was Bobby White?'

'Still drinks through a straw.'

'As far as I remember, we never found out who did it. But you're saying it was Bobby White?'

Curly fished the tea bags out of the cup, poured milk and offered Bill the sugar bowl. Then he pushed open the back door and reached for cigarettes from his jacket pocket. 'I always find a cup of tea is too wet without a fag.'

'You sure that was Bobby?'

'Course it was. Everybody knew that, except for you lot. In some ways, nobody round here minded that much. Skin-the-Cat was a cheeky little fuck and word was he was selling to school-kids.'

'Was that why he got assaulted?'

Curly lit a cigarette, took a puff and then started coughing. When he stopped, he said, 'Jesus, no. Bobby White wiped him out because he was stealing his business. Bobby's boys were into all that. Crack. Meth. Heroin. You must have known all that.'

'Serious Crime were always putting the underlings away, but they could never get Bobby White. Tell me about when you met him?'

'I never said I did, Bill. What makes you think that?'

'Because I was a copper and I've known you, what, thirty years? I know you did, just from the way you looked when I mentioned his name to you last week.'

Curly stood in the doorway so the smoke wouldn't linger in the kitchen. The back of the house was dark at this time of day. Old lobster pots held together by frayed blue rope filled the small garden behind his house.

'He wanted to use my boat to bring stuff in.'

'Bobby White? And by *stuff* you mean drugs?'

'I didn't ask, Bill. These two thugs turned up at my front door not long after the whole thing with Skin-the-Cat. They said that Bobby White wanted my boat. I told them I wasn't interested. They said they'd be back in a week to ask again.'

'One of them was a big guy? Don Swallow?'

'Correct. He was White's second-in-command. Tell you what,

Bill. At that point I seriously considered moving away, trying to start up fresh somewhere else.'

'Why didn't you tell me, Curly?'

'Don't be a twat, Bill. Bobby White. You didn't dick around with him. You're a sweet bloke and that, but you help old people across roads, remember?'

He dropped the cigarette and stamped it out on the concrete outside the door, then came back inside.

'A few days later they came back and told me to get in the car with them. I was wetting myself, no word of a lie. They sat me in the back of this big old black Merc – a 280, it was – and drove me up towards Rye. We stopped at that church in East Guldeford. Beautiful place. We sat in the car facing the grave-yard and all the time I was thinking, "Here we go." And then they put a blindfold on me and I was a hundred per cent sure I was dead.'

Bill shook his head. 'I had no idea.'

'Course you didn't, you knob. Ten minutes later I hear someone else getting in the car and this man said, "I want your boat."'

'Bobby White?'

'And he said he wasn't going to take no for an answer. But it was the only answer I could give him. I may be a bit shady at times, but I knew that if you get involved in that kind of shit, that's you for life. I didn't want any part of it, so I told him, and I said that he could kill me, but I wouldn't shift drugs for him.'

'That was brave.'

'Dungeness people. The real Dungeness people. It's what they say on this bit of coast. *We won't be druv.*'

'So what happened?'

'Nothing at all. The thugs drove me home and said, "If you know what's good for you, you'll keep your trap shut." Not that I needed the advice. And that was the only time I met him.'

'And what happened after that?'

'Nothing. Never heard from him at all. I kept waiting for the footsteps behind me in the dark but he never did a thing. I guess he took me at my word. I didn't want anything to do with him.'

'But you kept your mouth shut.'

'Because I'm not a total prannie.'

'So why you telling me now?'

Curly blew gently across the surface of his tea. 'Because he's gone, isn't he?'

'Is he?'

'So everyone says. Upped sticks and left years ago.'

'You sure about that?'

'Why?' asked Curly. 'You think he's back?'

FIFTY-TWO

The caravan was suddenly ablaze with blue and white light, and Alex was blinking.

Jill was keeling beside her. 'Are you all right, love?'

'You took your time,' said Alex. She stood shakily. 'He tried to get away. I ran after him but he caught me.'

'It's OK.'

'No it's bloody not,' said Alex.

She stepped into the door of the caravan. There was an ambulance and three police cars.

'How did you find me?'

'Found your car first, but you weren't anywhere near it. It was Charlie who spotted a line of wheat in the field. We tracked that down but lost the trail by the ditch. But then I found your phone.'

And then Charlie was there next to her. 'Proper freaked her out,' said Charlie.

'It was in the ditch. Lit up. Like some weird message from underwater. Charlie went down and fetched it—'

314

'There was a message on it. Must have just arrived. Lit up the screen,' said Charlie. 'Come on, then. Paramedics are here. They want to give you the once-over.'

Alex looked from one to the other. 'No. I've got to get home. I think we made a terrible mistake. I think Zoë's in trouble.'

'Kember's long gone now,' said another copper. 'Don't worry. We'll catch him.'

'No!' Alex shouted angrily. 'Zoë. My daughter. I need to get to her.' She noticed Jill shoot a glance towards Charlie at the mention of Zoë's name. 'What?' Alex demanded.

Jill said, 'Shit. I think the message on your phone was from Zoë.'

'Well? What did it say?'

'I couldn't see 'cause it died. It ran out of power. Or maybe the water got in. I've been trying to call her . . . but I can't get through.'

A police car took Alex back to the caravan site. 'We'll take my car,' said Jill.

Alex was grateful. She was too anxious to drive. All she wanted to do was get home as fast as she could.

'I'm sure she'll be all right, Alex.'

'Rose came here because she'd lost her job. Apparently she lost it because she'd assaulted a woman at work – as a result of a mental breakdown of some kind. She fell in love with her and when this woman didn't reciprocate, she lost it. So she comes down here with mental health issues and ends up being taken under Mimi Greene's wing. Mimi's kind to her and apparently she falls in love with Mimi.'

'Only, Mimi rejects her . . .' said Jill.

'Exactly.'

'Oh shit. So you reckon it was Rose who killed Mimi?'

'Rose is the best swimmer in the group.'

'Oh, Jesus.'

'And now Mimi has a thing about Zoë. And pretty much the last thing Zoë said to me was that she really likes Rose but she's not interested in a relationship.'

'Bollocks,' said Jill and she swerved off the road onto the track that led into the Dungeness estate, ignoring the 20 mph speed limit and rattling over the level crossing, headlights on full beam. A straggle of tourists walking towards the Pilot glared, raised their arms to shield their eyes, stood back from the track as Jill hurtled towards it, past the cabins, headlights catching the loops of telephone wire. The lighthouse blinked ahead of them. Jill had to slow to navigate an immense mobile home that was taking up half the road outside the Snack Shack, then she floored the accelerator again. She rounded the bend, and the bulk of the old power station was right in front of them and she was driving straight towards it, swinging into the lane that led to Alex's house and braking hard outside Bill's cabin.

It was dark. There were no lights on inside.

Alex jumped out all the same and banged on the door, then used her own key to open it.

There was no sign of Rose. If anything, the place looked strangely tidy.

'Well?' Jill said.

Alex looked up. 'Let's try the house.'

They jumped back in the car and rode the short distance to the back door. The house was dark too. Alex ran upstairs to

Zoë's bedroom and rifled through the clothes on the floor. Jill watched her from the doorway. 'What are you looking for?'

'Her swimming suit. I can't find it. She said she was going to go swimming with Rose.'

'Where?'

Alex stopped and looked up. 'I don't know,' she said. 'Shit. My phone is dead. I don't have Isobel's number.'

'Calm down,' said Jill, putting an arm around her. 'We'll plug it in and try and get it started. In the meantime, I'll try and find a number for her myself, and you need a cup of coffee or something.'

'Jesus,' Alex muttered.

Jill found a landline number for Isobel van Wees just as Alex's phone was restarting. Alex called it.

'Rose?' said Isobel. 'No, I haven't seen her. She's rather out of sorts. We were supposed to go swimming this morning and when she didn't turn up I was worried. I called her up and she just said she wasn't coming swimming with us any more and ended the call. She was rude. I was quite disappointed in her.'

'Christ. Can you check the beach? Please. It's important.'

'She's not there. I've just come back from a walk along the Parade.'

'You sure?'

She heard Isobel huff. 'Of course I'm sure.'

'Where else could she be? Do you have any idea of her favourite swimming places? She said she might go freshwater swimming.'

'There are so many, aren't there? Once you start, you discover them all over the place. What's wrong, Alexandra?'

317

'She's gone swimming with Zoë. I need to find them. It's important.'

'At this hour?' demanded Isobel. 'I don't know. We took a trip to swim in the Stour at Fordwich once. She loved that.'

Fordwich was in the north of the county. 'No. I don't think so.'

'So where else? Think. Please.'

'What about the bird reserves?'

Alex thought about it for a second. The lakes close to them were freshwater. 'No. Zoë wouldn't. She's obsessed with the wildlife. She wouldn't want anyone to disturb it.' Alex ended the call and said, 'Shit. I need a map.'

'Got one on my phone,' offered Jill.

'No,' said Alex. 'A proper map. A real one.' She ran into the living room, to where she kept her desk, and started pulling books off the shelves until she found the Ordnance Survey map for Dungeness.

After finding Mimi's body, Zoë would not want to swim anywhere off Dungeness. It was not safe water anyway. She wouldn't want to swim in the bird reserves either. But just inland, they were surrounded by lakes. The wildlife reserve was all lakes – around twenty of them – quarries that had filled with fresh water. To the west, there was a stretch of water used by pleasure boats, and another used by fishermen. Beyond Lydd there were huge stretches of water that marked the end of the shingle banks. She measured them with her finger and thumb. A ribbon of lakes four kilometres long. There were so many.

But there was nothing to do but look. 'What are you doing?' Jill asked.

'I'm going out. To look for Zoë.'

'Where?'

Alex looked at the map in despair. 'I don't know.'

'I can help,' said Jill. 'Please.'

'God, I bloody missed you,' said Alex.

She opened the door.

Zoë was standing there, and there, next to her, was Rose, both with their hair still wet. Lit up in the doorway, they were standing, hand in hand, smiling. 'We came here for the shower, because Bill's is rubbish.'

Zoë's smile vanished.

'What?' she said, looking from Jill's shocked face to her mother's.

FIFTY-THREE

It was after ten. Jill made a pot of coffee and two herb teas, then put the cups on the kitchen table and got out some digestives. Alex spoke: 'Right then. So you need to tell me why you lost your job in London, Rose.'

Sitting next to Zoë on the opposite side of the table, Rose looked mortified.

'Mum!' said Zoë. 'She was made redundant – weren't you? It sent her into a bit of a spiral.'

'They fired you, didn't they, Rose?'

Zoë looked at Rose, puzzled. 'What is all this, Mum?' she asked.

'I just need to get things straight. You had a falling-out, didn't you, Rose? I want you to tell me about it.'

Rose stared down at the table.

'It's OK,' said Alex gently. 'I just want to know what happened.' She reached her hand across the table and said, 'Just tell me.'

There was a tremble in Rose's voice when she spoke. 'OK. I

used to work for Hackney Council, in Finance and Corporate Resources. It was the kind of job my family thought was OK. They are evangelical. Nice people. Very straight. They never knew I was gay. It was hard for me to have girlfriends. There was a woman at work. We sat right next to each other. She was a wee bit older and really cool and popular and, you know, I thought she was nice. I never thought she thought anything of me at all. Plus, she was in a relationship with a guy in the Housing department and let me know about it. I was in love with her, I suppose.' She looked at Zoë shyly. 'From afar though. I never thought anything would happen because she was straight and in a relationship.'

'Go on,' said Alex.

'How did you know about all this?' asked Rose.

Alex took a sip from her coffee, then looked her in the eye. 'We found Mimi's boyfriend.'

'You arrested him?' Zoë exclaimed.

'Not exactly. I had a conversation with him.'

'But Malcolm killed Mimi . . . didn't he?' Rose said, frowning.

'I don't think so. I think it was someone completely different. I need you to tell me everything, Rose. I know it's difficult, but this is very important. This man – Mimi's boyfriend – said that you'd told Mimi about the trouble you had in London. And that's why you moved here.'

Rose winced. 'Mimi had no right to do that. I told her that in confidence.'

Alex watched Zoë lean in to hug her. 'She shouldn't have done. You're right,' Alex said quietly. 'But she did. What happened?'

'Go on,' encouraged Zoë.

321

'Should I even be here?' said Jill.

'You're fine. It wasn't Malcolm who killed him. I'm sure of that now. I need you to stay and listen, Jill. You need to hear this too.' She turned to Rose. 'What were you saying? Please.'

'This woman and me – all of us – we used to go for a drink after work. I'm not much of a drinker, but I liked her company. Only, one Friday she got drunk and she found me in the corridor on the way back from the toilets and she started kissing me. I was shocked. She told me she loved me, said she wanted me . . . you know. Wanted me. God. Know what? I admit I was flattered. She was beautiful and cool, and I never thought she even looked my way. My life has been a struggle. I wanted it to be true. It felt real enough. But when I went in on Monday, all excited to see her again, it was like nothing at all had happened. I said, "I really liked kissing you." She said, "I don't know what you mean," and then ignored me all week. So when it came to the following Friday I asked her out for a drink again and she said she was busy. So I asked for some kind of explanation.'

Alex said. 'Asked for?'

'That's when she started making out I was bullying her into sex. I swear I did not. She ended up talking to HR, saying I was harassing her. And because she was everybody's friend, they all believed her. That's why I left the job and came here. I became . . . unwell. I had to leave. Nobody believed me.'

'And what about Mimi? Were you in love with her, too?' asked Alex.

'Oh God. I can't believe this. Please don't.'

'Were you?' Zoë repeated.

Rose turned to Zoë. 'Kind of. But that was all a mistake. I

322

was really upset by everything. I didn't know anyone. She was kind to me. I came on to her. It was the most gruesome, embarrassing mistake I ever made and . . .' She pushed back her chair and stood. 'Oh God,' she said, reaching up and tugging at her braids. 'It was just the most cringe moment in my life, because I should never have done it when all I ever had from her was kindness. I fall in love. I can't help it.'

'So what happened?' asked Alex.

'It wasn't much. I just tried to kiss her one day. When we were out walking together. And she was really sweet about it, but she said she wasn't into girls. I just wanted the world to swallow me up. I genuinely wanted to die.'

'Were you angry that she rejected you?'

'No. No. Jesus, it was nothing at all like that, I swear. She just said that I should try not to be around her for a while.'

'What about Kimaya?' asked Alex.

Rose went quiet.

'What don't you like about Kimaya?'

'I didn't say I didn't like her,' Rose answered.

'Well?'

'I don't think Mimi liked her any more. Couple of weeks before she died, she asked me if I trusted her.'

Kimaya had told Alex she was one of Mimi's best friends. Alex took Rose's hand again. 'What was it that Mimi didn't like about Kimaya?'

'The reason she threw Malcolm out was that she couldn't bear it when people lied to each other. I don't know why, but she started avoiding Kimaya. Something happened that meant she didn't trust Kimaya any more.'

'What was it?'

'I don't know. I know she kept out of my way because she was trying to make it easier for me to move forward. But with Kimaya it was something else. It was weird. I think something had really hurt her. It had soured her about the whole swimming group.'

'She was uncomfortable with Isobel too, wasn't she? Why do you think that was?'

Rose frowned. 'I don't know.'

'This is important. I need to know you're telling me the truth. Have you invented any of this for any reason at all?'

'Mum,' muttered Zoë. 'Believe her. Please.'

'All this time, you thought I killed Mimi?' said Rose.

Zoë looked horrified.

'No. No,' wailed Rose, fear in her voice. 'Swear to God, no. I would never. I tell the truth. All the time. And nobody *ever* believes me. This is just what happened the last time.'

'It's OK,' said Alex. 'I believe you.' She remembered what Tom Kember had told her about Mimi, as he'd held the knife in the caravan: *She hated people who pretended to be one thing and then turned out to be liars.* It wasn't just Malcolm. 'I believe you,' she said again.

'You do?'

'I don't think you killed Mimi. Will you help me catch the person who did?'

'Of course I will.'

They sat around the kitchen table.

'OK then,' said Alex. 'Tell me about Victor.'

FIFTY-FOUR

The morning was bright and innocent. The eggs in the fridge were still OK, so Bill scrambled them for breakfast.

He was just eating them when there was a knock at the door. 'Bill?'

He opened the door and Jill Ferriter burst inside and threw her arms around him, clutching him so tight it hurt his bruised chest.

'Oh, Bill!' When she finally released him, she said, 'I called the hospital just now from Alex's. They told me you'd checked yourself out. Are you OK? Do you know who I am?'

'You're Jill. Jill Ferriter. The annoying one.'

She hugged him again.

'What are you doing here?' he asked.

'I spent the night at Alex's. She's gone to work now—'

'I went round looking for her last night. There was no one in,' he said, puzzled.

'We got back late. She was working on the Mimi Greene case. Something came up. It's OK now.'

'Mimi Greene?'

325

'The drowned woman up at Pen Bars. Listen, Bill. I have to tell you something.'

'You better come in,' he said.

They sat across the same table where they had been a week before. He made a pot of tea, which she pretended to like. 'It wasn't an accident, you falling in the water.'

'No,' he said. 'I don't think it was, either.'

'It was all my fault. I should never have asked you to do any of this. My dad even sent me a message warning you off. I didn't realise it at the time.'

He reached out and took her hand. 'It's all right, Jill. I knew what I was doing. I just got it wrong, that's all.'

'We talked to the man who fished you out, me and Alex.'

He sat, listening. 'Who was that?'

That part of his story was a void. She was filling in blank spaces for him. It helped. And she told him about the couple on the yacht, and the man from *Dizzy Rascal* who had disappeared soon after the fire.

'*Dizzy Rascal*?'

'Do you remember?'

He sat thinking for a long time and then realised his tea was cold.

The traffic was slow but they made it to Ashford by ten in the morning.

'Go and knock on the door,' said Bill, pointing to Katie Jordan's house. 'She doesn't like me.'

'Why not?'

'She doesn't like the police.'

'You're not a police officer any more. I am.' She explained as if talking to a child.

'I know all that,' Bill said. 'She doesn't though.'

Jill got out and rang the bell, stood there for a while, but no one answered, so he beckoned her back.

'Is that it?' Jill asked.

'She works at a food bank in Repton Avenue. We could try there too.'

'Who is she, Bill? Why do we need to talk to her?'

'She is Wayne Jordan's mother. I need to ask her something first.'

'What do you mean, first?'

They parked outside the small community centre. 'She'll be the one with the green thing in her nose,' said Bill. He pointed to where Katie's stud was. 'Tell her I want a very quiet word and then I'll never bother her again.'

Jill returned a minute later, alone. 'She told me to bog off else she'd call the police. I told her I was the police, which didn't help. You were right. She doesn't like us. What do we do now?'

'Wait, I guess,' said Bill. He looked at the community centre and saw Katie's face at the window, scowling at him.

After ten minutes she came out, looking hot from working in a glass-fronted building on a sunny day.

'Just a couple more questions, Katie,' said Bill from the open passenger window.

'Swear to God, I'd kill you now but I like working here,' said Katie. There was coral lipstick running into the wrinkles around her mouth. 'What is it this time?'

'You went to identify Wayne, didn't you?'

'Worst thing I ever done, Bill.'

'When you did, who was there?'

'Your mate, DI Christopher Tart.'

Christopher Tart, who for a while was known as Pudding. But one Christmas his nickname became Figgy Pudding and from then on just Figgy.

'And it was DI Tart who attended the scene of crime, too.'

'That's right. It was him who went to the farm and found Wayne in the boot of that car. Didn't have the decency to come and tell me, though. Left all that to you. I always reckoned it was Tart who told the press about my cannabis conviction too, thanks very much. Now can I go?'

'Wayne's body was badly burned. How did you identify him, Katie?'

'He wore these big signet rings on both hands. They had them in a little plastic bag, I remember. That's all I had.'

'And that was it?'

She nodded. 'I was hoping it was just a coincidence, but then it was dental records that confirmed it.'

Bill nodded. 'Which dentist did Wayne go to, Katie?'

Katie narrowed her eyes. 'What is this, Bill?'

'Was it the one on Faversham Road?'

Katie's eyes widened. 'That's right. How did you know?'

'The same one that Mandy French worked at?'

'Why, Bill? What's going on?'

Bill got out of the car slowly and stood next to her. 'Buried or cremated, Katie?'

Katie looked down towards Jill, sitting in the driver's seat. 'What's he on about, love?'

A young woman with dreadlocks tied on top of her head stepped out of the door of the community centre. 'Everything all right, Katie?'

Katie looked back at her, and then at Bill. 'Cremated.'

Bill reached down, took her hand, and she was so perplexed by what was happening, she didn't pull away. 'I'm sorry, Katie.'

'What are you sorry about now, Bill? This is all rubbish.'

'I have to go. I'll come back, I promise.'

'Don't,' she said, but she didn't let go of his hand.

'By the way, this woman here. You knew her mother,' said Bill.

Puzzled, Katie leaned down towards Jill again. 'What did you say your name was, darling?'

'Jill Ferriter.'

'Oh my God. You're Sandra's daughter.' Katie clapped her hand over her mouth. 'I thought you said you were a copper?'

'She is,' said Bill.

Katie's mouth was wide as Jill pulled away.

Jill pulled up a little way down the road. She banged the steering wheel with her palms. 'Oh my God. I get it. It wasn't Wayne Jordan that my dad killed.'

'I'm pretty sure it wasn't Wayne Jordan in the boot, no.'

Jill chewed on her lip for a while. 'Doesn't make any difference really. My dad was still a murderer.'

Bill nodded. 'Yes. He was.'

'Where are we going now?'

★

329

The route to Pevensey Bay was slow. Caravans clogged the roads, and when they got there, there was nowhere to park outside Figgy and Jenn's house, and they had to leave the car a couple of streets away.

'Wow,' said Jenn when she opened the door. 'And the dead shall walk the earth.'

'Figgy in?'

'Always. And who is this?' she asked, looking past him.

He stepped aside to introduce Jill. 'This is Sandra Ferriter's daughter, Jill.'

There was a small pause before she said, 'Wow.'

'Who is it?' Figgy called from the back room.

Jenn looked him up and down again and shook her head. She raised her voice. 'It's William South. And you are not going to believe who he has with him.'

She turned and led them down to the conservatory.

Figgy was sitting in an armchair reading a book. It dropped off his lap onto the floor. 'We were worried, Bill.'

'This is Jill,' said Jenn. 'She's Sandra Ferriter's daughter.'

Figgy looked at Jill, confused. 'You're kidding?'

Everyone was looking at Jill.

'Cool model railway,' said Jill, looking around.

'Isn't it?' said Bill. 'I wanted to see it again.'

'What?' Figgy put his head on one side, confused by events.

Bill went and sat down on the arm of Figgy's chair. 'There's real stuff in here, Figgy, isn't there?'

'In the layout? Just bits. That car accident was a car chase. Two lads coming out of a rave loaded on speed and coke. Silly arses never wore a seatbelt.' He pointed to the house that had real smoke coming out of its windows. 'That fire was the first time I ever had to deal with a dead body. Most of it's made up, but I put in little bits and pieces.'

Bill pointed to the beautifully made river and the oddly shaped boat floating in it. 'What about that boat?'

Figgy laughed. 'That's Micky. Jenn's brother. He's got a boat like that. Ugly bloody thing with a stupid name. What's it called, Jenn?'

Jenn stood in the doorway, arms crossed, saying nothing, lips tight. 'Don't talk to them, Figgy. Don't say anything else.'

Figgy looked puzzled. 'What's going on, Jenn?'

'I've come to talk to you about Bobby White,' said Bill. 'About what really happened.'

FIFTY-FIVE

When Isobel van Wees opened the door and saw the two uniformed officers standing outside, she looked indignant.

Alex stepped forward. 'May we come in, Isobel?'

'What is going on?'

'It would be better if we talked about this inside,' said Alex gently.

Isobel hesitated, then retreated down the hallway, allowing them to enter. 'I would prefer if you could take your shoes off,' she said to the two uniformed men.

'They'll only be a minute,' said Alex. 'Where is your husband?'

'Why do you want to speak to Victor?' She stood straight, a woman who knew how to hold her ground.

'Please, Isobel. Just tell us.'

'This is ridiculous, Alexandra. You have no right to just come in here without an explanation. They need to take their boots off.'

Alex said, 'I'm so sorry, Isobel. Believe me. But I think you've known there is something wrong, too.'

Isobel frowned. 'I don't know what you mean.' She waved a hand towards the garden behind her. 'He's in his writing shed.'

Alex pointed the officers towards the wooden shed at the far end of the garden and she watched as they made their way to it, rapped on the glass door. When Victor emerged, his face was apprehensive, and to her that seemed to confirm everything.

'Hello, Victor,' said Alex. 'We would like you to come with us to answer some questions in relation to the unlawful killing of Mimi Greene.'

'No. No. No. I didn't have anything to do with it,' he said.

'Victor?' Isobel looked puzzled.

Alex addressed Victor. 'We just need to ask you a few questions.'

'Can't you do that here?' Isobel demanded.

The upstanding English middle classes were innocent people. They had no idea about the law, thought Alex, or how it really worked. They felt it was intended for other people. 'It would be better if we did it at a police station,' she said simply. 'Will you please come with us now, Victor?'

'No, Victor. You don't have to go with them,' Isobel said as her husband stood, mute and pale, beside her. 'Alexandra. I thought you were one of us.'

Alex turned to the poet. 'Isobel. It's much better all round if he does this voluntarily. Do you understand?'

'Voluntarily? You mean if he doesn't go of his own volition you will force him to come with you?'

'Yes,' said Alex. 'We will.'

'This is unconscionable. My husband did nothing wrong,' she said firmly, then turned and looked at her husband and saw the expression of sadness on his face. Her own face changed too then, and the certainty that Alex had always seen there disappeared.

The two officers led him down the corridor to the car waiting outside.

'I'm sorry, Isobel,' Alex said. 'I'm sure Victor will explain everything to you in time.'

Isobel's face hardened. 'I genuinely thought you were my friend,' she replied.

The two officers took the front two seats, Alex sat behind, next to Victor. He looked scared.

He stayed silent until they were on the M20. 'Isobel is going to hate me,' he said.

Alex looked at him. Victor was a good-looking man. He had spent a life standing to one side of the spotlight that had shone on Isobel van Wees. Most men she had known would have found that hard. They were not used to being second-best.

'We'll talk at the station,' said Alex, and she turned away to look at the verge, absurdly green and full of flowers and life as the traffic hurtled by it.

They stopped just before the entrance to the station car park, standing in the full sunshine with the engine running and the air con on.

Victor looked around. 'What's going on?'

'We need to wait a few minutes before going in,' said one of the officers. 'They're not ready for us yet.'

'Still putting up the bunting?' said Victor.

'A bit like that,' said Alex.

'I didn't do it, you know,' said Victor.

'Let's talk inside,' Alex repeated, looking at her phone. There were no new messages. She would have to wait a little while longer. She called Toby McAdam. 'Yes,' she said. 'He's with me now. Any update on Tom Kember?'

McAdam told her that, no, there was no news. 'We have his car, now. We have two of his hideaways. It's just a matter of time.'

'I've got an idea,' said Alex. 'Something he said when we were in the caravan.'

'What?'

'I'll tell you when we're done here,' she said.

One of the officers reached inside his pocket and pulled out a packet of mints and offered them around. Victor gave a small shake of the head, but Alex took one and sucked in silence. The last sliver of it was on her tongue when her phone buzzed. 'One minute away.'

'OK,' she said. 'We'll get out now.' She opened her door, and hot air filled the car. Getting out, she walked round to Victor's side as he emerged.

The officers stood either side of him, but neither moved. 'I don't understand. Are we going inside?'

Alex saw the police car turning into the bottom of Church Road and making its way up the street towards them. Only when it was close did she say, 'OK. Let's go.'

DI McAdam was sitting in the front passenger seat. Kimaya Boyes was sitting in the rear. The driver slowed deliberately so she could get a good look at Victor before they turned down into the car park below the station. She waited on the pavement long enough to see the look of shock on Kimaya's face as she saw

335

Victor being led into the police station as her car disappeared into the underground car park.

McAdam interviewed Kimaya first. Alex watched the interview from a screen in the sweltering Portakabin. His first question was blunt. 'Were you sleeping with Victor Harris, the husband of Isobel van Wees?'

Alex watched as Kimaya stared for a long time at McAdam. 'I think I would like a lawyer,' she said.

FIFTY-SIX

'You're a copper, aren't you, love?' Jenn asked Jill, furrowing her brow.

'That's right. Detective Constable.'

'So have you come to arrest us?' Unshaven, pale, Figgy sat in his armchair looking used up.

'Bill wanted me to come here to talk to you first, so I could hear it all from you.'

Jenn and Figgy exchanged a glance.

Jenn said, 'Just let bygones be bygones, Bill, please. You of all people should know better than to go digging up the past.'

Bill looked down at Figgy. 'It's not exactly the past, though, is it? Jill's dad is still in prison for committing two murders, one of which I don't believe he's guilty of. Tell her, Figgy.'

Jill, still standing, looked at Figgy. 'What?'

'Wait,' said Jenn. 'You're not here to arrest him?'

'Who was in the boot of the Vauxhall, Figgy?' Bill asked.

'Please don't,' said Jenn. 'He's in no condition for this. Don't say anything, Figgy. You know the drill. She's not on duty. Bill's not even a copper any more.'

'Tell her, Figgy. Tell her who was really in the boot of the Vauxhall Chevette. She has a right to know.'

Figgy looked sadder than Bill had ever seen him. He looked from Bill to Jill and back again. He took a breath and spoke. 'It was Bobby White.'

'No. No. No,' Jenn wailed. 'All the good you've done for other people. You can't do this, Bill. Don't make him tell you this stuff, Bill. Figgy is a good man. He protected the community for years. He never made a bloody penny from all this. Look at him. He's dying of heart disease, Bill. There's no need to drag all this up any more. It'll kill him. Just let him live the rest of his life in peace.'

'Isn't up to me,' said Bill. 'It's up to Jill. It's her father who's the one in prison because of all this.'

Jill looked perplexed. 'Wait. What are you saying, Bill?'

'Get me a drink, love.' Figgy looked at Jenn. 'Get everyone one. Why not?'

'You know you're not allowed,' said Jenn.

'Yeah. I know,' said Figgy. 'I'm not supposed to do anything any more. I'm sick of it all. Get out the good one. That one your brother bought for me a couple of years back.'

'You don't have to do this, Figg,' she said.

'I'm bored of it all, Jenn. I'm bored of just sitting here day after day. Get us a bloody drink, love.'

She disappeared back into the house.

'Sit down, love,' Figgy told Jill. 'It's going to be a long day, so you might as well.'

★

Jenn returned with a tray, four cut-glass tumblers, a bowl of ice and a bottle of Knob Creek bourbon.

'I don't drink any more,' said Bill.

'Neither does Figgy,' said Jenn. 'Theoretically.'

'Your loss,' said Figgy, and he took the bottle and broke the seal and poured three big glasses and handed them out. 'Let me tell you about Bobby White, Jill. He was something else. There have always been drugs around here and there has always been violence attached to it. We weren't used to the scale of it then. We tried to stamp it out, only the smarter we got putting the dealers away, the worse they became. That was the trouble.'

Bill had never seen Jill's face look so hard. 'Why did my dad confess to killing Wayne Jordan when it wasn't even him anyway?'

'Wayne was a sweet boy, really, he just liked hanging round with the wrong kids. Your dad for one, Jill. First time I arrested Wayne for drugs, I tried to warn him what he was getting into. Caught him with a baggie of coke, I think it was. He was terrified I'd tell his mum what he'd been up to.'

'Katie Jordan,' said Bill. 'His mum, who thinks it was him in the boot of that car.'

'Yeah. Katie. Champion of the people. She hated me. Fair enough. So I told Wayne that Katie would be gutted, especially as she had a conviction for possession herself already. It wouldn't look good for her, now would it?' He took a big gulp from the whiskey and swallowed it with a wince. 'So I offered him a deal.'

'Oh, God. Wayne Jordan was your snitch?' Jill said, taking a lump of ice and adding it to her glass.

'Yeah. That's right. That's how we worked it back then. We'd all have our snitches on the inside. We didn't arrest them as long as they kept feeding us with information. Trouble was, it was like America against the Soviet Union. You get missiles, they get bigger missiles. And just like the Soviet Union, we could never keep up with the capitalists. The gangs started getting their snitches too. People on our side. They upped the game like they always do. And our snitches would end up disappearing, or mysteriously overdosing. They started using the fear. If you're caught, you don't just get hurt. Your whole family gets hurt. And a few of our colleagues in the Kent constabulary ended up with nice new houses in Spain. So you learned to go softly-softly and keep your snitches to yourself. Off the books. Wayne was my snitch. I had a few. You must have known that kind of thing went on, Bill?'

'I was a neighbourhood copper. You were in a different world,' Bill said.

'What I wanted more than anything was to use Wayne to take Bobby White down. Bobby White was the poison. He had arrived about a year earlier. At the start he was just another one of the lads, like Wayne Jordan, like Stevie Dowles. He lived in this old council house at the back of Ashford. I used to go and see him and he was always a charmer. Always polite. He was a piece of work, though. Everybody knew what Bobby was up to around here, but trying to prove any of it was another matter.'

'If you play by the rules,' said Jenn, 'people like him can run rings around you.'

340

Figgy reached out, took another bump of whiskey. 'To be fair, you have to understand, Bobby White was exactly the kind of criminal we created. They're like cockroaches. The poison only makes them stronger. Bobby White had everyone terrified of him. He understood the drama of it. How to scare people shitless. He used to drive round in this old Merc with black windows. Beautiful car. It was pure theatre. If he wanted to see you, he'd send the Merc to pick you up. Halfway through the journey, someone would stick a blindfold on you and so you never knew where you were going, whether they were taking you to somewhere he was going to kill you.'

Bill thought of Curly.

'The whole idea of it was to make you shit your pants. They'd hold a gun to your head and you'd never know if they were going to shoot it. And then the guys would get out, and Bobby White would emerge from the shadows, like, and would talk to you, tell you what he needed from you. Half the time you never even saw the bloody guy. That's how hard it was to get anything on him. Everyone knew it was him behind all the drugs round here, but he kept himself invisible. All we needed was one clear bit of evidence. I was such an arrogant little prick back then, I thought I would be the one to do it. Give me a fag, Jenn. Right now, I'd love one.'

'No,' she said. 'You don't smoke any more.'

Figgy sighed. 'So I forced Wayne to snitch, but he was pretty useless at it. Pretty useless at everything, poor Wayne. So I had to lean harder on him. I made him wear a wire, just one of them little recorders, slip it into your shirt, and as long as you don't move around too much, you can hear everything. Poor lad, he was terrified. The idea was . . . next time he went to buy his stash off Bobby White's men, he had to get them to mention Bobby White's name. That was all I needed. Or even better, if Bobby took him for a ride in the car, maybe I could get Bobby's voice on tape.'

'But you didn't,' said Jill.

Figgy sighed. 'Wayne Jordan was living in this run-down house on Bradstone Road. He didn't show up for our rendezvous so I went to check up on him. He was lying in the bath, naked with a bullet hole in his head, and carved onto his chest with a razor the words, "Figgy's grass". That's the thing. It was like being outplayed at every step. I couldn't afford anyone to know he was my grass. I hadn't cleared it. If I was found out to be running informants without clearing it with the powers that be, I would lose my job. Bobby White knew that. My other snitches would be in deep shit too. I was putting them in danger. That's why he bloody advertised it on Wayne Jordan's body.'

'Brutal,' said Jenn.

'So I dug a big bloody hole in the basement of that house and put our poor Wayne into it. Then I drove up to Bobby White's house in Ashford and knocked on the door and he gave me this great big smile, like he knew exactly what was going through my head. He didn't think I'd dare touch him. So he never knew what was coming when I hit him in the face with the spade I'd just buried Wayne Jordan with.'

Bill and Jill sat there, looking at each other, horrified. 'Jesus Christ, Figgy,' Jill exclaimed.

'Yeah. Well, I was under a lot of stress at the time.'

'What did he do?' Jill asked.

'Nothing. He couldn't. On account of how I hit him again. And again. Until he was dead.'

FIFTY-SEVEN

Jill's look of revulsion gradually turned into one of puzzlement. 'I don't understand. Bobby White was around for years after that. You couldn't have killed him.'

'Bobby White thought he was bullet-proof. More fool him. I'd stopped playing by our rules right then. Now I was playing by his.'

Jill looked around, confused. 'I don't understand.'

'Bobby White was dead. Only people didn't have to know it, did they? I didn't plan it. It just came to me. Who you going to miss more? A successful drug dealer, or a no-hope addict from the wrong side of Ashford?'

'Oh shit. That's why Bobby White's body was in the car,' said Jill, the penny finally dropping. 'Not Wayne Jordan's?'

'You catch on fast, don't you, darling,' said Jenn, stepping forward to wipe Figgy's mouth with a paper handkerchief. She turned to her husband. 'Stop it now, Figgy. They don't need to know any more than what you've told them.'

Figgy ignored her. 'Bobby White gets killed and there's going

344

to be all sorts of drama. So I made Bobby White disappear by letting everyone think the dead body was Wayne. I needed the dead body to be someone else if I wanted people to think Bobby White was still alive. It was just convenience, to start with. If someone's killed Bobby White, there's going to be a major bloody murder investigation. I didn't need that, so I stuck Wayne's rings on his fingers, put the body in an old car and set light to it with so much petrol that there would be nothing much left. I made sure I was the one who got to the farm first when he was found. Then I faked the dental records, just to be sure.'

'Mandy French,' said Bill. 'You got her to fake the dental records.'

'For an ordinary plod, you're not bad, Bill. Mandy was Jenn's brother's girlfriend at the time. Pretty girl. Lived in Brenzett, worked in a dental practice in Ashford. Always wanted money. I paid her to make it look like it was Wayne in the back of the car.'

'And then you set up my dad for the murder of Wayne Jordan,' said Jill.

'That came later. I never planned for that either. Everyone reckoned Bobby White killed Wayne, which was fine by me – at first. But then the rumours started. People started noticing Bobby White wasn't around. People thought maybe he killed Wayne and then scarpered. And if he wasn't around, that's when the real low life started crawling out from under the rocks. 1994 was anarchy, don't know if you remember it, Bill.'

'I'm amazed I remember anything at all after what happened to me this week.'

'Ha!' said Figgy. 'Nothing wrong with your brain, Bill – unfortunately. But it took a few days for me to realise what was

345

in the best interests of everyone. Bobby White might have been a violent bastard, but he kept the lid on it around here.'

'Bobby White was dead,' Bill said, 'but you kept the legend of Bobby White alive, because it suited you to. Even if it meant becoming a drug dealer yourself. That's right, isn't it, Figgy?'

'Remember a guy called Don Swallow?' said Figgy.

'Bobby's number two?'

'It was him who said it first. I was cacking myself he'd figure out Bobby was dead and start figuring out who did it, so I went to pull him in. Maybe I could even pin the Bobby White thing on him? He wasn't daft. He could see I was panicking. That's when he said, "Nobody hardly sees him anyway. Why don't we just make out he's back?" He was protecting his own skin as much as mine, but that's what we did. We kept the story going. That way, nobody knew Bobby was dead.'

'But you needed to make up an alibi to make sure Bobby wasn't in the frame for Wayne Jordan's murder.'

'That's when it starts to go wrong, see? I used Mandy French again. She was a looker. Just the kind of girl a thug like Bobby White would want to be seen on the arm of. I paid her to pretend she was Bobby's girlfriend. We set it up to look like he was in Paris with her at the time of the murder. I was Chief Investigating Officer so it wasn't hard. All that bollocks about them being in Paris. We faked that.'

'Beautiful bloody Mandy French,' said Jenn. 'Spiteful little girl.'

'She was an opportunist, just like I was,' said Figgy quietly. 'Pour us another one, will you, darling?' He held his glass out towards Jenn. Jenn scowled.

346

'Amanda French was the woman I was looking for when I went to the boatyard,' explained Bill.

'Did some modelling, that kind of thing. I paid her good money for the dental stuff and the alibi. That was the trouble. Give her some money, Mandy French wanted more.'

'You should have seen that coming,' said Jenn. She unscrewed the bottle and poured Figgy another glass.

'After Mandy did the witness statement for me saying she'd been in Paris with Bobby, she asked for even more money,' said Figgy. 'Said she was going to post the real dental records to the Chief Super unless I gave her ten thousand. Ten thousand. Jesus. I didn't think she had it in her. I told her that she would go down for perjury if she tried it on. I laughed in her face. That was my mistake.'

'Oh my God,' said Jill. 'You said she lived in Brenzett. That's where the post office was. She posted the dental records, didn't she?'

'Yeah. I knew I had to pay her something, but not ten grand. I let her stew for a day and then called her back to tell her I'd been hasty. I wanted to bargain with her, at least. She said it was too late. Mad bitch had posted the letter – anonymously – half an hour before I called. Special delivery, she said.'

'Oh God.' Jill put her face in her hands for a second. When she looked up, she said, 'It wasn't my dad in the post office. It was you. You were getting the letter back.'

'That's where you're wrong. It was your dad. I told him to do it.'

Jill looked disbelieving.

'You think your dad was an innocent man back then? He

347

wasn't. Your dad was a thug. Only reason he didn't have a record as long as your arm is I kept him away from that. He was my man. Your dad was another of my snitches. With Wayne, his weak point was his mother. He didn't want her being pulled in for taking drugs. With your dad, it was your mother. I mean, I had enough to arrest him twenty times over, but the thing that really made him do exactly what I wanted was that he would have done anything to protect her. Especially after he discovered she was pregnant with you.'

'Oh Christ,' whispered Jill.

Figgy took another gulp of the whiskey and washed it around his mouth before swallowing.

'That's why you had him kill the postmistress,' said Bill. It was another bit of the puzzle. The killing of Mary Spillett made sense now. Instead of her being killed as part of a botched robbery, the robbery was just a smokescreen to disguise the taking of the letter. If Figgy had let her live, Mary Spillett would have given away what he had really come for: the package that Mandy French had handed across the counter an hour earlier.

'I didn't plan it that way. I drove Stevie down there. He went in and asked her to give him everything behind the counter. She just thought he meant the cash. So he had to ask for the letter too. I was there outside. When he told me what had happened, I told him he had to go straight back in there and kill her because otherwise she'd have told everyone about the letter.'

'And that's what he did,' said Bill.

Figgy said, 'He didn't have much choice. And in return, I kept your mum out of prison.'

Bill stood. 'OK. We're done here, I think.'

'Back then, everything about our drugs policy was wrong,' said Figgy. 'We were never going to beat these guys the way we were supposed to do it. Every pound we spent on policing only made them stronger, more devious, more evil, more . . .' He erupted into coughing before he could finish the sentence.

Jenn handed Figgy a paper handkerchief. 'Before you fuck off, you should know this. For five years Figgy knew every bloody thing that was going on around here,' Jenn said. 'Bobby White kept a lid on it all. Other dealers were too scared of him to try and make a move. And if they weren't scared enough, Figgy would get Don to take them out in Bobby White's old Mercedes. Some of them he had to get a bit rough with, but that brought them into line.'

'He kept on dealing?' said Jill.

'Took a bit of doing at first.' Figgy nodded. 'Not all Bobby White's men were going to approve of the change of management. Don . . . Don sorted things out for me. One guy in particular.'

'Don killed him?' Bill pressed him.

Figgy didn't answer.

'As long as Don was making enough money, I made sure things didn't get out of hand.'

'You protected him as long as he protected you?'

'Shut up, shut up, shut up,' muttered Jenn.

'The only person who didn't deserve to die was that woman in the post office. The rest of them? Bad people, Jill. Bad people.'

'And nobody figured it out?'

'First couple of years I barely slept, thinking someone was going to figure it out. But I was the one who was in charge of finding Bobby White, wasn't I? So publicly I kept looking.

349

Besides, drug arrests were down. Violence was down. Why would anybody look at me? As far as everyone was concerned, I was doing a good job.'

'Yeah. You bloody were,' said Jenn.

'Got so good round here I was going round the country giving talks on how successful our drugs strategy was, believe it or not. All the time, I was shitting myself someone would catch on.'

'And you know what? Figgy didn't make a bloody penny out of it. Look at us?' Jenn waved her hand around at their bungalow. 'All the money from drugs. Figgy gave it all back in donations to community projects, to people like Wayne's mum. And they respected him for it. None of this was for himself.'

'That's bollocks and you know it,' said Jill.

'You're just another spiteful little girl,' said Jenn.

'Figgy paid people to shut them up,' said Bill. 'That's where all the money went. He dished it out because he had to.'

'You were saving your own skin, weren't you?' said Jill.

Jenn glowered. 'You don't understand anything.'

'And you paid Mandy French to keep quiet too?' Bill interrupted.

'God, no,' said Figgy. 'After what she pulled, I threatened to kill her next. See, she was scared of me now. Everybody was. Even your dad, Jill. Because I wasn't just pretending to be Bobby any more. I bloody became Bobby White. And she saw what I was willing to do. I never meant to become this person, Bill. I swear. Just, one thing led to the next. But I realised I had the power to scare people shitless. Know what?

It did more good than me going around acting like it was business as usual.'

'Is that how you persuaded Stevie Dowles to confess?' Bill asked.

'All he needed to know was that I would keep your mum out of prison. And I tried, believe you me. But after he went inside, she went fruit loops.'

'Jesus, no,' said Jill.

'I'm not proud, but maybe prison was the best place for your dad, I swear. He'd have killed himself on drugs soon enough.'

'You were practically a social worker,' said Jill.

'Yeah. Well. Fuck you too,' said Figgy. 'I'm trying to be honest here. Sandra was pregnant. If she went inside, we both knew they'd take the baby from her. So that's how I made him take the bow for the killing of Wayne Jordan too.' He took another mouthful of his drink and looked around the room. Jenn had moved to the door from the hallway into the conservatory and was looking sourly at her husband.

'Come on, Bill. Let's go. I hate it here,' said Jill.

Jenn turned away from Figgy and faced Jill. 'And you? What are you going to do?'

'What do you think I'm going to do?' Jill answered, staring her down.

'See? You've fucked us, Figgy, good and proper,' said Jenn. 'You think they're not going to run and tell their mates about all this?'

'So? Arrest me. Go ahead. I'm past caring, to be honest.'

'Fuck you, Figgy,' said Jenn. 'You may be be happy to go to prison, but not me.'

'You done nothing wrong. It's me they'll go for.'

'You so sure about that, Figgy?' And she reached behind her, behind the frame of the doorway she was standing in, and produced a shotgun, raised it and aimed it straight at her husband.

FIFTY-EIGHT

It didn't take McAdam long to get Kimaya to talk.

Alex watched the video from the Portakabin, the others crowding round watching over her shoulder.

'Yes, so, Victor and me had been sleeping together,' she said. 'It was nothing serious. Just a bit of fun. So Isobel was away somewhere . . . it was the Cheltenham Literature Festival, I think. It was the middle of the day. I must have fallen asleep in their bed when Mimi came around – she was dropping off a book she'd borrowed or something – Victor was downstairs in his dressing gown. It was just one of those things.'

'And?'

'Next thing, Mimi invited me to come swimming with her – alone. She wanted to talk. I suggested we go to Samphire Hoe. It's nice. It's private too.'

'She texted you. We found the message. *Let's meet. Need to talk to you xx*,' he read. 'Did you know what she wanted to talk to you about?'

'No. Not then.'

'So you agreed to meet at Samphire Hoe. How did Mimi get there? She didn't have a car.'

'I gave her a lift.'

'Right. So you picked her up from her apartment and drove her to Samphire Hoe.' Zoë had taken Alex there once. Samphire Hoe was a nature reserve on the coast just west of Dover, about twenty minutes' drive away.

'Anyway, we swam for a while and then she told me something was bothering her. She said she had been round to Isobel and Victor's house and she had been sure that Victor had another woman upstairs. And she said she recognised my coat on the hook.'

Alex watched the screen. Kimaya had her head bowed contritely as she spoke, but everything was very controlled. She knew there was no point lying about the affair. They had deliberately let her see Victor outside the police station.

'What next?' prompted McAdam.

'She said she was going to tell Isobel. And I begged her not to. I love Isobel. I love my husband. It was just . . . stupidity and boredom. Isobel always says that the sea makes people mad. I think she's right.'

'So you argued?'

'No! We didn't argue. I was just trying to persuade her not to tell Isobel. Not straight away, anyway. I promised I would break off the affair immediately. She didn't answer me, but I knew what she was like. She always thought everything should be out in the open. She had this thing about honesty.'

'What did you do to her?'

'Nothing. I swear.'

'You were angry with her?'

'Well, I dislike people who parade their principles around, as if they're better than the rest of us.'

McAdam nodded. 'Did you punch her or handle her in any way?'

'No. Absolutely not.'

McAdam removed the photographs of the body from the folder and put them on the table between Kimaya and her lawyer. Kimaya's expression didn't change. 'Can you explain the bruising on the victim's arms, shoulders and breasts?'

Kimaya didn't speak for a few seconds. 'I didn't do that.'

'Please look at the photographs,' said McAdam.

'I was just trying to get her to listen. But she kept trying to swim past me. I just wanted her to promise she wouldn't tell Isobel straight away. I didn't want her to get out of the water and leave until we'd sorted things out between us.'

'You didn't want her to get out of the water until she'd agreed not to tell Isobel that you were having an affair with her husband.'

Kimaya didn't answer.

'How long did it go on for?'

'I don't know. A minute. Two minutes.'

'Is that all?'

'Maybe longer.'

McAdam's voice was calm and even. 'How much longer? Ten minutes? Twenty?'

Kimaya raised her voice. 'I don't know!' Then composed herself again. 'I can't remember.' Evasion was her best strategy now.

'Then what?'

355

'I swam back to the shore and left her there.'

'At any time during your discussion with Ms Greene, did it cross your mind that a way to stop her telling Isobel van Wees about your affair would be to kill her?'

Kimaya looked horrified. 'God, no. What kind of woman do you think I am? I would never do a thing like that.'

McAdam just made a note on a page in front of him and nodded.

Watching the screen, Alex said, 'She made Mimi swim until she was exhausted and then held her head under.'

There was a murmur of assent behind her.

'Will we ever be able to prove it?' Charlie asked.

'I very much doubt it. But that's what happened.'

'Where was she when you got out of the water?' McAdam was asking.

'I don't know. I didn't look back. I just wanted to get away and go home. I should have stayed, obviously, but I was angry with her.'

'So you admit you were angry?'

Kimaya broke his gaze, looked towards the officer standing by the door.

McAdam made another note. 'Was Mimi Greene already in her swimsuit when you arrived at the beach, or did she change there?'

'I don't remember.' Her voice was sullen now.

'She had a dryrobe with her. She had something to change into when she got out of the water, didn't she?' The dryrobe that had been missing from her flat.

'Probably. Yes.'

'And she'd have had her phone with her.'

'I expect so.'

'Neither of those items has ever been recovered. Can you explain what happened to them?'

'Of course I can't! They were on the beach. Somebody probably stole them. A good dryrobe isn't cheap.'

'You didn't take them with you and dispose of them elsewhere?'

'No,' she said quietly.

She was lying. Alex watched the fight going out of her.

'Could you explain why, when DS Alexandra Cupidi told you that Mimi Green had drowned, you didn't tell her that you had been swimming with her the day before the discovery of her body?'

Kimaya didn't answer, still refusing to meet McAdam's gaze.

'And on the following Thursday, when DS Alexandra Cupidi interviewed you, can you explain why you made no mention of this?'

McAdam waited for an answer. The automatic sound level on the CCTV turned the silence in the room into a loud hum. Kimaya didn't speak again.

'Guilty as fuck,' said one of the coppers.

McAdam clearly thought so. He was picking up the papers that had been in front of him and straightening them before returning them to the folder and getting ready to terminate the interview.

Isobel was waiting, tight-lipped, in the reception area when Alex led Victor back from his own interview. The poet glared at her husband, and then at Alex.

357

It had not been a long interview. Victor had admitted to sleeping with Kimaya but seemed shocked to learn that McAdam had charged Kimaya with murder.

'I'm sorry,' he said when he saw his wife standing there, arms rigid at her side. 'I'm so sorry.'

'Go outside and see if the taxi is here,' she muttered. 'Is it true?' she asked Alex, when he had gone. 'You arrested Kimaya Boyes too?'

'Yes. We did.'

'I should probably offer her a lift too, I suppose,' she said. 'We'll have quite a lot to talk about, I expect.'

'We won't be releasing Kimaya just yet,' Alex told her.

'Oh.' Isobel seemed to absorb this information slowly. 'Oh I see. Oh my God.'

Alex had always felt intimated by Isobel. Now she felt sorry for her.

'And you're sure?' Isobel seemed disoriented. She had built a world she had been so certain of.

'We wouldn't be holding her if we weren't.'

'My God,' said Isobel again.

McAdam emerged from the security door just as a cab arrived to take them away, back to Hythe.

They watched the husband and wife drive away, both stiff and upright in the back of the minicab. 'Reckon we'll get murder to stick?' he asked Alex.

'Worth a try. Maybe Unlawful Act Manslaughter,' said Alex, 'but you never know. She's a cold one.' They turned to go inside. 'I've been thinking about Tom Kember. I think we should check with the Protected Persons Service.'

358

'You are kidding me? You think Tom Kember was in witness protection?'

They paused in the busy corridor. 'Ethan Johncock said he found a driving licence with Malcolm's ID on it. What if that was his original identity? It might explain why we found it so hard to track him down. Besides, something he said to me in the caravan. He told me he knew a thing or two about bad people. And he said he'd been involved with the police before.'

'I'll get on to it,' he said, checking his watch. 'I guess you better tell your friend Jill too, that we've found Mimi's real killer. She'll want to know. And no reason at all she can't come back to work now, is there?'

Alex called Jill's phone. She wasn't picking up. It was a hot day. She was probably on the beach, the lucky bastard, thought Alex.

FIFTY-NINE

Figgy looked puzzled. 'Put the gun down, Jenn. It's only me they're concerned about.'

But she stood there with the gun pointed across the room at her husband's chest.

'Always so sure of yourself, Figgy, weren't you?'

'It was you, Jenn,' said Bill, 'who warned Stevie Dowles to tell his daughter's mate to back off. And then when I didn't, it was you at the boatyard too. That boat.' He pointed at the model. 'That's your brother's boat, isn't it? *Dizzy Rascal*. When I started asking around at the boatyard about Mandy French, he called you up and you went over there and found me sitting on the jetty. What did you hit me with, Jenn?'

'What?' Figgy looked a little drunk now, and a little confused.

'He was asking after Mandy,' she said.

'Oh, Jenn,' said Figgy sorrowfully. 'Oh my darling. What did you do?'

'Yeah, well. I sure as hell don't want to see you rot in prison, my sweet, any more than I want to rot there.'

'And then a couple of nights ago you set light to Mandy's boat too, didn't you?' said Bill.

Jenn folded her arms. 'I'm not saying anything.'

'Jenn?' Figgy said. 'What'd you want to do that for?'

'To scare her into keeping quiet?' suggested Bill.

'Oh, Jenn.' Figgy looked at her sadly. 'Let it go, why don't you?'

'Don't do anything stupid, Jenn,' said Bill.

'I already did it, marrying that stupid bastard,' said Jenn. She gave a little smile.

'Give me the gun,' said Jill. 'You don't want to do this.'

'Course I don't want to do it,' snapped Jenn. 'Figgy was just trying to do the right thing by local people. People got hurt, but there were much less drugs around here as a consequence. That's all he was trying to do. Protect people. Nobody under-stood how bad it all was. It's not fair. None of it is. Bill's a copper. Used to be. He should have known not to go poking his nose into another copper's business. You should have all had each other's backs.'

'Oh, he was a bloody saint,' muttered Jill.

Bill was standing next to Figgy. Jill was still sitting in the chair by the doorway close to where Jenn stood holding the shotgun. 'Tell me what you remember about my mum, Figgy,' said Jill. 'I only knew her as a bit of a loser. Why do you think my dad was so nuts about her?'

Jenn said, 'She was a drug-addled whore. If it wasn't for people like her paying money for drugs, all this would have never happened.'

'She was a beautiful girl, Jill. Just in the wrong place at the wrong time,' said Figgy. 'Put down the gun, Jenn.'

'I'm not going to prison. Not with all those bloody criminals,' said Jenn. 'Not with you in that state. I'd rather we were both dead than that.'

Bill was standing in the line of fire, right next to Figgy, watching the barrels. Nothing he could say would reassure Jenn. She had tried to kill him at the boatyard. She would go to prison.

'It's over now, Figgy,' Jenn said, pointing the gun at him.

Figgy sighed. 'I guess you're right. Go down smiling, hey?'

'Please no,' said Jill. 'Don't do this, Jenn.'

'Oh, love,' he said, staring at her, and at the gun. 'I wasn't expecting all this to happen so fast. I wanted a little bit longer.'

'I know, darling.' Jenn smiled at him. 'Me too. We had pretty good times though, didn't we?'

'Not so bad,' answered Figgy.

'Don't,' said Jill. 'This is crazy.'

Figgy turned to Bill. 'You better stand back now, Bill. Knowing her fucking aim, she'll get you too.'

'Fuck you, Figgy,' Jenn said.

'Fuck you too, darling.'

'I'm staying right where I am.' Bill leaned a little to the right, covering Figgy with his body. He thought of his mother and father and remembered the unexpected smell of guns after you had fired them.

'I don't mind killing you too, Bill. I tried it once before,' Jenn said.

'Get out of it, Bill,' Figgy said. 'Warning you. She'll do it.'

'Not easy killing someone with a twelve-bore, Jenn. Chances are they won't die right away,' said Bill. 'Think about Mary

Spillett. She didn't die instantaneously. I've seen the photos. Remember, Figgy?'

'Come a little closer, Jenn. Head shot. I don't want it not to work.'

Bill saw the look of concentration on Jill's face. As Jenn stepped into the room, Jill made her move, lunging forward and grabbing the gun's barrel, but she was not quick enough. The railway layout disintegrated, trains jumping like snakes into the air. Glass flew out of the conservatory windows.

The air was thick; the smell a little like charcoal.

The dust fell on them all.

Figgy was screaming. It was a loud, desperate noise.

Bill watched from the other side of the railway layout as Jill continued to struggle to hold the barrel of the gun. Jenn was screaming at her, 'Give it to me, you bitch!' Jenn jerked back and tore the shotgun from her hands, and Bill looked on in horror as she swung the gun round and placed the barrels under her chin, scrabbling down to try and reach the trigger.

Jill threw herself at Jenn again and the two disappeared out of the door into the darkness of the corridor.

There was a second explosion and a crashing of bodies falling somewhere out of sight, and Figgy kept on screaming.

SIXTY

When Alex arrived in Pevensey Bay, the road was so full of cars and ambulances she had to park her Saab in the next street and run.

'Bill!' she shouted. He was sitting on a wall in the low evening light, being interviewed by a young fair-haired copper from Sussex police. There was blood on his shirt. 'Are you hurt?'

'No. This is Figgy's blood.'

There seemed to be a lot of blood. 'Who's Figgy?' Alex had no idea what had been going on.

'Long story,' said Bill. 'He's in that ambulance now.' He pointed to the closest ambulance.

'Badly hurt?'

She watched him take a breath. 'No. He didn't make it.'

'Shotgun blast in the femoral artery,' said the younger copper.

'I tried to staunch it,' said Bill. 'But he wasn't a well man. He kind of faded fast.' He raised an arm and wiped the sleeve of his shirt across his eyes.

Alex looked around. 'They said Jill was hurt too. Jesus, Bill. What's been going on?'

'The DC? Broken bones,' said the copper. 'They carted her off to Hastings hospital twenty minutes ago.'

Alex sat down on the wall next to Bill and put her arm around him until he was breathing more evenly. Neighbours filled the street around them, watching silently.

Alex drove Bill to the Conquest Hospital and they sat together in the waiting room, him still in his bloody shirt, covered by a jacket they had taken from Figgy's house. She bought him tea from the machine and put extra sugar in it. Jenn Tart was somewhere else in the hospital, being operated on. She had tried to blow her own head off, but Jill had tackled her to the ground before the gunshot, breaking her own bones in the fall. Instead of killing her, the shotgun pellets had torn the side of Jenn's face away. For the twenty absurdly long minutes it had taken for paramedics to arrive, Jill had knelt beside her, using her good arm to press a sofa cushion against her raw skin to try and staunch the bleeding. It must have been carnage inside the house, thought Alex, Bill trying to keep the other one alive a couple of metres away.

'What a day,' said Alex.

'Twenty-eight years he's been in prison, her dad,' Bill was saying. 'Maybe he deserved it. I don't know. He killed a woman, after all.'

Alex took a sip of the coffee she had bought for herself, and scowled. 'I'm so pissed off with you, Bill. You didn't share any of this with me. I'm supposed to be your friend.'

'You were busy,' he said. 'It was complicated.'

A nurse interrupted. 'Excuse me,' she said. 'Jill Ferriter. Are you the parents?'

Bill and Alex looked at each other. 'What?' Alex said indignantly. And then she realised that's what they probably looked like. Two anxious parents, bickering about who was to blame for their daughter's injury. 'No. We're not her bloody parents.'

'But you're giving her a lift, right? Because she's ready to go home now.'

Bill started laughing, which was something, at least.

They found Jill sitting on a gurney, wearing a sling and looking very pale.

'Did the woman make it?' she asked.

'Not pretty, but she'll live. Not much of a life though. She killed her own husband.'

Jill nodded.

Alex went and fetched the car and waited by the entrance till Bill emerged out of the automatic doors, leading Jill gently to the front passenger seat while he got in the back.

They talked all the way to Dungeness, each telling their part in the story.

'Kimaya Boyes?' said Jill, when she'd heard the news. 'That's awful. I liked her.'

'She was worried her husband would divorce her if he found out.'

'Well, that worked for her, didn't it? And Malcolm was just running away from tax and child support all this time? Jesus, the lengths some people go to avoid taking parental responsibilities. Have they found him?'

'No. They haven't. He's just vanished again.'

366

Back at the house, Zoë was waiting up. She had made soup. It involved green lentils and carrots but was actually not too bad. Alex desperately wanted a glass of wine, but held back; Jill wasn't allowed to drink because of her painkillers and Bill didn't any more anyway.

They talked for hours, all the same, sitting around the kitchen table. Without asking, as the sky darkened, Zoë got up and switched off the main light, but somehow that seemed right. There was something about darkness that made talking about it all easier.

Alex talked about the look on Isobel's face when she realised that her husband had cheated on her.

Jill talked about how she had secretly hoped that somehow she would discover her father wasn't a murderer after all.

'You can't pick your parents, Jill,' said Bill.

Zoë told them about how she had spoken to Rose for an hour on the phone that evening, Rose crying when she heard what had happened and how Mimi had died.

'She was devastated. I felt so bad telling her.' This time, it was going to be Zoë's turn to persuade Rose to come back to swimming in the water. They had planned to meet on the beach at Hythe in the morning.

There was going to be a funeral for Mimi in a fortnight. Rose had asked Zoë to go with her.

'Is she your girlfriend?' Jill asked.

'Why does everyone always want you to have a boyfriend or a girlfriend anyway?' said Zoë.

Bill talked about how sad he had felt when he thought he was going to die with the water over his head. 'It was just this

367

sadness,' he said. 'I felt that I've only really started to come alive these last couple of years, and I thought it was all over.'

In the darkness, Alex stood and put her arms around him. 'It must have been weird coming round. You didn't have any idea who I was, did you?'

'I kind of knew I liked you. Jill not so much.' They laughed.

And then they looked at Jill. It was getting light already. They had talked their way through the darkness. The sky was pale grey behind the black lighthouse. Beyond that, out of sight, the water was still. Everything seemed to have stopped. 'My dad . . . you know. He was my dad. All this time.'

In the dawn light, Alex walked Bill back to his house. He was still slow on his feet, finding his way again.

When she got home, Jill had gone to sleep in the spare room. Zoë had disappeared upstairs too.

Unable to sleep, she sat on the shingle bank by the side of the terrace of houses and watched the headland come to life. The bin lorry had arrived and was slowly working its way down the line of cottages when she called DI McAdam. 'Is it too early?'

He answered the phone so fast she guessed he had been awake too. 'Is Jill OK?' he asked, his voice low. She heard him getting up, leaving the bedroom and walking downstairs to where he could talk more easily. 'You were right about Tom Kember, you know?'

'At least I was right about something,' she said.

'Don't beat yourself up. We all thought it was Malcolm, not just you. We tracked down his Protected Persons Service handler yesterday. Apparently, the eighteen-year-old Malcolm had been a witness to a drug-gang-related murder in Feltham in 2009. To protect his safety, he had been offered a new identity and an apprenticeship as a builder, the handler said. A couple of years after his conviction, the murderer Malcolm's evidence had helped convict died following an epileptic seizure.'

'So Malcolm wasn't scared of him any more.'

'Looks like he drifted back to using his old ID to lead a double life as God's gift to women. Even did some building work under the name to avoid paying HMRC. Would have probably got away with it for a while longer if Kimaya Boyes hadn't murdered one of the women he'd been sleeping with.'

SIXTY-ONE

Two days after Figgy is shot dead, Bill takes Katie to the house in Bradstone Road in Folkestone, where a forensics team has been digging out the basement. They have discovered bones.

'I still don't like you, Bill,' Katie says as she looks at the hole they've dug in the earth and the pale dome of a skull they have recently exposed.

It turns out, though, that there are two bodies there. One is almost certainly Wayne Jordan. It is too early to say to whom the other bones belong, but Bill reckons it's probably another of Bobby White's men. Before he was shot, Figgy had hinted that there had been at least one other member of the gang who had got in the way of his takeover.

On a quiet avenue in Dartford, big Don Swallow's sixteen-year-old granddaughter opens the door to discover four policeman standing outside. 'Granddad?' she calls up the stairs.

Jenn is still in hospital. She's refusing to talk, but when she recovers she'll be tried for killing her husband, and for the attempted murders of Mandy French and Bill South.

Whatever Zoë said about Rose, she has been spending half her time over at her flat in Hythe. Alex is surprised how much she misses her. The house feels too big and empty. She's been spending the evenings with Bill. He's working on building up his strength.

Yesterday, Rose and Zoë came round to pick up Bill. They dropped in to say hello, like Zoë was a guest, visiting. 'Where are you lot off to?' asked Alex, trying not to sound offended for not being included in whatever they were doing.

'We're taking Bill up to the pool at the campsite in New Romney,' said Zoë. 'Rose is teaching him to swim.' And Bill stood there, embarrassed at having to be taught by two young girls.

'Good for you,' said Alex.

When Alex picks Jill up from her flat in Ashford, the first thing Jill says when she steps out of the lift is, 'You heard the news?'

McAdam called Alex first thing. Tom Kember had been sleeping rough in Mitcham, begging outside the Co-op. By pure fluke, a woman whom he'd slept with and then ghosted had recognised him. She had got into an argument with him, which had escalated into a fight when her boyfriend arrived, and store security had called the police.

'Poetic bloody justice,' says Jill. 'Men who have kids and then abandon them.'

She looks shaky, thinks Alex. 'Yeah,' she says. 'I know. You need a hand to the car?'

She takes her by the arm and leads her to the Saab. It's a two-hour drive. Alex regrets taking the coast road the moment she

371

realises she'll be driving Jill towards Pevensey Bay, close to the house, but when they drive past the turning, Jill says nothing, just looks doggedly out of the windscreen.

When they get to their destination, they park outside. Jill is sitting in the passenger seat of the Saab. The seat is pushed all the way back so there is room for Jill, with the cast on her leg and the plastic shell that protects it. There is a thin, grey drizzle falling and Alex has switched off the windscreen wipers. Droplets dot the glass. Ahead, the outside world loses focus.

'You good to do this?'

Jill says, 'I don't know.' She holds the printed email with the prison visit details in her lap. There is a low, modern brick building on the other side of the road. They saw the sign on the railings when they pulled up: *Visitors: Enter by Gate*. There's an arrow under it pointing to the right. Jill's father will be in there somewhere, waiting to see her for the first time.

'Take your time,' says Alex.

'I forgot to ask, Jill,' she says after a while. 'How was your dinner date with Charlie and Guy?'

Jill smiles. 'Actually not the worst date I've been on, by any means. I know that's not a high bar. Funny really. Me on crutches. Guy in his chair. But I'm inviting them round to the flat next week. Charlie's all right once you get to know him.'

'Nice,' says Alex.

Jill sits, left hand on the door handle of the Saab. Alex is ready to get out, help her out of the car, to fetch her crutches from the back the moment she opens the door.

'If you want,' says Alex, 'I can bring you back another time.' Or we can just go home to mine, she thinks.

There is wine chilling in the fridge.

Jill has her eyes on the gate. Alex says nothing more, just waits for her friend to choose what to do, to make up her mind whether she's going to go in or not.

THANKS

A few years ago a reader from Hythe asked me if I would write a story in which something bad happened there, because she felt Hythe probably deserved it. I hope this fits the brief. Thanks to her and the Hythe Sea Swimming Group.

Thanks also to Jules Swain, Graham Bartlett, M. W. Craven, Susi Holiday and Colin Scott for advice, much gratitude to Elly Griffiths for wise words and to Caroline Maston, Samantha Brownley, Kett's Books, the Steyning Bookshop, the Kemptown Bookshop, City Books and to all the many other booklovers and booksellers who've given me so much support.

Thanks massively to my editor Jon Riley at riverrun for his faith – and to Jasmine Palmer, David Murphy, Ana McLaughlin and Elizabeth Masters – and to my agent Karolina Sutton. Thanks also to Nick de Somogyi yet again for the tactful way he reminds me that there are only seven days in one week and they must come in the right order.

Finally, thanks to Jane, Tom and Ellen for keeping me afloat.

I originally came across the enigmatic concrete man in Keith

375

Swallow's excellent history Nanny Goat Island. He is not easy to find. It took me and Jane two days to track him down. If you want to spend less time tramping stones by the nuclear power station you can find him on what3words///celebrate.brambles. quaking.